Praise fo

'I enjoyed this book immensely . . . I don't have words to describe exactly how excited I am to read the second book in this trilogy next year. I loved being on Stringybark Creek with the Callahan family and just want to dive back into it.' —Noveltea Corner

'I loved this book, I connected with the characters and I enjoyed the journey . . . *The Wrong Callahan* is a well-paced tale of love, betrayal, family, PTSD and small town communities. Another five-star read from me!' —Beauty and Lace

'Just in time for Christmas, Karly Lane returns with another winning read . . . Although *The Wrong Callahan* is here to entertain rural romance readers, Karly Lane would love the audience to take away a small sense of appreciation of the work our agricultural workers commit to, day in day out. It truly is tremendous and worthy of our attention in this current challenging environment for our Aussie farmers.' —Mrs B's Book Reviews

'Lane's research is impeccable, and rings true.' —Compulsive Reader

'Karly's novels are always full and rounded; reading one is like stepping into a new community for the duration and being welcomed in with open arms.' —Theresa Smith Writes

'Karly Lane has an uncanny knack for truly capturing the spirit of rural communities . . . She clearly has a love for rural Australia.' —Read the Write Act

Karly Lane lives on the mid north coast of New South Wales. Proud mum to four children and wife of one very patient mechanic, she is lucky enough to spend her day doing the two things she loves most—being a mum and writing stories set in beautiful rural Australia.

ALSO BY KARLY LANE

North Star
Morgan's Law
Bridie's Choice
Poppy's Dilemma
Gemma's Bluff
Tallowood Bound
Second Chance Town
Third Time Lucky
If Wishes Were Horses
Six Ways to Sunday
Someone Like You
Mr Right Now
Return to Stringybark Creek

KARLY LANE

The Wrong Callahan

Book 1 of the
Callahans of Stringybark Creek series

ALLEN&UNWIN
SYDNEY • MELBOURNE • AUCKLAND • LONDON

This edition published in 2019
First published in 2018

Allen & Unwin
83 Alexander Street
Crows Nest NSW 2065
Australia
Phone: (61 2) 8425 0100
Email: info@allenandunwin.com
Web: www.allenandunwin.com

A catalogue record for this book is available from the National Library of Australia

ISBN 978 1 76087 623 4

Set in Sabon LT Pro by Bookhouse, Sydney
Printed in Australia by McPherson's Printing Group

10 9 8 7 6 5 4 3 2 1

The paper in this book is FSC® certified. FSC® promotes environmentally responsible, socially beneficial and economically viable management of the world's forests.

To my brothers, Darren and Brad.
I wouldn't trade you for the world . . .
for horses maybe, but not for the world.

One

Lincoln Callahan pulled the car over to the side of the road and turned off the engine as he stared at the sign on the front gate. *Stringybark Creek*. Paddocks stretched out in front of him as far as the eye could see, and in the distance loomed the mountain range, casting its afternoon shadows over the valley. This was his home. Stringybark Creek, which was situated outside Rankins Springs in the dry heartland of the New South Wales Riverina, had been in his family for five generations. He came from farmers—hardworking, salt of the earth people who'd carved this property from the bush. Their blood, sweat and tears had been the soil from which the crops and cattle had grown for one hundred and thirty years.

Lincoln could have flown from Brisbane to Griffith and hired a car, or even asked his parents to pick him up from the airport, but he'd needed the solitude of the long drive.

It was late November and already the heat was unbearable. It wasn't Afghanistan-unbearable, but it was bloody hot all the same. Summer was just around the corner and he knew it was only going to get worse. He rolled down his window and felt the cold air rush out, to be replaced by the oven-like heat from outside. A crow let out a dismal cry somewhere nearby, and in the distance he could hear cattle, but other than that there was only the rustle of the long grass and the buzz of insects.

Lincoln slowly leaned forward and turned the ignition. He always got an anxious rush of adrenaline as he drove through these gates. Part of it was excitement to be back home, but another part was knowing what was to come. His parents always made a fuss about his career in the army. He had to admit that this used to make him puff his chest out just a little—praise from your dad was always a big deal, no matter how old you were. It was not what he needed now though. He craved only peace and quiet. He didn't want to be reminded of his work while he was here. He wanted to be plain old Linc. He wanted to do everyday farming jobs, the stuff he never thought he'd miss but did. The stuff that his younger brother, Griffin, thought he was mad for volunteering to do when he was home on leave.

He missed this place when he was away, which was weird considering he couldn't wait to get away from it when he was younger. His heart had never been in farming the way

Griff's was. He'd always had his sights set firmly on the military—just like his great-grandfather who fought in the First World War. He'd wanted to see the world . . . okay, and blow things up, but mainly he'd wanted to get as far away from Stringybark Creek as he could. Life was too short to stay stuck on a farm all his life. There was more to living than fixing fences and planting crops. It was ironic now, then, that when he did have time off, that's exactly what he looked forward to doing the most.

Dirt billowed up around the car as he headed down the driveway. As he rounded the next bend, he felt a smile tug at the corners of his mouth when he saw the sprawling homestead come into view. *Home.*

He hadn't told his parents he was arriving today—he'd told them a vague 'probably next week'. Even though he knew his mother would read him the riot act about not giving her notice so she could make up his room, he knew she'd already have it prepared for him. She'd cottoned on to his surprise tactics years ago.

By the time he'd pulled the car up beside one of the three large machinery sheds across from the house, his parents were already on their way over to greet him.

'Lincoln Callahan! How many times have I told you about sneaking up on us like this?' Lavinia Callahan called out.

'Hi, Mum,' he said, swooping her off her feet and twirling her around. It was the only way to stop the lecture in its tracks. It still gave him a bit of a shock to see her with grey hair; last time he'd come home, she'd informed him that she was tired of fighting nature, so she'd decided to embrace it instead. It didn't mean any fewer visits to the hairdresser though—she still looked as stylish as always, with a sculptured cut, shorter at the back and longer on the sides. Over the top of her squeals of protest and threats of bodily harm, Linc swapped a knowing grin with his father. After setting down his mother, dodging her playful smack, he put his hand out. 'G'day, Dad.'

'Good to see you, son,' his father said, dragging him in for a bear hug, and even as Linc braced himself for it, the hearty slap on the back still almost sent him sprawling.

Bob Callahan was a big man. He was as tough as they came. Linc had always admired his father's strength, not only physical but also mental. His hair may be silver now, but he was still a powerful man. There'd been times that Mother Nature and banks had tried to break his old man—but they'd never succeeded. Although it had come close on a few occasions. They all knew families in the district who hadn't been so fortunate. Life on the land wasn't always kind.

'You're home!' his mother said.

Her hands fluttered up to her mouth and Linc gave a moan. 'Don't start crying, Mum.' While it had been two years since he'd been home, his parents had made several trips to Brisbane during the last eighteen months to catch up with him, although anyone looking on would think she hadn't seen him for a decade.

'I can't help it. My baby's home,' she sniffed.

'Oh, for the love of God, woman. He's a grown man,' his father said, rolling his eyes skywards.

'He'll always be my baby, Robert Callahan,' she snapped, before turning her gaze back to Linc. 'I can't believe you're here so early. We weren't expecting you until closer to Christmas.'

'Change of plans,' Linc said with an offhand shrug. 'The opportunity came up so I took it.' Well, it wasn't really a lie.

'What are we doing out here in this terrible heat, anyway? Come on, let's go inside. I was just about to put the kettle on.' It didn't matter what time of the day or night you turned up, Mum was always just about to put the kettle on. It was one of the familiar things he'd been counting on.

Linc pulled his large duffle bag from the car and they made their way across to the house. 'So how's business, son?' his father asked.

'Good. We're picking up some big contracts now. Signed an insurance company that's going to be a big turnaround for us. We're looking at expanding into Papua New Guinea. Our name seems to be getting out there.'

'Good,' Bob grunted. 'A reliable reputation makes all the difference in the world.'

After leaving the army a year and a half ago, Linc had thrown in with two mates to start a crisis management company. Their aim was to provide emergency management to businesses with staff travelling overseas or into high-risk environments, offering assistance with incidents from car accidents and sudden illness to kidnappings and terrorist attacks.

His father was right, in this business reputation *was* everything. It only took one mistake—one tiny balls-up—and the business you'd worked so hard for would be gone. No one wanted to hire a firm who'd failed to protect their clients.

Linc dropped his bag inside his old bedroom and gave the room a quick once-over. While his mother hadn't kept it as a shrine to his teenage self—there were no posters on the walls or trophies on the dressing table—she hadn't turned it into a sewing room or gym either. There was a new queen-size bed with a dark blue doona and fancy curtains on the windows, but it still felt like his room. He headed down the hallway, past his brother's old room, and two more bedrooms that used to belong to his sisters, one of which now housed his gran, and out into the kitchen.

'Gran,' Lincoln said, greeting his grandmother.

'It's so good to see you home,' the older woman smiled, clasping her cool, soft hands around his, before reaching up to kiss his cheek.

His grandparents had been part of his life for as long as he could remember. They'd moved from the main house when Linc's parents had outgrown the smaller farm house at the end of the dirt driveway after having all their kids. Griff lived there now. After Grandad's passing, Gran had decided she didn't want to live by herself anymore and had moved back into the main house with his parents. So now Gran was back in the home she and Grandad had raised their family in. She'd come full circle. He knew she missed Grandad. He did too.

His grandad had been the toughest man, besides his own dad, he'd ever known. He'd worked on the property until the day he'd died. It had been in his blood the same way it was in his father's and Griffin's.

'You're looking more like your grandad every day. He was so handsome,' his gran sighed wistfully. 'Is it time for afternoon drinkies?' she asked, leaving Linc blinking at the rapid change of topic.

'I'm making a cuppa, Ida. How about we start with that first?' his mother said.

Linc hid his smile as his gran muttered beneath her breath. Gran was known for her love of an afternoon Scotch; she claimed it was the reason her father and older brothers had all lived to be over one hundred.

'I might take a drive out and find Griff after this,' Linc said, pulling out a chair.

His father gave a grunt as he reached for a side plate. 'He'll probably be over at the boundary fence to Pommy George's. He's been spending a lot of time over there recently,' he said dryly, and Linc raised an eyebrow curiously.

Pommy George, as he was known locally, was a quiet bloke who'd appeared one day and bought the small property that bordered part of Stringybark's eastern boundary. He'd kept to himself for a few years, running a landscaping business, then headed off to Bali one day and returned with a bride.

His mother gave a cluck of her tongue and frowned at her husband as she placed a plate of scones on the table. 'Your brother's taken a bit of shine to the new girl who's running the spa while Savannah's away.'

'The spa? You mean that hippie joint next door?'

'It's not a hippie joint,' Lavinia said briskly. 'It's a day spa, and quite luxurious too. It's put us on the map.'

'What map would that be?' Linc asked, taking a scone and reaching for the butter.

'People come out here from all over. You wouldn't believe it. It's won all kinds of awards.'

'Don't get your mother started,' Bob groaned. 'She's been on about starting up a flamin' B&B.'

'What? Here?'

'As I've told your father, there's a huge market for boutique accommodation, especially now that we get people coming out here for spa treatments. They're always looking for somewhere to stay when they book their appointments. At the moment the only place available is the pub. Savannah mentioned that she's looking into adding more accommodation at her place to try and cater for them. It's a good opportunity to get tourism happening in the district.'

'All this from women getting waxed?' Linc asked dubiously.

'They don't just do waxing, dear,' his mother corrected somewhat impatiently. 'Savannah did her training in all kinds of exotic places and she offers treatments that practically no one—not even in the big cities—offers. I've been trying to get your father to go over. He would benefit from a massage and detox wrap.'

'Not bloody likely,' Bob muttered as he took a bite of his scone—practically fitting in the whole thing in one bite.

Linc tried his best to blink away the image of his father in a detox wrap, even though he had no idea what it was. 'So Griff has a thing for day spas?'

'More like the sheila running it.'

'Robert!'

'What?'

'Honestly,' she said with a weary roll of her eyes. 'She's a delightful young woman. Her name's Cash and she's running the spa for the next few months.'

'So is it serious?' he asked, reaching for a second scone. No one made scones like his mother.

'Doubt it,' Bob put in from across the table.

'Why?'

'He hasn't even asked her out as far as I know.'

'There's nothing wrong with taking your time about these things, Robert.'

'Well, he wants to hurry up or he'll miss out. I reckon half the bloody town's circling the poor girl.'

'She's not a piece of meat,' Lavinia snapped.

'She may as well be. Not many single women left in town. His options are running out.'

Linc bit back a smile as he listened to his father. Not much changed around here. His brother really had left his run a bit too late. Most of his friends from high school were either married or had left town, and the pickings *were* pretty slim. It was the story of any small country town.

'Told him he'd waited too long. He should have snatched up young Olivia Dawson when he had the chance.'

'She's a lawyer now, you know,' Gran put in proudly. The Dawsons were the family from the neighbouring property. His youngest sister, Hadley, and Olivia had been inseparable growing up, and Olivia had been his brother's high-school sweetheart.

'Yeah, I think Hadley told me about it,' he said. 'Hey, speaking of Hadley, are the wedding preparations all on track?'

'You know your sister,' his mother said drolly. 'Nothing would dare *not* be on track.'

'Enjoy the peace while you have it, son. Once your sister gets here, this place will make downtown Afghanistan look quiet,' his father added.

His sister's wedding was one of the reasons he'd decided to come home early. He'd been booked in for Christmas, followed by the New Year's Eve wedding. Relatives from far and wide were set to converge on Stringybark. His mother had been planning this family reunion for months. He was hoping he'd get a bit of peace and quiet before all hell broke loose.

'I don't trust that fella of hers,' Gran announced, reaching for a scone. 'His eyes are too close together.'

'There's nothing wrong with Mitch's eyes,' his mother assured her.

'Mark my words. He's not the one for her.'

'He's won a Logie for TV personality of the year, he can't be that untrustworthy,' Bob said, reaching for another scone but changing his mind when his wife lifted an eyebrow at him in silent reprimand.

'Logie smogie,' Gran tsked.

'Well, we're not the ones marrying him, so we'll have to trust that Hadley's making the right decision,' Lavinia said diplomatically.

Linc couldn't say he hadn't had doubts about his sister's choice of husband himself, but this was based on one encounter with the guy. He'd had the annoying task a few years earlier of escorting the pretty boy journo into a combat zone where the idiot had almost got them killed. Still, maybe he'd changed over the years. Nowadays he had his own TV show and rarely worked in the field, except when some huge international story broke and every man and his dog in TV news had to report 'live from the scene.' But his mum was right—they weren't the ones who had to live with the guy, so if Hadley wanted to marry him, who were they to call her on it?

Linc grinned as his mother passed the plate of scones across to him, then pulled it away when his father went to grab one. 'You have your cholesterol to think about, Robert.'

'And I will think about it, dear . . . as I'm eating one of your delicious homemade scones smothered in jam.'

'But without the cream,' Lavinia smiled sweetly, moving the small bowl of fresh cream away from her husband.

It was good to be home. For a moment Linc was filled with a calmness he hadn't felt in a long while. Then his happiness began to waver. How long would it last?

Two

Cash Sullivan locked the door after her last client of the day and hurried to clean everything up. Stripping the sheets off the bed, she bundled them up in her arms to dump into the washing machine on her way back up to the main house. It was hard to believe she'd been here for three weeks already.

The offer to take over her best friend's day spa while she went on an extended visit to the UK had been too good to refuse. Besides, it couldn't have come at a better time for Cash. She'd just got out of another doomed relationship and had been eager for a change of scenery.

Rankins Springs wasn't exactly the kind of place she would have chosen, though. It was a small, sleepy town in the middle of nowhere—not a place you'd immediately think of when opening a day spa, but Savannah was booked solid most days.

Naively, Cash had thought the pace out here would bore her to tears, but in fact she'd never worked this hard in any salon before, and that included the resort island she'd been working on up in the Whitsundays.

Cash stepped outside onto the gravel path that led from the Bali hut Savannah's husband, George, had built for her. The gentle, hollow sound of large bamboo wind chimes floated through the air, accompanied by the soothing sound of trickling water coming from the Balinese water feature.

It was hard to believe that only a few metres away was a quaint little farmhouse hidden from the hut by a thick wall of bamboo planted to give the salon privacy from the rest of the farm.

Cash had been blown away by the whole place when she'd first arrived. The Sacred Spirit Day Spa was more suited to a luxury resort in some exotic tourist destination than a small community the size of Rankins Springs. Savannah never did anything by halves, though, and when she married her farmer she refused to give up her passion for the beauty industry just because she was following her heart from Bali to rural Australia. She set about bringing beauty therapy to the country, and now she had people travelling hours for spa treatments.

It was a little over a month until Christmas and already the silly season had started. It was a relief to walk inside the farmhouse and take out the chilled can of beer she'd been thinking about all day.

She glanced at her mobile on the benchtop and knew immediately who the missed calls and text messages were from: Dale Monstrato. An image of him lying naked in bed with the receptionist from the gym where he spent his every waking moment flashed through her mind, and she deleted the messages without bothering to read them. 'Idiot,' she muttered darkly, not entirely sure if she were referring to Dale or herself.

At first he'd seemed perfect; his exotic good looks and devil-may-care attitude had all the hallmarks of a Cash Sullivan kind of guy. He'd travelled extensively and they'd been to many of the same places, so they hit it off instantly. But then, after a few months, it lost its shine. The things she'd found attractive began to irritate her. His travel stories began to grow repetitive, his devotion to his workout and diet routine drove her nuts, and that sexy, rebellious streak that had been a turn-on at first lost its appeal when it translated to 'I do whatever the hell I want to do'.

Sometimes she imagined that she chose these types of men on purpose, knowing they were shallow and self-absorbed. Maybe because she knew they'd be easier to leave. She always left. Even when she thought that this time she'd stay and make a go of it, she never did. When it came to the crunch, when things began to look like they might get serious, she would start to panic. It was almost like claustrophobia. She'd start to imagine a life in one place and her feet would get itchy. Moving kept her free. It gave her independence. Whenever she got tired of a place she just packed up her few belongings and left. She liked not being tied down to anyone or anything. At least she *had* liked her life that way. Until lately.

Savannah had never weighed in on Cash's love life in all their years of friendship. She took the 'live and let live' motto seriously, but when Cash had told her about Dale, instead of the expected 'plenty more fish in the sea', Savannah had given her a stern lecture. *A lecture*.

'How long are you going to continue down this path, Cash?' Savannah demanded. 'Do you seriously want to end up a lonely old woman?'

'Hey!' That was uncalled for. 'Go easy on the old.'

'I'm serious, Cash. You're so determined not to become your mother that you've lost all sight of what's normal.'

'It's got nothing to do with my mother,' Cash said stiffly.

'It's got everything to do with her, Cash,' Savannah said, her voice softening slightly. 'You don't want a relationship because you think it'll just end up the same as your parents.'

'Do you blame me? You know how bad it was.'

'And if you keep choosing these men—the ones with no substance, the guys who you know aren't worth the time of day—then you'll be right, you'll have a terrible relationship just like your parents.'

'What the hell, Sav?'

'That's what you're doing, Cash,' Savannah said, not giving an inch. 'You're choosing men you know aren't ever going to settle down. You're deliberately sabotaging any chance for a normal relationship.'

'Oh, please!' Cash rolled her eyes on the other end of the phone. *That was so dumb . . .*

'You have to stop, Cash. It worries me to see you lonely.'

It had taken a few days for Cash to get over her hurt and call her old friend back to accept the job. However, her words had hit their mark. She *did* need to make better choices; she was twenty-eight and where had she got in life? She'd travelled all over the world, sure, but she had no meaningful relationship with anyone except Savannah, and she hadn't stayed in one place for more than twelve months. Meeting new people, seeing new places, all of it had been exciting and fun, but lately it had begun to lose its appeal.

A faint noise outside drew her attention and she smiled a little as she changed out of her smock and work pants and into a loose cotton dress, pulling out the ponytail she'd worn for work, allowing her long, chocolate-coloured locks to fall down past her shoulders.

Her bare legs felt cooler out of her work uniform, and she caught the flash of colour from the intricate tattoo on her foot that wound its way up around her ankle. She spent much of her day covered up. In the beauty industry it was important to present a serene, almost clinical image to clients. Her tattoos were barely visible when she wore work clothing. The majority of her clients wouldn't even be aware she had them. They were not something she flaunted—they weren't for show, they were for her. She wasn't ashamed, she just didn't need to impress anyone with them. The ones on her back were usually hidden, but she had one quote that wrapped around from her shoulder to her upper arm, and another on the inside of the other forearm, which were more visible. She knew she stood out like a sore thumb around here, but she was relieved to find most people were welcoming and friendly.

She took a cold beer from the fridge then headed out onto the front verandah. The front of the house couldn't have been more different to the back. Where the rear of the house was an oasis of tropical plants and water features, the front was a quaint cottage garden, complete with white picket fence and a cobbled pathway—the advantage of having a landscaper as a husband. Savannah's excuse for the two strikingly different areas was that she spent all day surrounded by serenity. After work and on weekends she liked to unwind in a different environment. There were days when Cash had to agree there *was* such a thing as too much serenity.

The sound she'd heard earlier grew louder and she looked across at the paddock that bordered her friend's place. The Callahans owned one of the largest properties in the district and it was very much a working concern.

The tractor came into sight a few minutes later and rolled towards the fence, coming to a stop. The silence that followed was almost deafening. This was nothing like the old rusted tractor George had parked out in his wonky timber shed. This was a monstrosity of a machine, Kermit-green, and it screamed 'serious farmer' like nothing else could.

She watched the graceful ease with which the driver hoisted himself over the fence. Her gaze swept across the denim jeans and long-sleeved checked shirt, taking in the masculine physique beneath.

Griffin Callahan was easy on the eye, that was for sure. He took off his hat as he approached and Cash noticed he'd had a haircut since the last time she'd seen him. His caramel hair had been trimmed on the sides and kept slightly longer on top. He'd even shaved. He looked clean-cut, handsome and respectable.

'Hey,' he said, stopping at the bottom step and looking up at her.

'Hey,' she replied, smiling. 'You must have been reading my mind,' she said and saw his eyes widen slightly in surprise. 'It's beer o'clock,' she elaborated, holding up the can. 'Want one?'

'Oh. Right,' he said, clearing his throat a little. 'Yeah, sure. That'd be great.'

'Take a seat. I'll be right back,' Cash said over her shoulder as she headed inside to grab another can from the fridge. As she went to shut the door, she hesitated before taking out the container of dip and cheese and snagging a box of crackers. Why not? It was Friday, after all.

'Wow, looks like a feast,' Griff said, jumping to his feet to hold open the screen door for her.

'Thanks,' she smiled, placing the goodies down on the small table and taking a seat. She was getting used to Griff dropping by. Over the last few weeks he'd been stopping in most afternoons. The last few times he'd arrived with presents from his mother, who was a client of Savannah's, and a woman Cash liked a lot, even though they were about as different as two women could possibly be. Lavinia Callahan looked like she'd stepped from the pages of a stylish country-living magazine. Her hair and makeup were always impeccable, but natural and not over the top. Her nails were well maintained but short and practical. Cash knew Savannah adored her neighbour, who'd become a mother figure to her friend, and had been integral in the day spa's success, thanks to her mind-boggling network of contacts around the area. After meeting her, Cash understood her friend's affection. Lavinia Callahan was warm, friendly and had a natural way of mothering people, something Cash had had limited exposure to in her life. Lavinia was always sending little care packages that she brushed off as nothing: a carton of eggs, or containers of lasagne or casserole she'd *accidently* made too much of and would send over with Griffin. Cash suspected this was Lavinia's way of making sure she was eating. It was strange having someone do these little acts of kindness for her. Cash had to admit, she'd grown fond of the gesture.

'Well, you're always bringing me things,' Cash said to Griffin. 'The least I can do is offer you a drink.'

'I've been thinking about a beer all day,' he said, making her smile at his comment as he opened the can and took a long swallow.

Cash tried not to stare as the tanned neck tipped back. It was a nice neck, thick like a football player's, as were his shoulders. Cash gave the man a covert glance, trying to work out why she didn't get that little lurch of attraction. There was a definite kindling, a bit of a flicker—he was a good-looking guy; hell, he was *very* good-looking—but, she thought sadly, despite his good looks, he was *nice*. He was well-mannered and clean cut. *This is the kind of guy you need.* She heard Savannah's voice in her head and resisted the urge to roll her eyes.

'How was your day?' he asked, and Cash realised that while she'd been busy chiding herself, silence had fallen between them.

'It was good. Busy,' she added quickly. 'How was yours?'

'Same,' he said, then dropped her gaze and stared down at the can cradled in his hands.

'How's your mum?' she asked brightly and hoped it didn't sound as forced as it felt.

'Yeah, good.'

Alrighty then. This was going swimmingly. 'I had a booking for your sister and her bridesmaids today. She must be getting excited?'

'Hadley? Yeah. If it goes ahead this time,' he added dryly.

'Why? Did something happen before?'

'They've postponed it twice already. Apparently it's one of the drawbacks of marrying a celebrity TV journalist—if a big story breaks, they have to drop everything, including their wedding.'

'Wow, that's a bit . . .' She wasn't sure what it was. 'Frustrating,' she said, coming up with a polite enough word. Why would they even bother getting married if either of them could ditch their wedding for a story? Didn't bode well for their commitment. Then again, with her relationship track record who was she to judge? 'Your sister must be very understanding,' Cash said doubtfully.

'She's as bad as he is. The first postponement was his, the second time was hers.'

'Huh,' Cash mused thoughtfully as she sat back in her chair. It didn't sound like a great foundation for a marriage. Not that she had any kind of experience of what made a strong marriage. Her role models hadn't exactly been the happy family types.

She gave a mental shrug. *Not my circus, not my monkeys.*

Her eyes followed Griff's tanned forearm as he reached across and took a cracker from the plate. There was nothing wrong with this guy—and yet something didn't feel *right*. They didn't click in a way that made her go all gooey inside. She knew from a combination of Savannah's lectures and a little bit of experience, that less gooeyness and more clean-cut dependable was needed if she wanted a lasting relationship. But while Cash found Griff's polite, quiet ways a pleasant change from the ego-driven men she usually dated, she was finding it increasingly difficult to get the guy to open up. He seemed quite happy to let her talk about herself, to tell stories of her travels, without feeling the need to reciprocate.

'I was wondering—'

The phone interrupted Griff's question, and Cash paused, waiting for him to finish.

'Go answer it. It's okay,' he said, pushing to his feet. 'It wasn't important.'

'You don't have to go,' Cash said as he turned to leave.

'I've got to get back to it anyway. See you around, Cash. Thanks for the beer.'

Cash grabbed the phone, looking over her shoulder through the screen door as she followed Griff's departure with a frown. 'Hello?'

'Were you in the middle of something? I was just about to hang up.' Cash couldn't help but grin at the sound of Savannah's voice.

'Is it just me, or are you sounding more and more English every time I talk to you?'

'It's just you,' Savannah said in a dry tone. 'Everyone here keeps asking me to say weird words like "crikey" and "bonza". Apparently I sound Australian enough to them.'

'No, there's a distinct upper-class English pronunciation thing happening with you. I'm sure of it.'

'You didn't tell me why it took you so long to get to the phone. Did I interrupt something hot and heavy with Farmer McHottie?' Ever since Cash had mentioned Griffin's visits, Savannah had been having a field day with helpful advice on how to snag him.

'As a matter of fact, you did.'

'Really?' Savannah yelped on the other end of the line.

'Okay, maybe not the hot and heavy bit. But Griffin was here briefly.'

'That boy's got it bad. Can't say he ever parked his tractor in my paddock before.'

'I should hope not. You being a happily married woman and all.'

'If Griffin Callahan offered to plough my pasture . . .'

'Savannah!'

'What? I'm married, not dead.'

'Was there a point to this call? Or are you just homesick?'

'No point. I was up and thought I'd call.'

'All good. No dramas. The Callahan wedding party is all booked in.'

'I'm so grateful you were able to take over for me. I swear if I'd had to pass on this wedding, I'd never have lived it down.'

'Well, it wouldn't have been your fault. You and George had this trip booked for months,' Cash said calmly. That was the main reason Savannah had practically begged her to come out and keep the spa open. Hadley Callahan's wedding.

'I just hope there isn't another last-minute cancellation like last time. Anyway, best go.'

'Best go!' Cash mimicked in a chirpy English accent.

She chuckled as her friend muttered a few less than savoury comments before hanging up. Cash turned back to look out through the screen door as she listened to the sound of the tractor fading into the distance.

She hadn't actually considered *actively* searching for Mr Right, but when Griffin Callahan had turned up on her doorstep, it had almost seemed as though fate was throwing her a bone. Or maybe—and much more likely—this had been Savannah's plan all along. Put her in a place where the only single man for miles around was decent and wholesome and she was bound to fall for him sooner or later.

Well, that was ridiculous. You didn't just change the type of person you were attracted to like you changed your brand of shampoo. But the more she encountered Griffin, the more she began to reconsider her stance on the subject.

Maybe she should give it a try? If for no reason other than to prove to Savannah she was wrong.

But she hadn't expected it to become so confusing. She was sure Griff liked her, and yet he hadn't made a single move. Was she reading the signs wrong? Maybe she was losing her touch.

She sighed as she collected the cans and headed into the kitchen. Maybe Savannah didn't have a clue what she was talking about.

Three

Lincoln heard the screen door thump shut and looked up as his brother walked out onto the verandah.

'You're a bit early for the wedding, aren't ya?' Griffin said after the briefest moment of surprise, eyeing him with a curious tilt of his eyebrows.

'Figured I better get out here while I had a chance, in case they called it off again,' Linc drawled.

Griff gave a short grunt, before easing his large frame down into the chair across from Lincoln and stretching out his long legs with a weary sigh. Linc had always been taller than his little brother, until Griff had hit high school. There was something fundamentally wrong about your kid brother being taller than you. Griff took after their mother's side of the family in height and appearance—he'd inherited the Thorncroft good looks, with his chiselled jawline and aristocratic features, as well as the thick eyelashes his sisters had always hated him for. Lincoln still liked to rub that in whenever the opportunity came up, although he secretly envied his brother's well-shaped nose—his own had taken a few hits over the years. What it lacked in prettiness, it made up for in character—at least that's what he told himself.

Lincoln was more like his father's family. The Callahans were darker haired, with a stockier build—the streetfighter to the Thorncrofts' more gentlemanly refinement. A throwback to their Irish descendants.

'How you been?' he asked, handing across a second beer he'd brought out with him a few moments before.

'Same old, same old,' Griff said as he reached out to take the beer. 'Same shit, different day. Someone has to do it.'

'It must be torture, sitting in that airconditioned cabin all day, drivin' backwards and forwards,' Linc grinned.

'Not my fault you choose to go runnin' around in jungles and all the arse-end places of the world.'

'Yeah, well, I spend more time in the frequent flyers' lounge than in the jungle nowadays.'

'So how's that going, being a big-shot businessman?' he asked, downing most of his can in a long swallow as he waited for Linc to answer.

While a large percentage of his daily life involved an office or airport, it was a small company, which meant they were all still boots-on-ground for some of the time. His thoughts automatically went to his last assignment and the near disaster there, but he quickly shifted his focus back to the conversation at hand. 'It was a bit shaky there for a while, but it's starting to pick up now. You looking for a job?'

'Not much call for drivin' tractors in the jungle, I wouldn't think.'

'You never know,' Linc said, taking a sip of his own beer. 'You've got skills that could transfer into a lot of fields.'

'Yeah, right,' he scoffed. 'And leave Dad here unsupervised?' They shared a grin. 'Nah, I only just managed to get him to stop watchin' over my damn shoulder every minute of the day. I think I'm good right where I am, thanks.'

'I reckon there might be another reason why you wouldn't want to move in a hurry.' Linc's grin widened as he saw his brother's eyes narrow suspiciously. 'I heard you've been very neighbourly to a certain newcomer in town. Anything going on there I should know about?'

'Nothin' that's any of your business,' he said calmly, but Linc had more experience than most reading people, and he knew he'd hit a nerve. If it was anyone other than his baby brother, he'd probably back off.

'So the rumours are true then,' he said thoughtfully.

'If by rumours you mean what Mum's been saying, then you should know by now she's clutchin' at straws. Ever since high school she's had me married off to anyone I've happened to look at twice.'

'Yeah, but you're not getting any younger, Griff,' Linc said, rubbing his chin with mock concern.

'You can talk. You're closer to a midlife crisis than I am.'

'Midlife crisis,' Linc scoffed, throwing his brother an irritated glare. *Bloody young upstart,* he thought indignantly, then almost groaned when he realised he sounded exactly like their father. *Shit.* Maybe he *was* getting old. 'Shut up,' he told Griff, who gave a chuckle.

'Ah, brotherly love.'

Lincoln glanced up as his elder sister, Harmony, walked towards them. Tall and slender, she was another sibling who'd inherited the Thorncroft genes. Actually, the reason he'd got so little was probably because Harmony had taken most of them before he was born. Her hair was a much lighter shade than both the boys'—it was a honey brown, but with lighter blonde highlights which he noticed now, surprised, were actually grey. When had that happened?

'Hey, Mon.' He stood up and greeted her, noticing how fragile she seemed in his embrace. She pulled away quickly and gestured to the two teenagers standing behind her. 'Payton. Holder. Say hello to Uncle Lincoln.'

The two sullen-looking youngsters shuffled forward reluctantly. 'Hey, kids. Wow, you've both shot up since I last saw you.' Actually, it shocked him how much they'd changed. The last time he'd been home they'd still been little kids. Now they were . . . he quickly did the sums in his head and realised they'd be fourteen and twelve. How did they change so much in such a short space of time?

Payton rolled her eyes before mumbling a bored, 'Hi,' and Linc felt his eyebrow rise in response. *What was with the attitude?* He took in the T-shirt that left her midriff bare and the skimpy denim shorts and wondered what the hell was wrong with his sister. Why would she let her daughter leave the house half-dressed? Inside his head, his younger, cooler self asked if he'd like a walking frame, and he swore silently. He was *not* getting old, damn it!

'So do you, like, still kill people and stuff?' The comment snapped his attention onto the boy. Holder had his mother's lighter hair and hazel eyes and, while he didn't have the same bored expression as his sister, there was still something about the kid that rubbed Linc the wrong way.

'Only when they annoy me,' he said and heard Harmony give an exasperated sigh.

'Don't tell him that. No, your uncle does *not* kill people.'

Beside him, Griff nodded at their nephew before giving a grimace and making a slicing action across his neck with a finger.

'Griff! Stop that,' Harmony snapped, turning her son away. 'Go inside and see if Nan needs any help. You too, Payton, and stop rolling your eyes!' she called as her daughter turned and walked away.

'Wow, Mon. They've sure grown up. When did that happen?' Linc said in the quiet that followed the kids' departure.

'While you've been away,' his sister said, and he didn't miss the slight edge to her tone. He knew over the years he'd disappointed his family more times than he could count by not being able to make it home for the usual celebrations. More than once he'd been left feeling like crap after making the phone call home to break the news that he wouldn't be there after all. His mother's understanding voice on the other end of the line always hit him harder than if she'd broken down and cried. The fact she would never allow him to hear her disappointment only made it worse. He loved his family, felt a fierce protectiveness towards them, but he'd let them down because serving his country had always had to come first.

That, in part, had been the driving force behind starting his own business. He'd realised how much he'd missed. He was basically a stranger in his own family.

'Well, I'm home for a while this time.'

'How long?' Mon asked.

'Four weeks or so,' he shrugged.

'Just in time for harvest,' Griff said, eyeing him thoughtfully.

'I figure it's about time I pulled my weight around here. I'm sure you'll find me something to do.'

'You remember how to drive a chaser bin?' Griff drawled.

'It hasn't been *that* long,' he protested, although, truthfully, it had been a while since he'd been home during the crazy season. It was always a race against the clock or the weather. Anything that could go wrong usually did, and inevitably there was a machinery breakdown or several, no matter how much preparation you put into maintenance beforehand.

'What about your business? Surely you can't take off that much time?' Harmony asked, her frown almost identical to the one Griff was wearing.

Her tone instantly set him off. 'Jesus, Mon. What are you, the freaking CIA?' The instant he snapped at her, he regretted it and made an effort to soften his tone. 'That's why I have partners. Besides, they have the current jobs under control and I can still run stuff from this end. Technology, people,' he said, forcing a grin. 'You pretty much control everything with a mobile phone and laptop nowadays.'

Harmony still didn't look convinced, but Griff didn't seem overly perturbed.

'Do Mum and Dad know?' Griff asked just as the screen door opened and their parents came out.

'Do Mum and Dad know what?' Bob Callahan asked, carrying a platter of food for his wife.

'How long Dumble Dork here's staying,' Griffin said, sending a swift nod at his older brother.

'Isn't it wonderful?' Lavinia beamed at her children. 'And as soon as Hadley gets here I'll have all my babies home. The first time in . . . I don't know how long.'

'You'll be beggin' to go home in a week,' Griffin predicted, sending his brother a doubtful look.

'You're just scared I'm gonna show you up,' Linc shot back.

'Yeah, right,' his brother scoffed, folding his arms across his chest.

'That's enough, you two. Here, eat something,' Lavinia said, thrusting a plate of tiny quiches between the men.

'So where's Don?' Linc asked, looking up at his sister as she took a seat beside their father.

'He'll be here a bit later.'

'Still at work?' Griff asked, and Lincoln wondered at the undercurrent he was detecting between his siblings.

'I would assume so,' Harmony replied, but her smile seemed brittle and Linc made a note to ask his brother about it later. 'How's Cash today?' she asked, reaching for her wineglass but not before she sent her younger brother a too-innocent look.

Griff's mouth hardened slightly but he gave an offhand shrug. 'She's all right.'

'When am I going to meet her?' Linc asked as he reached for another quiche.

'Probably never. Griff still hasn't asked her out yet,' Harmony informed him.

Normally Lincoln would have jumped all over that piece of news, paying out on his brother unmercifully, but Griff's tight-lipped expression warned him that this was a sore point. He must be getting soft. Once upon a time he'd never have let a little thing like his brother's feelings get in the way of making fun of him. It was what siblings did.

'You'll get to meet her tomorrow night,' his mother piped up, causing Griff to almost give himself whiplash as he turned and stared at his mother.

'What?'

'I invited her this afternoon. I forgot to mention it to you to ask her, and when I called she said you'd just left.'

'You did *what*?' Griff stared at their mother in alarm.

'She asked your girlfriend out on a date for you,' Harmony explained without disguising her glee. Clearly these two had no qualms about walking on eggshells.

'Harmony,' Lavinia cautioned lightly. 'I did nothing of the sort, darling,' she said, soothing Griffin's growing horror. 'I simply invited her to dinner. She's a neighbour and I thought it was the right thing to do. Besides,' she added, 'if you're interested in someone, I think it would be nice if everyone got to know her a little bit better.'

'Jesus, Mum!'

'I don't know what you're getting all huffy about. I promised Savannah we'd take care of her. She must be lonely over there by herself.'

'You should thank her, Griff. She did you a favour. It's not like you were ever going to work up the nerve to ask her out.'

'Shut up, Mon. It's not like you're an expert on relationships,' Griff snarled and instantly an uncomfortable silence fell on the small group.

'Considering everyone else seems to know her, it'll be interesting to see what all the fuss is about,' Linc said, before changing the topic. 'How much rain you had lately, Dad?'

From the corner of his eye he saw that Griff still sat stiffly, and Mon's cool demeanour spoke volumes. Something was definitely going on there. If his parents were aware of the problem, they didn't show it, other than a confused frown they'd swapped during the brief exchange. For now, the conversation stayed on safe topics, but whatever was going on between Griff and Mon needed sorting out before things got out of hand. This wasn't what he'd been expecting. Becoming a negotiator between his siblings didn't sound like the kind of R&R he'd been hoping for.

Four

Cash swore under her breath as she tossed yet another outfit onto the bed. This was ridiculous. 'It's just dinner with the neighbours, not an audience with the damn Queen,' she muttered to herself, but somehow it was more than that.

She liked Lavinia Callahan, but she'd been trying to play matchmaker with her son since the first day they'd met and, while things were moving along slowly with Griff, Cash wasn't actually sure how she felt about tonight. What if the whole family tried to push them together? She could only imagine Griff's reaction to that. He'd seemed oblivious to his mother's blatant attempts to organise meetings between them by getting him to drop things over to her—his shyness surprised her. He was a good-looking guy, and in her experience attractive men were usually confident—if not overly confident a lot of the time. Not Griffin Callahan though. Not for the first time she wondered what his story was. There had to be one. And it wasn't from lack of trying to get it out of him—he wasn't much of a talker.

A quick glance at her watch and she let out another frustrated groan. If she didn't leave now, she'd be late. Cash snatched up the first top she tried on, a white lacy blouse with loose three-quarter sleeves, and grabbed the long floral skirt from its hanger. She slipped her feet into a pair of white sandals and headed out to the kitchen to grab her handbag and car keys.

The Callahans might be her next-door neighbours, but the entrance to their property was six kilometres further up the road. Distances still astounded her out here, and this wasn't even as remote as some of the towns further west. The gate to Stringybark Creek wasn't elaborate—she'd seen a few on her drive out here that were grand stone structures or beautifully stained timber and curved brick walls with property names in gold-plated signs. Not Stringybark Creek. It surprised her. The Callahans were an old established family and their property one of the largest in the area, but there was nothing ostentatious about them or their place. As she drove up the long dirt driveway, she took in the bush that lined the narrow road and realised that once, a long time ago, this bush would have covered the entire region. It seemed almost impossible to imagine how difficult the job would have been for those first settlers, clearing so much of this land by hand in order to build their homes and graze their livestock.

As she rounded a bend, the house came into view and Cash caught her breath at the sight. The sprawling home sat in a clearing surrounded by an oasis of green. Lush manicured lawn was bordered by brightly coloured gardens. The house itself was similar to an old Queenslander, but not as high. A sweeping double staircase led to a massive front door, and the tin roof drooped low to cover the timber verandahs in traditional bullnosed fashion. It was breathtaking.

She parked the car beside two other vehicles and walked around to take out the cake she'd baked for dessert. As she closed the passenger side door, she heard footsteps on gravel and looked up to see Griff.

She smiled at him. *He really did have a nice face.* 'Here, let me carry that,' he said, taking the plastic container from her.

'Oh, thanks. I hope I'm not late.'

'Nope, I only just got home myself.'

'You've had a big day,' she said, glancing at her watch. She knew he started at some ungodly hour of the morning—he'd told her so during one of their limited conversations.

He gave a nonchalant shrug. 'Had to get some stuff finished before it rains.'

'It's going to rain?' Cash gave the sky a quick glance but it didn't look particularly cloudy.

'Supposed to, but I'll believe it when I see it. Come on in. Mum's been cooking up a storm all day.'

She followed him along the path towards the five or so steps that led onto the verandah and then came face to face with a large number of Callahans seated on various outdoor chairs arranged around a massive rectangular table.

Idly she wondered what the collective term for a group of Callahans would be—a gaggle? A mob?

'Cash!' Lavinia greeted her warmly, hugging her and then leading her over to meet the others. 'Everyone, this is Cash. Cash,' she said, turning her beaming smile upon her, 'this is my daughter, Harmony, and her husband, Don. Their children, Payton and Holder. I'm not sure if you've met my husband Robert?' She indicated the well-built man who stood up from his seat and came across to shake her hand.

'No, I haven't,' Cash said, smiling. 'Hello.'

'G'day, love.' Cash instantly liked the man. There was a gruff warmth to him.

The screen door opened and Cash glanced up. She felt a sudden weird flutter in her chest. Blue-grey eyes met hers and Cash felt a prickling sensation of awareness glide over her body.

'There you are, Linc. Cash's here,' Lavinia's voice was the sensible splash of cold water she needed. 'This is Griff's brother, Lincoln. He surprised us by arriving yesterday.'

Cash forced a smile to her lips, nodding a hello, unable to trust her voice. Linc seemed momentarily caught off guard too, but recovered quickly enough, his own smile crinkling the corners of his eyes attractively. Although in looks he was very different to his brother, more like his father, with a rounder shape to his face, she saw a resemblance in their chin and jawlines. His short shaven hair was darker than his brother's, and the stubble on his lower face gave him an unyielding, dangerous appearance. A little light inside her head began to flash in alarm.

'I've heard a lot about you, Cash. Nice to finally meet you,' he said, holding out his hand. Cash hesitated only briefly before reaching out. His skin was hard, not callused like Griff's, but toughened by the elements. They were not office hands.

'What would you like to drink?' Griff stepped up beside her and Cash blinked away the strange sensation that had fallen over her. 'Wine, beer, soft drink?'

'A beer would be fine, thanks. Can I help?' She hoped that didn't sound as desperate out loud as it had in her head.

'Nah, it's fine. Take a seat.'

Lavinia fussed about, taking the cake from Griff and nodding towards the chairs scattered around in an informal cluster. Cash slipped into a seat next to Harmony, and avoided taking a look at the other man, who had taken up position leaning against the verandah railing.

'I've been hearing amazing things about you,' Harmony said, taking a sip of her wine, tilting her head slightly as she studied Cash.

'Oh?' What could she say to that? The woman looked friendly enough but there was a coolness beneath the surface that made Cash wary.

'Everyone in town's been raving about your massages and treatments. I'll have to make a booking.'

'I'm really enjoying the spa.'

'How do you know Savannah?' she asked, taking another delicate sip of her wine.

'We're old friends. We used to work together up in the Whitsundays.'

'Is that where you came here from?'

'No. I've been working overseas and, more recently, in Sydney.'

'I wouldn't have thought working in a place like Sydney you'd be interested in coming out here.'

Cash gave a nonchalant shrug. 'I was ready for a change.'

'So how long are you here for?' Linc asked, and Cash was grateful for the reprieve from his sister's interrogation.

'Until Savannah and George get back. Sometime after the new year.'

'What then? Back to Sydney?' Harmony asked.

'I haven't decided yet,' Cash admitted. The truth was, she had no idea what she was going to do next. Usually she had some kind of rough plan, but the whole Dale thing had caught her off balance, and with Savannah's offer coming almost straightaway afterwards, there hadn't been time for making plans. All she knew was she needed to get away so she could lick her wounds in private. Once upon a time, after a break-up, she would have had a cry, thrown her belongings in a bag and moved on. This time, though, she was finding it harder to make a decision about where she wanted to go next.

Griffin came back and took the seat beside her before handing her a glass of beer—no beer in a can today.

'Do you live nearby?' Cash asked Harmony, feeling a need to redirect the questioning.

'We live in Griffith.' Harmony sipped the last of her wine and reached for the bottle to refill her glass.

'What line of work are you in, Don?' she asked, realising the man seated beside his wife hadn't said a word yet. He was dressed in a button-up white shirt and camel-coloured chinos. The other men were dressed in an assortment of denim and T-shirts, and Don's casual boat shoes were a stark contrast to the work boots.

'Real estate,' he said, eyeing her curiously. 'Not in the market to buy a place of your own, are you? I have one or two properties that might interest you.'

'No, not at the moment, thanks,' she declined politely.

His phone started ringing and he pulled it from his pocket. 'Let me know if you change your mind,' he told her, standing up to take the call without a backward glance.

'Don't be long,' Harmony told him with an annoyed frown as he walked past her, disappearing around the side of the verandah. Cash watched her take a long sip of her wine, almost downing half the contents.

'So you're settling in all right over there?' Bob asked, breaking the small lull in conversation.

'Yeah, It's great. I'm really enjoying the peace and quiet.'

'Can't be too quiet over there with this fella doin' so much work over that way,' Bob said, giving his youngest son a dry glance.

Cash saw Griff's face tighten slightly, and a small blush creep up his neck. 'I hardly hear him,' she said, feeling sorry for the poor guy. 'But I was pretty glad he was nearby that day the cattle got through the fence.'

'Yeah, sorry about that, they're buggers for breakin' through fences when they set their minds to it,' Bob said.

'I haven't heard this story,' Harmony said, refilling her glass again. 'Tell us.'

Cash looked at Griffin and he gave a *sure, what the hell* shrug. 'It was the first day I'd been there by myself. I walked out the back and there were all these cows.' Cash remembered the panic she'd felt seeing a herd of cattle happily grazing in George's orchard and gave a shake of her head. 'I tried to shoo them all back through the fence, but apparently I don't speak fluent cow, so they weren't being too cooperative,' she said dryly. 'Luckily Griff was working nearby and came over to see what was going on. He managed to get them back home and fixed the fence for me.'

'Our hero,' Harmony gushed, toasting her little brother silently.

'He was a hero. To me,' Cash said, suddenly irritated by his sister's sarcastic tone. 'I had no idea how I was going to get them out.'

'Thank God you were there, Griff!' Harmony continued with a mocking, wide-eyed glance.

'Knock it off, Harm,' Griffin told his sister, and surprised Cash when he casually dropped his arm across the back of her chair.

'What? I'm happy for you two,' Harmony continued.

'Harmony, can you come and give me a hand in here for a moment, darling,' Lavinia called from inside, and Cash breathed a sigh of relief when the other woman rose to her feet and excused herself. She wasn't sure what her problem was, but clearly there was something going on between brother and sister. Harmony didn't seem to be a very happy person.

Conversation turned to general questions about the weather and farming. Cash found Griff's dad funny and easy to talk to. His brother, on the other hand, was a very different story. He didn't contribute to the conversation much, and although he didn't say or do anything to make her uncomfortable, there was something disconcerting about him, something she couldn't quite figure out.

Five

Linc leaned back against the railing and tried to get his head together. When he'd walked outside a minute ago, he hadn't been expecting the swift kick of attraction he felt when he set eyes on Cash—*his brother's girlfriend*. He wished the last reminder was enough to cool his roaring libido. It wasn't. What the hell was his brother *doing* with a woman like that? She wasn't even his type. Griff did serious relationships; he'd had the one steady girlfriend all the way through high school until they broke up after going away to uni. Then he'd met Tiffany at ag college and they'd been together almost four years until she'd taken off on an overseas job. Ever since then, Griff hadn't had a steady girlfriend as far as he knew. He liked the quiet, studious ones. The girls that you took home to meet Mum. Although Cash seemed to have won over his mother, from all the gushing he'd had to listen to since arriving yesterday.

And yet here Griff was with Cash. Cash with the tattoo and a smokin' hot body. She was nothing like the sweet, Sunday-school-teacher kind of girl Griff usually went for. Admittedly, Cash probably wasn't *trying* to look hot, but there was just no denying the woman's curves under that outfit. His gaze fell on her crossed legs and the way she casually swung one strappy-sandalled foot every now and again. *Christ, even her feet were sexy.* The delicate black and red spiral that graced the top of her foot and wrapped around her ankle in a vine did things to him he wasn't sure a foot was supposed to do. There was a free-spirited, rebellious streak about her, and he somehow suspected that underneath her fresh-faced appearance there was a wild side to Cash Sullivan.

As she lifted her long hair, he caught the briefest glimpse of black lines at the base of her neck. More tattoos. He itched to find out just what else she was hiding under those clothes. The thought excited him more than he cared to admit.

'I like your piercing,' Payton was saying. His gaze zoned in on the tiny glitter of a stud in her nose that he'd missed.

'Thanks.'

'Do you do them at the spa?'

'Yes, actually, I do. I'm a qualified body piercer.'

She didn't look like any body piercer he'd ever seen. The ones he'd seen looked like walking advertisements for their trade, with huge holes in their earlobes and studs in every conceivable body part. Cash looked clean-cut and wholesome in comparison.

'Cool,' Payton said, looking wistful.

'What is?' his sister asked, coming back outside.

'Cash does piercing over at the day spa.'

'Don't even think about it, young lady.' Harmony narrowed her eyes at her daughter.

'I like your tattoo too.'

Cash smiled graciously at the younger girl, but after noticing the less-than-thrilled look on Harmony's face, she dropped her gaze back onto her drink.

'Once I'm eighteen I'm getting my nose pierced and a tattoo,' Payton informed everyone in general, but clearly it was aimed at her mother, who looked anything but excited by the prospect.

'Go right ahead if you want to look like a delinquent. Good luck finding a job,' Harmony said, and instantly Linc's hand tightened around his glass of beer as he saw Cash flinch slightly.

'I've got tats and I've managed to work ever since leaving school,' he pointed out.

'It's different with men,' his sister shrugged.

'Cash has both,' Payton pointed out, oblivious to the backhanded insult her mother had just given the woman.

'Your mum's right, Payton,' Cash said calmly, and Linc was impressed by how dignified she sounded. 'You should think very carefully before getting a tattoo. They last forever and people can be very quick to judge you once you have them,' she added, taking a sip of her beer before coolly holding his sister's gaze.

He bit back a smile.

∽

'When did you get yours?' Payton asked.

Cash followed the girl's gaze to the finely scripted ink words written on the inside of her lower forearm. She remembered the day she'd walked into the small back room of the tattoo parlour and given the handwritten quote to the burly tattoo artist. 'I got this one when I was about nineteen, I guess. But you should take your time and think about what you want to put on your body—make sure it's important enough to live with for the rest of your life.'

'What does that one mean?' the girl asked, still looking at the quote on her arm that read: *Rise and rise again, like the Phoenix from the ashes, until the lambs have become lions.*

'It's a reminder about never giving up.'

The teen pursed her lips and gave an approving nod of her head.

'Robert, the roast is ready to be carved,' Lavinia called and began directing everyone to take a seat at the large timber table.

'Ignore my sister. She's not usually like this. I don't know what her problem is lately,' Griff said quietly as they stood up to walk across to the beautifully set table further along the verandah.

'It's okay.'

'It's not.'

Cash saw that he was genuinely angry about it and put her hand on his arm gently. 'I'm a big girl. I can handle your sister,' she smiled. 'She's probably just having a bad day. It's no big deal.'

His brother pulled out a seat on the other side of the table and Cash caught his eye. It was only brief, but it made her pulse leap automatically in response, and she dropped her hand from Griff's arm, busying herself with taking a seat to cover the fact she was uncomfortably flustered.

What was going on? She'd known Griff for weeks. Why would she be acting like this over his brother, who she'd known all of two damn minutes? Griffin was reliable and kind. *Focus on Griffin. You do not need to be sidetracked by hormones and a pair of blue eyes that do unnerving things to your heartbeat.*

Dinner was a unique experience for Cash. Dining with a large family wasn't something she'd ever done. Her own family was about as opposite as you could get to this. She listened with interest as Bob and Lavinia spoke about the area and the neighbours, how the community pulled together and the mind-blowing number of committees they were both involved with. Bob had been a member of the local rural fire brigade for almost thirty years and she was surprised to discover that Griff was also. It made sense, she supposed. After all, out here, who else was going to defend their properties and the town?

Throughout the conversation and meal, Cash noticed that Don left the table twice to take business calls, making her wonder if there was some kind of sudden boom in the real estate market in Griffith. There was something a little too slick about Don. Harmony didn't speak, she just drank more wine and seemed to withdraw inside herself, while the two teenagers ate their meal in sullen silence, sneaking glances down at their laps to the phones they were trying to discreetly play with.

'Payton. Holder,' Harmony snapped when she finally glanced over and caught the two children playing on the devices. 'Put those phones away, right now.'

'But Dad gets to use his,' Holder whined.

'Your father's working. Put them away.'

Cash thought Payton was about to argue, but one glance across at her grandparents and she wisely closed her mouth, sliding her phone into her pocket and picking up her cutlery to resume eating.

Don returned a few moments later without bothering to apologise for the interruption, and Cash wondered if anyone else was picking up on the distinct chill coming from the far side of the table where Harmony and her family sat. It was none of her business—she didn't even know these people—but clearly there were some major issues going on in Griff's sister's marriage. *Not my circus*, she repeated firmly. She had enough issues of her own to deal with without taking on anyone else's.

After dinner, Cash pushed her plate aside and stifled a groan. She couldn't think when she'd last eaten so much food. 'Thank you, Lavinia, that was amazing.'

'I'm so glad you enjoyed it, Cash.'

'You've outdone yourself, Ma,' Griff agreed, leaning back in his seat and dropping his arm across the back of Cash's chair once again.

'You say that after every meal,' Lavinia chided him lightly, but Cash saw a warm glow in the woman's face and knew she loved taking care of her family. She tried to imagine what growing up with a mother like Lavinia would have been like, but couldn't. 'Well, I hope you saved some room for dessert.'

Cash almost groaned at the thought of more food but smiled bravely. She could only imagine what dessert would be like following the delicious meal she'd just eaten. Maybe she had a little more room to squeeze in a taste of whatever culinary delight Lavinia had whipped up.

Cash rose from the table as everyone started gathering the plates but was waved back into her seat. 'You just sit there and relax,' Lavinia said. 'Griffin will keep you company while we get dessert ready,' she added, and Cash tried not to cringe at the blatant attempt to orchestrate some alone time for them.

Griff happily handed his plate across to his brother to take inside and added a 'Thanks, mate' just to add insult to injury.

'I hope they haven't scared you off tonight,' he said quietly, looking into his beer after they'd all gone.

'Your family's great,' she said and honestly meant it, although she wasn't sure what he was trying to ask by 'scaring her off'—that sounded a little more serious than the neighbourly drop-ins they'd been sharing over the last few weeks.

'You're a hit with Mon's kids.'

Cash gave a small smile. 'I'm pretty sure your sister thinks I'm a poor role model.'

'Nah, she's just going through some stuff right now. Don't take it personally. It's the first time I've seen Payton actually have a conversation that didn't involve one-word answers and eye-rolling.'

'Anything that a mother wouldn't approve of will always be something a teenager thinks is cool.'

'Mon's just a bit of a . . . perfectionist. I think she's struggling with her kids becoming teenagers.'

Somehow Cash thought there was a bit more to it than a stressed-out mother of teenage children, but, again, it wasn't any of her business.

Lavinia came back out carrying plates and everyone else soon followed with an assortment of dishes, including Cash's cake. This wasn't a simple dinner, this was a feast of gargantuan proportions. Oh, dear God, the food.

Cash refused to sit while everyone else cleaned up after dessert and helped carry in the last of the plates. The kitchen was a chaotic traffic jam of bodies and clinking cutlery, and with no idea where things belonged, Cash was actually in the way and didn't argue when she was ushered outside once again.

'I just need to borrow Griff for a minute though,' Lavinia said, grabbing hold of her son. 'Linc'll keep you company for a few minutes, won't you, darling?' She smiled up at the startled face of Griff's older brother.

'I'll be fine, Lavinia,' Cash tried to protest, feeling more than a little awkward that she somehow needed to be babysat, particularly when this guy clearly didn't feel like being the babysitter.

'Nonsense, out you go,' she said, shooing them from the kitchen, and Cash went, feeling like a naughty child that had just been banished by the grownups.

Six

Linc knew he was playing with fire the moment he made the decision to go outside. He should have said no, but then, who was he kidding? As if anyone ever said no to Lavinia Callahan. He walked across the timber floorboards, leaning back casually to rest his back against the verandah post.

For a long moment they stood there in silence, listening to the sounds of the night all around them as the clinking of crockery and the low murmur of conversation went on inside the house. He figured his mother wanted some serious talk time with Mon and Griff. After their exchange earlier, he'd seen her frowning and knew that look would be followed by *please explain* at some stage later. Cash leaned forward, resting against the verandah rail with her arms draped across the top as she stared out into the darkness, drawing Linc's gaze to the inscription on her inner arm.

'"And when they seek to oppress you, and when they try to destroy you, rise and rise again and again, like the Phoenix from the ashes, until the lambs have become lions and the rule of Darkness is no more",' he quoted softly.

Cash looked over at him in surprise, then a slow smile spread across her full lips.

'It's by Maitreya, from the *Holy Book of Destiny*, if I'm not mistaken.'

'Or Russell Crowe from *Robin Hood*,' she added with a grin. 'Do you know the entire quote?'

'Not really, I vaguely remember it says something about casting stones and building churches. I thought I'd impress you with the bit I *did* know.'

'Yeah, that *was* pretty impressive,' she grinned.

'What drew you to that particular quote? You said it meant something to you, earlier.'

For a moment he didn't think she was going to answer him. He saw the smile slowly melt from her lips, replaced by a reflective sadness. 'I came across it one day. I'd just lost my brother, and my mother the year before, and then my father . . . left,' she said, and he got the feeling she'd amended what she was going to say. 'I'd just decided I was going to make some pretty big changes in my life, and I think this felt like a mantra of sorts, you know?' She looked up at him quickly, before dropping her gaze to stare at the writing. 'I wasn't going to give up and I wasn't going to be a meek, frightened lamb anymore. I was going to be a lion.'

'Well, it seems to have worked.'

'I don't know how much of a lion I became, but it helped me stay focused. Griff said you were in the military?'

'Used to be. Now I'm in business with two mates and we run a crisis management company.'

'I'm guessing you handle a particular kind of crisis . . . not like wedding plans going awry because of a double-booked venue or something?'

Linc chuckled and shifted his weight a little. 'We handle things for companies that have employees in foreign countries who get themselves in trouble—car accidents, trouble with the law, illness . . . that kind of thing.'

'And what do you do to help?'

'We either contact people we have in that particular country or we go over there ourselves and try and untangle whatever mess the client's got themselves into,' he said, liking the way her head tilted slightly as she listened to him. 'We also handle things like risk management and travel briefings. We inform clients about how to keep their staff safe in hostile environments. We provide security and medical assistance if needed. All kinds of stuff.'

'It certainly doesn't sound boring,' Cash said. 'Was it hard getting out of the army and becoming your own boss?'

He looked at her curiously, surprised by the question.

'I assumed after so many years being told what to do, it would be strange to suddenly be making all the decisions yourself.'

He'd never been asked that before and it threw him off kilter a little. It *had* been a weird thing to get used to.

'It was, but we've pretty much got the hang of it now,' he said with a ghost of a smile.

'That must be very rewarding.'

'It's a relief that I can put the skills I've learned to practical use outside the army.' That had always been his biggest concern whenever he'd contemplated life out of the military. What would he do? He couldn't imagine doing anything else. He'd been sick of spending so much time away from home and being at someone else's beck and call, day and night, and the pay was lousy compared to what some guys were getting working civvy jobs, but he'd never complained about risking his life for his country—defending Australia was one of the values he held sacred. Maybe it was cliched to some people nowadays, but to him it had always struck a deep chord.

Then the decision about leaving had been pretty much made for him. A flash of memory forced its way into his mind and he heard the roar of the explosion followed by a barrage of rubble that rained down around him, biting into his skin, the dust billowing and filling his mouth and lungs with the chalky debris. He hadn't been able to stay in any longer. So he'd got out.

'Do you miss it out here?' she asked, dragging him back from the past.

'Yeah, I do. Which is funny, considering I couldn't wait to get out of this place when I was a kid.'

'I know what you mean,' she agreed as she looked out into the darkness. 'I was the same, I couldn't wait to leave either.'

'Where did you grow up?'

'Mount Druitt. A lot of people get stuck there in a kind of vicious circle. I wasn't going to let that happen to me.'

'Do you still have family there?'

'Not anymore,' she said, and he could tell she was done talking about it by the steely edge to her tone.

'Everyone's different, I guess. Just look at me and Griff. He's the complete opposite—he couldn't wait to get back here after uni and he's been here ever since.'

'Could you ever see yourself moving back here?' she asked.

'I don't know. Not really. I mean it's always going to be my home—I guess as you get older you see things differently than when you were a kid. I can't see myself farming for a living. That's Griff's thing, and in case you haven't noticed, unless you're a farmer there's not a whole lot else to do out here.'

'Unless you're a beautician,' she pointed out.

Linc chuckled. 'Somehow I can't see myself becoming a beautician either.' She smiled at that and he felt a strange warm sensation spreading through his chest.

'Has he bored you to death with all his war stories yet?' Griff asked as he came out to join them, and Linc was surprised by the momentary flash of annoyance his brother's appearance caused.

'Nope, not yet,' he heard Cash say as she eased back from where she'd been leaning, to face Griff. 'We were just discussing career options out here.'

'Must have been a long discussion,' Griff said dryly.

'I don't know, I think your mum and Savannah are onto something with the B&B idea.'

'Just think, Griff, you can deliver the breakfast trays to the rooms before you head out for the day.'

'Oh yeah, like that's gonna happen.'

'Mum sounds pretty keen,' Linc said, eyeing his brother.

'She's still gotta sell Dad on the idea yet.'

'Yeah, it's not like Mum usually gets her own way about anything . . .' He smirked at his brother's forlorn expression. Their mother *always* managed to talk their father around. It was just a matter of time.

'I think I better be getting home. I'll just go in and say goodbye to everyone,' Cash said, and he tried to ignore the disappointment her leaving sparked in him.

After Griff and Cash walked away, he let out a long, frustrated sigh. What the hell was happening to him? Whatever it was, he needed to get it in check fast. For everyone's sake.

Seven

The night was cooler than the day, but there was still a warmth to the air. Cash didn't think she'd ever get tired of the country smells. It wasn't always the clean, fresh air you always read about in books; at times the smells weren't exactly pleasant—cows and mud and fertiliser were hardly romantic—but to Cash there was something wholesome about the smells of animals and dirt. A rustic grittiness that made her senses come alive. Tonight she could smell hay and grass and climbing jasmine that was growing on a fence nearby.

'I hope that wasn't too painful,' Griff said as they reached her car.

'I had a good time. Your family's great.'

'They have their moments, I guess.'

'I'd have given anything to have grown up in the kind of family you have.'

'You never talk much about yours.'

Cash fought the familiar dread that always followed questions about her family. It was easier not to talk about it. Over dinner she'd managed to evade the issue. She'd given vague answers to questions about where she'd grown up and where her parents were. It was just simpler to say they'd both passed away when she was young. She hated the sympathetic looks that always prompted, but it was better than the flinching, mouth-dropping horror that followed her telling the truth. There just wasn't a pleasant way of saying, 'My mother killed herself and my father was involved in gang warfare and is currently in prison for murder.'

'Like I said, if I had a family like yours, I'd be very happy.'

Griff's eyebrows dipped slightly at her comment and he watched her intently, one arm resting along the top of the roof of her car, blocking her access to the driver's door. There was nothing threatening about his position, but there was something different about him. He'd always kept a friendly distance between them when they'd been together—non-threatening and comfortable. Tonight, just like earlier when his arm had gone across the back of her chair, he seemed to be making some kind of statement.

Griff was different to any other man she'd ever been interested in. His laidback, almost shy nature was something she didn't have a great deal of experience with. The men she'd grown up around or usually found attractive were confident, dominating types—like her father. They didn't tend to be the sort to waste time on taking things slowly or putting people at ease. Griff confused her that way. It was refreshing, and it made her feel differently about herself, but it also made her worry that maybe she was doing something wrong too. Why hadn't he kissed her yet? Was he aware there wasn't quite that spark between them? Maybe she was really screwed up and just didn't get 'normal'. Damn Savannah! This was all her fault. If her friend hadn't put the idea into her head about giving someone different a try, she'd never be in this position. She wouldn't be second-guessing every little thing.

Maybe people weren't supposed to suddenly change the type of people they dated? Maybe you were attracted to the kind of men you were attracted to for a reason? She'd always made excuses to herself—that real life wasn't like a movie or a book; men didn't really treat you as though you were their queen and something to be cherished and respected. Real life wasn't a fairytale. Then she saw Savannah and George together. Her best friend—the one person who had consistently been there for her, the one person who had seen her at her worst and still loved her—had found a man who treated her like the most precious, rare and beautiful thing on earth.

Cash had received a call from Savannah, begging her to come to Bali for her wedding. Cash had gone without a second thought, but more with the intention of talking sense into her friend. Only once she'd seen the two of them together, she'd realised there was no need.

The love she saw in this man for her best friend stunned her. Maybe love wasn't just for fairytales, after all?

Maybe if Savannah found it, then she could too?

As soon as the thought entered her head she shook it away. She couldn't imagine it. She couldn't see any of the men she'd ever had a relationship with making her want to give up her life—her freedom—to settle down. And yet . . .

'I'm glad you came tonight, Cash,' Griff said, and Cash held his gaze as well as her breath as he leaned closer slowly.

She lifted her head slightly to meet his lips as they gently touched hers, warm and surprisingly soft. He didn't deepen it and their bodies didn't touch anywhere else, but she could feel the heat from his body where he stood. It was the softest of kisses, undemanding yet pleasant, and when he slowly pulled away, Cash was left feeling strangely unaffected. She'd been waiting for something more. It was their first kiss, he was holding back and being considerate; she sensed that was just the way Griffin was, but she'd wanted more. A spark of fire, a swirl of excitement in the pit of her stomach, anything, and yet it hadn't come. What was wrong with her? Why couldn't she fall in love with a nice gentle guy like Griffin Callahan?

'I'd better get home,' she said, mustering a smile that she hoped hid the conflicting emotions and disappointment that were threatening to leak out through her eyes. She had to get away from here before that happened. 'Thank you for tonight.'

She sent a brief glance up at his face and wished she hadn't. She knew he'd sensed what she was feeling. She saw the hurt written across his handsome features before he managed a grimace-like smile and stepped back to allow her to get into the car. She wanted to explain that it wasn't him, it was her, but she knew that would only make it worse. How could she explain that she just wasn't attracted to him? He was perfect. And yet there was no spark.

'Watch out for roos on the road,' he said as he carefully closed the door, which only made her feel more terrible. He even worried about her driving home!

She turned on the ignition and waved. As she took a last glance in the mirror she saw the dark silhouette of Griff watching her, his shoulders hunched slightly, his thumbs hooked in the front belt-loops of his jeans as he stared after her.

'You're a bloody idiot, Cash Sullivan,' she muttered, switching her eyes back to the road ahead.

Eight

Linc sat outside and watched the first faint pinks of the sunrise touch the horizon. He loved this time of the day when everything was fresh and full of promise. There was optimism in the start of a new day. He hadn't slept well last night—not that *that* was unusual, but the nightmares had started again. They seemed to come in waves, as though waiting for him to let down his guard before they rolled in.

It didn't take a genius to work out why they were back again now. It was because of Baghdad and the fact he'd almost lost a client to a stupid mistake. He'd lost his concentration for a split second, but it had been long enough for everything to have almost gone to shit. He still couldn't believe how close they'd come. He'd been distracted by a face from his past—a face that haunted him.

A cold sweat had broken out on his back and forehead as he'd gazed across the road at the young boy standing in a doorway. The black-eyed stare had pierced through Linc's body like needles. It was impossible. The kid was dead. It wasn't real. On some level he knew his mind was playing tricks on him, and yet the image held him transfixed. It was only for a second, but it felt like hours. Long enough for the guy he was supposed to be protecting to be shot at. At the very last minute Linc came to his senses and tackled his client to the ground, saving him from injury. It should never have happened. He should have noticed the car slowing down as it passed by them, the gun at the window. He would have, had he not let his mind play tricks on him.

Linc squeezed his eyes shut and massaged the bridge of his nose as he clamped down on the memories. The squeak of the screen door hinge made him open his eyes and ease back in his chair.

'You look like shit,' Griff said as he walked past, carrying his own cup of steaming coffee to take a seat beside him.

'Thanks.'

Griff leaned back in his chair and looked out over the shadowed landscape, cradling his coffee. 'How'd you sleep?'

Linc glanced over at his brother. 'Not great.'

'So I heard.'

Linc glanced up warily. 'What do you mean?'

'I heard you wake up a few times.'

Great. 'So much for privacy.'

Griff grinned and threw him a sarcastic glance. 'Not much has changed, especially the thickness of the walls. It was almost as bad as being next door to you as a teenager.'

'Pervert.'

'Well, they were wrong about one thing. It clearly doesn't make you go blind.'

'Shut up,' Linc grunted in surprised amusement. 'You can't talk. Anyway, don't you have your own house? Why are you sleeping here?'

'It's only temporary. Mum's in the process of repainting the bedrooms in my place. Apparently I'm giving up the old house for the Samualses when they get here for the wedding.'

Her sister's fiancé, Mitch Samuals, and his family were from Sydney's North Shore and their mother was on a mission to make sure everything was spick and span before their arrival.

The brothers sat in silence, distracted by memories of growing up in the old house. Sometimes Linc wished they could go back to those days, back before he knew the horrors humans were capable of inflicting on one another.

'You have nightmares often?' Griff asked, breaking the silence.

Linc didn't feel comfortable talking about the dreams with anyone, especially his younger brother. He hated that they made him seem weak or messed up in the head. It didn't match the image his family had of him and he felt like a fraud.

'Nah,' he brushed off Griff's concern, feeling panic begin to raise its ugly head. He needed a distraction. 'How come you didn't go home with the sexy neighbour last night? You losin' your touch or something?'

He knew he'd hit a sore spot as soon as his brother's expression hardened and his hand tightened around his mug. 'It's not like that,' he muttered.

'Like what? You like her, don't you?'

'Yeah. But we're not . . .' He let the sentence fade and Linc frowned a little in confusion.

'Why not?'

His younger brother leaned forward abruptly, rubbing a hand across the back of his neck. 'I don't know. She's . . .'

'What?' Linc tried not to evaluate why he was so eager to find out what the problem was. He had a feeling it wasn't entirely in his little brother's best interests.

Griff was shaking his head slowly as he stared at the wooden floorboards beneath his booted feet. 'She's so . . . she's hot as hell.' He gave a sigh. 'When I'm around her, I can't even speak—I'm like a goddamn mute. Then last night . . .'

Linc tried to focus on staying nonchalant but his own thoughts were a mess of conflicting emotions. He felt like an arsehole for hoping his brother and the hot neighbour hadn't hit it off, which just proved what a shit he really was.

Griff gave a low, mournful groan before putting his cup down and rubbing his hands briskly across his face.

'What about last night?' Linc prompted after Griff stopped talking.

'Never mind.'

'No, really. What happened?'

He watched as his brother leaned sideways and picked up his cup once more, slumping in his chair and staring moodily out across the paddocks. 'I kissed her.'

'And?'

Griff slid him a sideways glance. 'You practising to be a relationship counsellor or something?'

Shit. He must have sounded desperate. *Get a grip, dickhead.*

'Nothing,' Griff finally said, sounding defeated.

'What do you mean, nothing?'

'I mean,' he said after tossing down the remainder of his coffee and getting to his feet, 'I kissed her and . . . nothing. She wasn't into it. She practically ran away.'

A silent cheer went up inside his head before he tackled it to the ground and pushed its head into the dirt to shut it up. 'Maybe you misread the situation,' he said.

'Yeah, maybe. Who knows. Anyway, I got work to do.'

Linc stared after his brother thoughtfully. He felt bad for him—no one ever liked rejection—but what the hell was he doing chasing after a woman like Cash anyway? They had nothing in common—nothing *he* could see anyway. She had more in common with—*No.* He wasn't going to make a play for his little brother's girlfriend . . . or whatever she was supposed to be. Maybe coming back home for this long was a mistake after all.

Linc let out a long breath and cleared his thoughts. Coming home was exactly what he needed. A few weeks of good, honest hard work and he'd be back to his old self again. He just needed to keep busy and stay out of trouble—which meant staying away from Cash Sullivan. That woman was trouble with a capital T.

Nine

Cash had spent the night tossing and turning and woke up feeling out of sorts. After her second cup of coffee on the front verandah, she felt slightly more human and ready to face clients for the day, but she couldn't shake a lingering uneasiness. She'd been curious to see if anything would happen with Griff. She really liked him, but if the bazinga wasn't there when they kissed, then there wasn't much hope that it was going to appear any time soon. Sadly, attraction, the feel-it-in-your-bones kind of attraction, was something that was either there or it wasn't.

An image of Lincoln Callahan flashed through her mind and she clenched her jaw. *No. No way.* She'd spotted that guy a mile off. He was trouble—a heartache waiting to happen. She knew it as certain as she knew her own face in the mirror on the wall—the one that was glaring at her now. He was exactly the kind of man she needed to stay away from. Him and his sexy stubbled jaw and sleeve-busting biceps. And those perceptive blue eyes, the kind that seemed to strip back her layers and see everything she wanted to hide.

Nope, she wasn't going to shake that particular apple tree. There had to be plenty more decent, nice . . . *normal* men out there if she wanted to pursue this stupid theory of Savannah's and try a decent guy for a change. This was the country, for God's sake!

❧

Linc pulled up outside the farmhouse and blew out an irritated sigh. This had not been his idea. Griff was taking last night's flop badly. It wasn't something Linc really understood—so there'd been no chemistry? What was the big deal? If he'd had a less than thrilling experience with a woman, he wouldn't be moping about it the next day. He'd be putting it down to a lesson learned and moving on. Clearly Griff didn't work the same way.

There were plenty more women in the sea; at least, there always had been . . . although now he thought about it, this was Rankins Springs and maybe the area had been overfished in recent years . . . Maybe Griff *did* have a reason to pout after all.

When their mother had asked Griff if he'd mind dropping off some baking to Cash this morning, he'd stood up from the table and walked away, muttering some excuse about being too busy, leaving their mother to turn her baffled expression onto Linc. Seeing as he didn't think his little brother would appreciate him explaining what the problem was, Linc had ended up agreeing to the chore just to keep the peace. Not that seeing Cash was exactly a chore. Still, he wasn't sure why it was so important to deliver the woman biscuits . . . today.

When he went to knock on the front door he noticed the sign that instructed any enquiries to be directed to the day spa through the side gate. He was tempted to leave the goods on the bench seat next to the door, but he didn't want to be in trouble with his mother if any of the contents weren't supposed to be left out in the sun. Dropping his head in silent defeat, he headed towards the side gate and followed the path that wound through a gravelled garden. Inside he could hear the low murmur of voices and again hesitated. Was it frowned upon to interrupt whatever the hell they were doing in there? He really didn't feel like getting yelled at. He was just about to place the container at the door when two women came out from a back room, stopping at the front desk.

He saw the surprise cross Cash's face when she saw him, but she managed to smile and finish her farewells without skipping a beat. He nodded at the woman who exited the salon; she smelled like coconut oil and was very shiny. She also wasn't from around here if the silver Audi she got into was any indication.

'What are you doing here?'

Cash's irritated tone snapped him from his pondering. 'It's nice to see you again too,' he said, cocking an eyebrow at her. 'Mum's been baking.' He held up the container.

'Sorry,' she muttered, rubbing her arms before crossing them defensively across her rather delectable chest. 'I didn't sleep well last night.'

Interesting, he thought, watching her body language. His presence seemed to make her feel threatened. 'Yeah, well, Griff's been walkin' around like a bear with a sore head too, thanks to you.'

'How is that my fault?'

'He's got it in his head that you're not interested in him anymore.'

'Excuse me?'

'He told me what happened last night. Put the poor bloke out of his misery and call him or something.'

Cash lifted an eyebrow at him, jutting out a hip with her arms still crossed. 'I'm pretty sure that's none of your business.' Then she turned abruptly and headed into a nearby treatment room.

'Normally I'd agree with you,' he said, following her into the room and watching as she began tidying up, 'but you're not the one who has to live with him, and it's really starting to bug me. So what's the deal with you two anyway?' he asked, reaching out to pick up a bottle of something that was labelled *face exfoliant* and inspecting it curiously.

Cash took it off him and put it back down on the table. 'There is no deal.'

'The way everyone's been acting, you two should be just about ready to tie the knot.'

'Oh, for goodness sake! Doesn't anyone have anything better to do around here than gossip?'

'You're really *not from here,* are you?' he said with an amused shake of his head.

'What gave it away?' she asked sarcastically.

Linc braced his arms on the side of the bed behind him and gave her a slow grin. 'The fact that you're surprised people are talking about you. Haven't you ever lived in a small country town before?'

'No.'

'Huh,' he said, as though turning this unusual prospect over in his mind, before pushing away from the bed and moving across to the table as something else caught his eye. 'What the hell kind of kinky torture instrument is this?' he asked, looking perplexed at the plier-shaped plastic gadget.

'It's a sculpturing tool for brows. Look, thanks for dropping this over, but I have to get the room set up for the next client.'

'Okay, fine,' he said, replacing the instrument before turning back to face her and catching a subtle blend of lime and vanilla, 'but just do me a favour.' She looked up at him, and her eyes seemed more muted today, the colour more fern-tree green in the centre. He swallowed and tried to concentrate on what he'd started saying. 'Don't write off Griff so fast. He's . . . he deserves a shot at—' He stumbled on his words all of a sudden. No, Griff didn't deserve a shot at her, he'd had his shot and blown it! *What the hell?*

Linc shook his head slightly and winced when he saw her eyes squint a little as she regarded him curiously. 'He's one of the good guys,' he hurried to finish.

He saw her expression soften and then sadden. 'I know he is.'

All of a sudden Linc wished he hadn't witnessed this moment of vulnerability, hadn't seen how much this woman cared about his brother's feelings. It made him feel even worse for having a moment of complete disregard for anything else other than his own selfish interests. Her tone told him everything he needed to know. There was no hope for Griff. Linc cleared his throat. 'You should probably tell him. So he knows.'

'Yeah. I will.'

Linc gave her a sharp nod before turning away. He was a basket of mixed emotions himself. He felt shitty for his brother who was about to get the 'It's not you, it's me' speech, but he also felt a strange anticipation beginning to fill him. Cash would soon be free again.

Yep, he was most likely going to hell . . .

Cash was a little surprised when she heard a car pull up outside late the next afternoon and opened the door to find Griff standing there. He cleared his throat after saying hello, shifting his weight from one foot to the other.

'Would you like to come inside?' she asked, opening the door wider.

'Ah, yeah, sure.' He took hold of the screen door as she turned and led the way into the kitchen, automatically going to the fridge to grab some drinks. As she handed Griff a beer, she watched him stare at it silently for a while before saying in a rush, 'About the other night . . .'

Cash swallowed nervously and put her own beer on the table in front of her as she waited. She really didn't want to have this conversation, but it needed to happen. It wasn't fair to let him hold out hope, but she felt terrible and she genuinely liked him.

'I wanted to know if you'd like to go out to dinner with me . . . Being thrown to the wolves like that with the family wasn't really fair . . . I think it kinda had something to do with what happened . . . later.'

'Griff, I—'

'If we had a chance to do it over again, it'd be different, I reckon,' he said finally as he looked up at her.

'I had a lovely time with your family the other night . . . it wasn't that,' she said slowly. 'Griff, I really like you, but—'

'No. It's okay. You don't have to say it.' He quickly got to his feet. 'It was a stupid idea anyway.'

'Griff, wait. It wasn't.'

'Yeah. It was. I was kidding myself that someone like you would be interested in a guy like me.'

'What? No, that's not true. Griff, I really like you. You're funny and good-looking and kind . . .'

'And not your type.'

'I didn't say that.'

'You didn't have to. I might be from the country but I'm not stupid. I could tell you weren't interested after we . . . You don't have to spell it out for me.'

'If you knew there was nothing there, then that means you didn't feel it either, Griff,' she said quietly, hoping he'd lose that kicked-puppy look.

'That's the problem, Cash. I did feel it. I've felt it from the moment I set eyes on you. It was always there for me.'

Cash felt her heart sink at his quiet words, unable to say anything to stop him as he calmly let himself out of the house. Why couldn't she just be a normal person who fell for normal men? She felt too miserable to make any dinner for herself, instead taking her unopened can into the bedroom and switching on the TV to let the mindless babble drown out the lecture she was giving herself inside her head.

Ten

Lincoln reversed the ute into the machinery shed, turned off the engine and grabbed his hat from the passenger seat. He'd been out fixing a neglected length of fencing that had been placed in the 'one day when we get the time' basket. There were a lot of those jobs around the place, the kind of things that needed doing but weren't urgent. While he was home he hoped to clear a few of them off the list for his father and brother.

He'd never seen the appeal of farming for a living. When they were kids they'd been expected to do their fair share of the work and it had been intense. By the time he was old enough to leave school, he was well and truly over it. But now it was different. He didn't see the work as tiresome and boring, it gave him a chance to unwind. He craved the peace and quiet of the land, and working with his hands gave him a quiet sense of achievement.

As he headed into the house he heard voices out on the verandah, indicating his parents had visitors. He washed up briefly before heading out to make an appearance, hoping to make a quick exit afterwards. He really didn't feel like company tonight and hoped it wasn't anyone he'd feel obliged to stay and talk to for too long. His hopes were dashed when he saw it was the Dawsons, long-time friends and neighbours. He bit back a groan, fixing a smile to his face as he came forward to greet them.

'Here he is!' Bill said, shaking his hand heartily. 'It's good to see you.'

He greeted the man and then turned to kiss his wife, Sue, before taking a seat and gratefully accepting the can of beer his father handed him.

'Your dad's been telling us about your new venture. Bloody interesting.'

Griff appeared around the corner, having finished up for the day as well. He took a long swallow of his beer as he listened to the conversation, his arrival seemingly going unnoticed by the others. Linc envied his brother—they didn't all look at *him* so expectantly, hanging on his every word as though he was some kind of celebrity. This was what he hated the most about coming home to visit. He knew his parents and friends were proud of what he'd done in his years serving in the military, but he hadn't done it for the accolades. It was his job. It was what all those years of hard work and pushing himself to the limit, both physically and mentally, had prepared him for.

It'd been the damn medal that had changed everything. It didn't matter that it had been years ago, all everyone ever remembered was the bloody medal. Good men had died that day. Friends. It'd been one of the worst combat fights he'd ever been involved in—a veritable blood bath. He hadn't done anything that every single man there wouldn't have done given the opportunity. His actions may have saved the lives of the majority of his unit, but he couldn't save all of them and that's what hurt the most.

When he'd joined the army, he'd already known he wanted to be a commando. He'd had a plan fixed firmly in his head even back them. He'd wanted to be part of something bigger. He'd wanted to challenge himself. He'd wanted to be the best of the best. Even though he knew what was ahead of him, what it would take. When he'd finally gotten selected for the commando course, it was much harder than he'd expected. Nothing had prepared him for the absolute limits he'd be pushed to and the strength it would take to overcome the fears and physical pain in order to push himself and make it through selection. But he'd done it for himself—not to become some kind of hero. Although maybe in the beginning he'd had a bit of an ego, and knowing how proud his dad was of him after he'd been such a disappointment to him as a farmer had been pretty huge, but that was before. Before the years of dealing with the reality of war and witnessing the very worst of humanity.

'You've done so well, Linc,' Sue added, nodding in agreement with her husband. 'You should be very proud of yourself.'

Linc forced a weak smile, even though his insides were recoiling. Proud was the last thing he felt. His gaze fell away from Sue's beaming face and landed on his brother's, catching the silent snort he gave before downing the remainder of his beer. Griff was the only person *not* caught up in the hype and praise. It should have annoyed him that his kid brother thought he was an absolute tool, and maybe it did a bit, but strangely it was refreshing. Around Griff at least he didn't have to pretend. It was as though Griff could see through all the bullshit. He didn't enjoy the feeling, but at least he didn't have to feel like a fraud, the way he did right now.

'I better go and have a shower,' he said, backing away.

'I can't believe you're putting him to work, Bob!' Sue exclaimed. 'He should be resting.'

'Yeah, Dad. War heroes can't be expected to lower themselves to work around here like the rest of us mere mortals,' Griff drawled, eyeing Linc cynically as he crumpled his empty can and brushed past him on the way inside.

Linc stared after his brother as the screen door shut behind him, the words replaying in his head. Linc thought they'd gotten past this. Griff's resentment had started slowly. At first Linc had thought he was just being the usual pain-in-the-arse kid brother he'd always been, but with each visit over the last few years, it seemed to grow. He'd thought this visit would help change that. He'd thought that by coming home to work, it'd show Griff he was serious about wanting to help out, but apparently even helping pissed Griff off.

ஃ

'You wanna tell me what's got you so ticked off?' Linc said later as he went into his brother's room.

'Not really, no.'

'Well, do me a favour and stop being such a dick.'

'Me? Look who's talking.'

'What did I do wrong?' Linc demanded.

'Nothin'. You never do anything wrong. You're the golden child, remember.'

Linc stared at his younger brother. Not this old argument again. 'Give it a rest.'

'Yeah. Whatever. We don't want to upset the hero.'

'If you've got something to say, man up and say it. Stop poutin' like a freakin' kid. I've had a long day and I don't need your shit.'

'Long day?' Griff gave a snort and shook his head and Linc immediately bristled.

'I came back to help you and Dad out. I don't have to, you know. I could sit out there on the verandah and watch you bust your arse if I wanted.'

'So what? You want a medal for that too?'

'Okay. You keep being a miserable arsehole, I've got better things to do than waste my time here.' Linc left the room, barely containing the urge to hit the wall.

One day Griff was going to push him too far. Most of his visits home in the past had been relatively short and he'd managed to keep a rein on his temper, mainly out of the knowledge that it would break his mother's heart if her two boys fought. This time, however, he was home a lot longer and his temper was a hell of a lot more volatile lately. Turning the other cheek and cutting his younger sibling some slack was not going to be as easy when he'd have to do it for weeks on end. Nope, the time was definitely drawing near when he and Griffin would need to take a little drive and sort things out once and for all.

Cash pulled into the petrol station on her way back from a daytrip into Griffith. She'd put aside most of today in order to stock up on groceries, get a haircut and pick up some supplies for the salon. She hadn't seen a real shop in weeks. Although she missed the convenience of big retailers and having a multitude of outlets on her doorstep, just getting into the regional town of Griffith had been enough to brighten up her day. However, after the first few hours Cash had found herself strangely craving the peace and quiet of the little farmhouse. Even Griffith's laidback hustle and bustle felt a little too busy for her. It was something she wasn't about to tell Savannah, though, or she'd never live it down.

She listened to the pump ticking over as it filled her thirsty tank and let her eyes roam the quiet street before her. The main road through town was wide and straight. The shady park across the street beckoned invitingly to the few tourists who'd pulled over in their caravans, and the sound of birds and insects provided a gentle backdrop to the sleepy little town. Old houses and shops, which had long since closed, lined one side of the main street. There was still a quiet charm to the little town, despite the fact there were very few services available. Lavinia had told Cash that the greatest concern for the town was that there were fewer and fewer families staying here. The primary school numbers had been dropping significantly over the last few years, and without a surge of young families with children, it was at risk of closing.

The pump clicked off and Cash took out the nozzle, hanging it up before reaching for the petrol cap she'd placed on the roof of the car.

A vehicle pulled up on the other side of the bowser and Cash muttered a curse as she dropped the petrol cap and watched it roll under her car.

'Looking for this?' a deep voice enquired from beside where she was kneeling on the ground.

Cash glanced up, seeing the crooked smile on Linc Callahan's face as he held up the petrol cap.

'Yes. Thanks,' she added, getting to her feet and dusting off her knees.

'Back from a bit of retail therapy?' he asked, and Cash frowned, wondering how he could have known where she'd been.

He nodded towards the back seat of her car where a heap of plastic bags sat.

'Salon supplies,' she told him as she finally managed to tighten the cap into position.

'How's things in the world of beauty?' he asked casually, leaning an arm on her roof.

'Fine,' she answered, tilting her head to consider him carefully. 'You're one of those men who thinks beauticians are a waste of money, aren't you?'

'No,' he said, sounding surprised. 'I guess I always picture them as pampering rich women who have nothing better to do. Seems a bit of an extravagance.'

'Maybe in some places, but usually it's ordinary women who come in to de-stress from their lives.'

'So you really enjoy the job?'

'Yeah, I do. It's a great feeling to know you've made someone feel better after they walk out of your salon. Everyone deserves to feel more confident and better within themselves.'

'It's not all a bit too . . . I don't know . . . self-absorbed?'

It wasn't an unusual attitude, but thankfully it was becoming rarer. In the city, a fairly large proportion of her clientele were male. But there were still some places where men were sceptical of the beauty industry. 'It's not only waxing and pampering. We get lots of people coming in with skin problems. They're probably the most rewarding clients. Some people live all their lives with bad skin or facial hair that robs them of their confidence. Helping them gives them their confidence back and the freedom to go out and enjoy life again. It's not defending the country, but it's what I do,' she said with a shrug.

She saw him frown and straighten at her comment. 'I wasn't trying to put you down,' he said, and she got the feeling he was bothered by the thought.

'Well, I can see how it pales in significance compared to what you do. Then again, I guess most jobs would.'

He opened his mouth to reply but a loud crash and bang cut through the quiet as a woman across the road dropped the metal lid of a garbage bin. Cash's gasp caught in her throat as she found herself bodily slammed into the side of her car, with Linc plastered against her, shielding her . . . from what, she had no idea. It happened so quickly she didn't have time to protest, but within seconds he was pushing away from her and scanning the street.

Cash felt her heart still pounding in her ears. *What the hell just happened?* Hesitantly she straightened her T-shirt and tucked a stray strand of hair behind her ear, keeping a wary eye on the man who was now standing, shoulders hunched and hands shoved into his pockets, staring down at the cement beneath his feet.

'Sorry about that,' he muttered. 'Instinct.'

'Instinct?' she repeated faintly. 'You often instinctively throw yourself at strange women out of the blue?'

'I just heard . . .' He stopped abruptly. 'Look, I'm sorry.' He rubbed his hand across the back of his neck. 'Sometimes noises like that catch me off guard. Are you okay?' he asked, looking at her directly for the first time.

'I'm fine. Are *you*?'

She saw his concern hastily slip away and he dropped his gaze once more. 'I'm fine. I better let you go.'

'Yeah,' she said, making to move towards the service station to pay for her petrol.

'Cash, wait,' he said, stopping her. 'Look, I'm about to head up to the pub before I go home, come up for a drink?'

'I should probably get home . . .'

'Come on, just one? I don't want you goin' off thinking I'm some weirdo.'

Cash quirked an eyebrow at that but smiled. 'We couldn't have that, could we.' She was relieved that the earlier awkwardness seemed to have vanished. 'Okay, I'll stay for a quickie,' she said, before adding quickly, 'a quick drink.'

Linc chuckled as he inserted the nozzle into his tank. 'I'll meet you up there in a sex . . . I mean sec,' he added with a wink.

'In your dreams,' she muttered, although for some reason it may have sounded more wishful than disdainful.

❧

The double-storey pub curved around the corner of the street and upstairs boasted a huge wrap-around verandah. A few years earlier the only pub in Rankins Springs had closed, but then it had become the centrepiece of a massive event when a couple of enterprising young men got two celebrity radio hosts to launch the reopening after a group of local families joined together to buy it. Looking around at the almost deserted street, it was hard to imagine the crowds of thousands the event had drawn, but Cash wished she'd been here to see it.

'What can I get you?' a friendly-faced bartender asked as Cash took a seat at the bar.

'A lemon squash, thanks,' she said and looked around the hotel.

'Here you go, love,' he said a few moments later, placing the tall glass of pale lemon drink before her.

'You can add a beer to that too thanks, Mal,' Linc said, coming up behind her.

'Hey, Linc! I heard you were back. How's things?' Mal beamed, reaching across the bar to shake Linc's hand firmly.

'Yeah, good. Only been home a few days.'

'Back for the big shindig?'

'Yeah. Things are getting pretty hectic.'

'I can imagine. Still, it's good business for us. We're booked out with your sister's bigwig guests, and I hear they're even running a bus into Goolgowi and Griffith for accommodation. Sounds like one hell of a party.'

'You know Hadley. She never does things by halves.'

'Found the pub okay, I see,' Linc said after Mal turned away to get his beer.

Cash grinned at that; even she couldn't possibly get lost here. 'Lucky I had Google Maps on my phone,' she told him.

'How's your old man? Haven't seen him for a while,' Mal asked as he took Linc's money and hitched a foot up on something on the other side of the bar, settling in for a yarn.

Linc sent a quick apologetic glance across at her. If his constant stream of questions were any indication, Mal was delighted to see Linc. Or it could be that the man just liked a good chinwag and they were the first customers he'd seen all day. Either way, Cash didn't have to worry about anymore awkward chat with Lincoln—she couldn't have gotten a word in sideways if she'd tried.

Over the course of the next ten minutes or so, more people came in and joined the conversation. It didn't take long to realise just how well thought of Linc was in his home town. He was like a mini celebrity, albeit a reluctant one, holding court with a small crowd of bright-eyed fans—they genuinely loved him. She knew he'd received some kind of medal, she wasn't sure of the details. Griffin had mentioned it briefly and she hadn't thought to ask more about it, but clearly it was a big deal.

The incident at the car earlier played through her mind. He'd called it instinct. It made sense, she supposed—as a soldier he'd have learned to respond instinctively to danger. It may have only been a harmless garbage lid dropping, but in another place and time that sound could have been a gunshot or a landmine going off. Who knew what kind of havoc that would play with a person's nerves. It spoke volumes about the guy that when he'd sensed danger he'd thrown himself in front of her instead of taking cover himself.

He seemed to know everyone in the pub pretty well, but there was something about the way he held his body—his shoulders were stiff and his hand seemed to be clenched around his beer glass—that gave Cash the impression he was not at all comfortable.

She finished the last of her drink and slid from her bar stool, lightly touching Linc's arm and ignoring the hardness of the bicep beneath her fingers.

'I'm sorry to cut in, but I need to get going . . . Did you want to get that thing out of my car before I leave?' she asked, holding his confused gaze for a moment before leaning closer. 'You know the thing your mother wanted you to take home . . .'

After a moment the confusion dulled and was replaced by a flash of relief and Cash knew she was correct in suspecting Linc was not enjoying the swarm of attention he was getting. 'Oh, yeah. That . . . Sorry Mal, everyone, I have to get going. Great to catch up,' he added, standing and backing away from the bar.

'You're back for a good while, so we'll catch up again,' Mal said with a wave farewell as they walked out the front door.

'There isn't actually a thing . . . is there?' he said, breaking the quiet as they walked towards their cars.

'No.' She smiled.

'Just checking. Thanks.'

'I had a feeling you were looking for an escape.'

'Yeah. Big time. Sorry about that. So much for going for a quiet drink.'

'That's okay. Your friends miss you.'

'I don't get home all that often, and I haven't been in there for a couple of years.'

'Well, they all seem to think a lot of you.'

'Yeah. I don't know . . . I've known them all my life.'

'It's more than that. They're proud of you. You're like the homegrown hero.'

She saw his mouth turn down slightly at that and a small twitch in his cheek gave her pause. 'I'm not making fun of it. I think it's awesome how much your town loves you.'

'It's weird. It happened years ago and they still all want to talk about it. That's why I stopped going out when I came home. I never know what to say to people . . . I'm just me, you know, and they expect me to be something, I don't know, special.'

'I don't think you have to be anything other than yourself,' she said, watching him as he fiddled with the keyring he held in his fingers.

'Yeah, well . . . it's a bit hard when everyone thinks your one thing and you're not.'

Cash wasn't sure what to say to that. The guy was a hero. He'd won a medal. He'd risked his life fighting for his country. That wasn't your everyday average bloke. But she really didn't know him well enough to argue the point and so she let it go. 'Well, thanks for the drink. I guess I'll see you around.'

'Thanks for what you did back there . . . seriously, I'm grateful,' he said.

Her eyes roamed across the taut face before her. He was so . . . intense. And then she made the mistake of locking eyes. His gaze pulled at something deep inside and it scared her. This wasn't just attraction. It wasn't even knee-shaking lust. It was something primal—a need for . . . something. It was the *something* that terrified her. She wasn't sure she was brave enough to find out what it was.

He moved forward the slightest bit, barely half a step. Cash froze. Her breath caught momentarily before resuming normal function, only he was so close that each time her chest expanded they almost touched, and the warm, clean male smell that filled her senses only made her breath quicken again. There was no way he was going to believe he didn't affect her. He didn't move, he just stood there, watching her, waiting for her to make the first move, and damned if she didn't want to.

Swallowing hard over a suddenly dry throat, Cash eased away, and with only the tiniest of spaces between them, she felt commonsense begin to return. She tried to ignore the loud protest of regret as she fumbled for her car keys and unlocked her door.

'I have to go,' she said, forcing herself to calm down and act like the normal, rational adult she wanted to be.

'See you around, Cash,' he said, and his gravelly voice sent unexpected goosebumps along her arms.

As she drove away she felt the bands of attraction loosen, and she was able to breathe again. She hadn't been expecting a reaction like that, and it only reinforced her earlier thoughts that the man was off limits. She'd been down that track before—her commonsense sideswiped by lust. Men like that only ended up breaking your heart. Well, not this time. Nope, she was going to stay well away from Lincoln Callahan.

❧

Linc parked the car in the shed and dropped his head back against the headrest as he thought back over the incident at the service station, letting out a long, slow breath. He clenched his hands around the steering wheel while the memory replayed.

Of all the times for him to have a reaction. He'd felt like an absolute moron afterwards. He was just lucky he hadn't copped a smack across the face. While in his head he'd been back in the thick of it, doing what he was trained to do, civilians going about their daily business were hardly likely to understand why they were getting jumped on.

It wasn't so much the noise that had made him react, it was the *unexpected* noise. When you were in a firefight, it was loud. That went with the territory. But when you heard an unusual crack or bang or pop it was only ever a prelude to something bad—a bomb or a gunshot . . . getting messed up or, worse, getting *dead*. It was hard to turn off the instinct that reacted to danger when you got home. After a while, it didn't happen so often, but now and again it liked to sneak up on you, to remind you.

He resisted the urge to groan out loud. He could only imagine what a screw-up Cash must think he was. When he was done feeling sorry for himself, he realised she'd been pretty cool about the whole thing, considering. His spirits momentarily lifted, before an annoying little voice in the back of his head reminded him that making a play for his brother's girl probably outweighed anything bad she could possibly be thinking about him.

As far as days went, this one was turning out to be pretty bloody shit.

Eleven

Cash wasn't sure what to expect when she first met Hadley Callahan—she'd seen her on the news of course, but she'd never really paid that much attention to her—not that she'd ever admit that out loud around here. But it was true—she never paid much attention to the actual person reporting the news; she just watched the story, often with a sad shake of her head and an uneasy feeling in the pit of her stomach.

However, the woman who appeared in the salon was nothing like she might have imagined. She was tiny for starters. She wasn't sure why but she'd thought someone risking her life in one war-torn country after another would be bigger . . . tougher, somehow. Hadley Callahan was neither of those things to look at. She was stunning. Thick blonde hair fell in bouncy curls around her face and down to her shoulders. Her amber-coloured eyes were studying Cash curiously, with a lingering amusement that made Cash wonder what the woman had heard about her.

'You must be Cash,' Hadley said, sticking out her hand in a brisk businesslike gesture.

'I am. And you'd have to be the famous bride-to-be.'

'That would be me, yes,' she said dryly but flashed Cash a smile. 'I think everyone's waiting for me to announce it's called off again, though.'

'Oh well, it's good to keep them all guessing,' Cash shrugged, leading the way into the small sitting room that was used for consultations. 'Can I get you something to drink? Tea, coffee, water?'

'No, thanks. I've just come from morning tea with Mum and the aunties. I had to leave before they fed me anything else. I don't know how they think I'm going to fit into my wedding dress if they keep up all that food.'

'They certainly do like to cook,' Cash agreed. She sat down across from Hadley and picked up her notebook to start making arrangements for the wedding day makeup schedule. 'So how many bridesmaids are you having?'

'Seven,' she sighed.

Cash didn't say anything as she wrote it down in order to calculate the time and cost.

'Yeah, I know, bordering on pretentious. But there's certain protocols you have to follow around here,' she explained with a roll of her eyes. 'You have to have your immediate family, so that's Harmony, then cousins, and only *then* can you ask your actual friends.'

Cash bit back the smile at Hadley's weary explanation. It seemed no one was immune to Lavinia Callahan's influence. As she stared down at the numbers on the page she bit the side of her lip. This was going to take some creative juggling to fit everyone in. It looked like she would be needing Savannah's backup beautician from Griffith. They discussed colours and preferences, and Cash tried some shades on Hadley until they were both happy.

'So, I have to ask, what's going on with you and my brother?'

Cash was glad she wasn't in the middle of applying eyeliner or she would have probably poked the woman's eye out as she gave a small start at the unexpected question. 'Nothing,' she said quickly, and immediately regretted it when she saw Hadley's shrewd gaze zero in on her face. *She's a reporter, you moron! She's trained to sense fear!*

'I'm not interested in . . . I mean, he's not here for long and neither am I, so it's kind of pointless really.'

When the blonde's eyebrow raised slowly, Cash snapped her mouth shut and stopped talking.

'Actually, I was referring to Griff . . . but apparently I haven't been updated on the situation.'

'Griff? Oh. Yes, I really like him. It's just . . .' *Oh, dear Lord, would you shut up!*

'Linc arrived,' Hadley finished for her with a knowing grin.

'No, it isn't like that. *Really*,' she stressed.

'Relax, Cash. I'm not judging you,' she shrugged lightly. 'I was a little surprised to be honest. You're not exactly Griff's usual type.'

'His usual type?'

'He normally goes for the sweet and meek,' she explained dryly.

'Oh.' Okay, so she wasn't sweet or meek . . . apparently.

'Don't get me wrong,' Hadley said quickly, 'I'm not saying there's anything wrong with you—I'm hardly the sweet-and-meek type myself. I was just surprised, that's all,' she nodded thoughtfully as she considered Cash. 'It makes more sense that Linc would be the one.'

'Linc is *not* the one,' Cash said, then remembered who she was talking to. 'I mean he's not my type.'

'Really?' Hadley asked doubtfully.

'Well, not anymore. I'm done with . . . his type.'

'Don't let appearances fool you. Linc's one of those still-waters-run-deep kind of guys. I wouldn't write him off too soon.'

'I'm afraid I'm done with complicated alpha men. I'm looking for someone a bit more low maintenance. That is *if* I were actually looking . . . which I'm not.'

Hadley gave a chuckle, her eyes lighting up. 'Then you probably should stay away from all the Callahans.'

'Yeah, I kind of figured.'

'Actually, it would do Linc the world of good to have his world shaken. Don't be too quick to dismiss him,' she said kindly, before standing up to leave. 'Oh. Actually, I almost forgot,' she said, turning back to face Cash. 'Mum said to come over for afternoon drinks. Something to do with wedding preparations and help you offered, I don't know.' She lifted her hands helplessly, as though she had no idea, and Cash might have believed it a little more if she hadn't caught the flash of mischievousness in the woman's eyes before she turned away.

Cash was too surprised to protest immediately, and then it was too late, Hadley had already walked out and Cash was left to stare fretfully at the empty doorway. *Great.* Another Callahan gathering, and this time she'd have to face Griff after their awkward last meeting. And then there was Linc. This was a bad idea on so many levels, but she'd had to go and open her big mouth to offer help, hadn't she? It wasn't like she could just not turn up. Lavinia would probably come over and pick her up. *Note to self, don't open your fool mouth ever again!*

~

Linc watched the car pull up and felt something a lot like excitement kick him in the gut. He hadn't been aware that Cash was coming over and, judging by her wary expression, she didn't really want to be here.

'Oh good. She came,' Hadley said, coming up beside him. He was standing with his arms folded across his chest and she slipped her arm through his.

'You knew she was coming?' he eyed his sister warily.

'I invited her,' she said, looking rather smug.

'What are you up to?' Hadley had that look in her eye, the one that always led to trouble. Like the time she'd decided to write her own newsletter and distribute it around town, taking on animal rights in the meat industry . . . That had gone down a treat with Dad and every other farming family in the area.

'Nothing,' she smiled up at him sweetly, before letting go of his arm and walking over to greet Cash.

Linc looked around for his brother and spotted him talking to Olivia Dawson, his sister's best friend. Griff hadn't seen Cash yet, and Linc inwardly winced at what his reaction might be.

'Cash!' his mother said, gracefully getting up and coming over to greet her guest. 'What a lovely surprise.'

The realisation that Lavinia had had no idea she was coming seemed to be a shock to Cash as well, if the colour draining from her face was any indication, but Hadley, as always, was smooth to jump in and defuse the situation. 'I roped her in to coming along to help. You must be rubbing off on me after all these years, Mum,' she said, sending a bright smile at Lavinia.

'Lovely! The more the merrier, and thank you, Cash, you're already so busy.'

As Lavinia walked away, Cash gave a bewildered look to his sister. 'You said your mother invited me,' she said in a low tone.

'Did I? Oh well, doesn't matter, you're here now,' she smiled. 'Linc, keep Cash company while I get her a drink.'

'Is everyone in your family this bossy?' Cash asked, some of the shock wearing off to be replaced with disbelief.

'Pretty much. You get used to it after a while.'

'I shouldn't be here.' She looked around casually enough, but he detected the nervous energy beneath the surface.

'Strangely enough, my sister also invited an old school friend of Griff's along as well.' Cash followed his pointed glance across to the other end of the long verandah and spotted Griff in conversation with a pretty brunette, and after a moment he saw the tension in her shoulders relax a little. 'So it's all good.'

She gave him a brief sideways glance at that. 'You think so?'

'Not much else you can do about it, is there?'

'I just don't want it to be uncomfortable for Griff. Everyone's been so determined to push us together. I shouldn't be here.'

'You should. You're a neighbour and everyone likes you. You have a right to be here.'

'This is his home.'

'It's also mine, and I want you here,' he said and when she looked up at him, he quickly added, 'And so do Hadley and Mum.'

With Christmas just around the corner, Hadley wanted to get the wedding preparations done before the silly season well and truly took over. There was no messing about with this little get-together—after a table full of finger food was brought out, they were all given an assortment of jobs to do. There were sugar-coated almonds in delicate pastel shades that looked like baby robin eggs, to be placed in small gift bags tied with fancy ribbon. Jars had to be wrapped in material for table centrepieces, and burlap banners painted. And then there were the tissue-paper pompoms that were going to decorate branches of potted trees Hadley wanted to dot around the reception area.

'Seriously, Hads, with the amount of money you and Mitch make, couldn't you just pay someone to make these for you?' Linc complained good-naturedly as he contorted his big fingers into strange positions to fold the fragile tissue paper.

'I could, but then they wouldn't have been made with love,' she said, flashing a sweet smile at her brother. 'Look at you go.'

'I cannot believe you managed to con us into this,' he muttered.

'Just think how proud you'll be when you look at these hanging on the trees around the marquee.'

'If you tell anyone I helped make these things, I'll have to kill you.'

'Oh, so you don't want this uploaded onto Facebook then and all your big tough army mates tagged in it?' she said, holding her phone up and snapping off a shot, before cackling evilly.

'Hadley, I think you're pushing your luck, darling,' Lavinia warned, carrying out a tray of drinks.

'Mum, take her phone off her, will you?' Linc said wearily from across the table and Cash bit back a grin.

'How come all the other men got to do painting?' he asked, looking over his shoulder.

'Aww, diddums,' Hadley crooned, but it was clear that she adored her eldest brother and that had Linc truly not wanted to be there, he wouldn't have stayed.

'Seriously though, Hads, I would never have picked you for a cheapskate. Why the hell are we doing all this stuff? And how come Mitch isn't here helping?'

'I'm not being a cheapskate,' she said defensively. 'I know exactly what I want, and I can't find it anywhere, so we have to make it. And Mitch is tied up with his show. Besides, I meant it when I said this feels so much more meaningful. It's fun,' she added, looking around the table at everyone.

Seated beside Linc was Hadley's best friend Olivia, whom Griff had been talking to earlier. Other than a brief smile when they'd all taken a seat, the woman had barely glanced in Cash's direction. Cash got the feeling Olivia wasn't her number one fan at the moment—probably because Griffin had told her how horrible she was. Cash glanced across the verandah to where the majority of the men were gathered, doing more drinking than actual painting, and knew she was being unfair. Griff wouldn't have told Olivia anything nasty about her; after all, they hadn't even dated. She knew she was only feeling guilty because, well . . . she was. She should have stopped their little get-togethers on her front verandah before Griff had gotten his hopes up.

'So, Olivia, what do you do?' Cash asked, trying to make conversation.

The woman beside Hadley looked up in surprise. 'Me? I'm a corporate lawyer.'

'So we know who to call if we need bail,' Linc added.

'Ah, no. I specialise in mergers and acquisitions. If you need to be bailed out of jail, you'd probably need a criminal lawyer,' she told Linc dryly.

'Right. Noted for future reference.'

'But on the other hand,' Hadley interjected happily, 'if you ever take over a multimillion-dollar company, Olivia is your gal. She's been steadily climbing up the corporate lawyer ladder of success over the last few years.'

'Well, it's not as exciting as the threat of having a bomb dropped on you at any time,' Olivia said, kinking an eyebrow at her friend, 'but I like it.'

'I'm very proud of you, you've put in the long hours and hard work and you're now where you want to be.'

Cash saw the small half-smile that crossed Olivia's face and wondered at the slight hesitation she read there. Maybe she was just uncomfortable in the spotlight, she thought, before conversation turned back to the wedding.

Twelve

'Why are you stirring up trouble, squirt?' Linc asked his youngest sister as she came over and took the seat beside him after the party had wound down.

'I'm not.'

'Really?' he said doubtfully. 'You invited Cash over because . . . ?'

'I like her,' she shrugged before letting out a long breath. 'Look, I love you and Griff both dearly, and of course I want to see Griff happily settled with someone, but I want to see you happy as well. You need some stability in your life, Linc. I worry about you. Besides, Blind Freddy can see that Griff and Cash are not in the least bit compatible.'

'And you think she and I are?' he asked curiously.

'I do. I agree the timing's not ideal, with Griff and all, but a woman like Cash doesn't come along very often. You've got to seize the opportunity when you can.'

Linc gave a noncommittal grunt at his sister's logic. 'Speaking of opportunities,' he said, holding his sister's frank gaze, 'how are you feeling about this wedding?'

'Well, that's an odd question,' she said with an abrupt chuckle, but he saw her eyes dart away and his suspicions were confirmed.

'Listen, I know everything's kinda crazy right now, but you know you can put things on hold if you want to, right?'

'Oh yeah, sure. Like the last two times. Everyone would be so thrilled with that.'

'Just reminding you that you still have options.'

'You're as bad as everyone else. You think this marriage is going to fail too, don't you?'

'I didn't say that,' he said calmly.

'Oh, come on, Linc. I know you can't stand Mitch. You've never hidden the fact.'

'I'm not the one who's marrying him,' he said, taking a sip of his beer.

'No, you're not. *I* am. So I wish everyone would just stop with the "it's not too late" talks.'

'Who else has been talking to you?'

'Mum and Dad, Harmony; she's got it in for everyone and everything lately.'

'So it's not just my imagination then.' Linc said.

'Nope. Something's going on with her. For the perfect wife, she's acting very anti-marriage. Not that long ago she was hassling me that I was leaving it too late to get married and I should be giving up my career to concentrate on starting a family before I got too old.'

'Nice change of topic,' Linc said, eyeing his sister levelly.

Hadley tipped her head back and gave a strangled groan.

'Look, you're my kid sister. If you're happy, I'm happy. Just make sure you're doing this for the right reasons, that's all.'

'You think I'm not?' she said in a deadpan tone.

'Just make sure you're making decisions for you, and not to keep everyone else happy.'

'I know you all think you're helping, but I wish just once everyone would try and remember that I'm a grown adult. I'm capable of making my own decisions.'

'Okay,' he held up his hands in surrender, 'just wanted to make sure.'

'Maybe you should take your own advice,' she said, tilting her head slightly to study her brother's face carefully.

'How so?'

'Are you happy?'

'Course I am,' he said, trying not to shift uncomfortably under her eagle eye. Of all his family, Hadley knew more than most about what his life had been like in the service. While she'd never served in the military, she'd been close enough to the action to know the kinds of things he'd been through. It wasn't as easy to hide things from her and that scared him a little. He liked control, and she threatened that with her knowing gaze and gentle probing.

'Everything okay? You seem a little . . .'

'I'm fine,' he snapped, then bit back a frustrated growl. 'I'm good,' he said in a less abrasive tone. 'Just getting used to being back under the parental roof again.'

'Last time we talked you were heading to Baghdad. I thought you were going to be over there until just before Christmas. Then Mum tells me you're back home.'

'There was a change of plans,' he shrugged, ignoring the trickle of sweat starting to prickle down his back. He could feel her studying him in that annoying way she had with an interview subject when she was trying to find the right angle to tackle a particular topic.

'You can talk to me, Linc,' she said gently. 'Or better still, go see someone trained to help. Those appointments—'

'Were a waste of time. I'm fine,' he said firmly, putting a stop to that line of conversation. He knew his sister meant well. She'd tried to line up an appointment with a psychologist when he left the army. He'd gone to one session and never returned. He wasn't into talking about his feelings with a stranger. 'Just drop it, Hads. The business is going great and life's good.'

He saw her chew thoughtfully on her lip, as though considering whether or not to continue, but she obviously took the hint and managed a small smile. 'That's good. I'm glad. So what are you going to do about Cash?'

His relief that she'd stopped questioning him was short-lived. 'I don't know.' His gaze drifted across to the other end of the verandah and settled on his brother.

'She was never his,' Hadley said quietly.

No, Cash was never his brother's girlfriend, but then he doubted Cash would ever really belong to anyone. There was a wild streak inside her—that was probably one of the first things that had attracted him to her. She was mysterious and exotic and she stood out like a brightly coloured flower in the desert, and he wanted her . . . badly.

❧

Cash had a strange feeling as she watched the ute heading up the driveway the next day. Stringybark Creek was written across the driver's door, but because the windows were slightly tinted, all she could make out was the outline of the driver. She found herself holding her breath as the door opened. The hat threw her at first. For the briefest of moments she thought it was Griff, until he straightened and pushed the faded old hat back on his head and she caught a glimpse of dark stubble. A shot of white-hot longing went through her and she swallowed. *Dear Lord.* Previously she'd only ever seen him dressed in cargo pants or casual gear; today he was in denim jeans, a white T-shirt and dusty boots and Cash couldn't seem to drag her eyes away from him.

'Hi,' he said, coming to a stop at the bottom of the steps.

'Hi.' She knew she should probably say something else, but for the life of her she couldn't string two words together.

'Apparently you have a fence that needs fixing?'

'A fence?' He was eyeing her strangely, and for good reason—she was acting like an idiot.

'Dad said to come over and fix the fence.'

'Oh! That fence,' she said, giving her head a quick shake. What was *wrong* with her? 'Yeah, there's a fence down, but I didn't . . . I mean, I wasn't expecting anyone to come and fix it. You've probably got a million other things you'd rather be doing.'

'All good. I'm happy to be away from the three-ring circus that's going on at home.'

'Pretty crazy?' she asked, already suspecting that chaos would be unfolding with so many strong women under the one roof.

'Griff's runnin' around trying to sort out the last-minute details for harvesting and Dad's driving him crazy, and then there's Hadley and Mum deciding that they practically want to renovate the shearing shed for the reception, so at this point I'll take any excuse to get out of the place for a while.'

Cash gave a chuckle of commiseration. 'Well, in that case, I guess it's only neighbourly to give you an excuse to stay away.'

'If you point the way, I'll go take a look.'

'I'll show you,' she said, checking her watch briefly. She still had half an hour before her next appointment arrived. 'It's just behind the house yard. You can drive through if you like.'

'I'll take a look and then come back for the gear. See what I'll need.'

She led the way around the house, through the Balinese garden and out the back through the tall bamboo screens.

Linc gave a low whistle. 'This is really something, isn't it?'

'It's pretty amazing. I keep telling Savannah that George would make a killing in the city.'

'You're not wrong. This is crazy.'

Cash gave him a smile over her shoulder, happy that he found the gardens as incredible as she did. She opened the gate and stepped through into a fenced paddock. 'That's where the fence is down.' She pointed to a length of sagging wire nearby.

'Ah, that's a piece of cake to fix. Won't take long at all.'

'I noticed it the other day. I think the cows decided they like this side of the fence better.'

'Grass is always greener?' he asked cocking an eyebrow.

'Looks like it.' She didn't often venture further than the backyard, so she wasn't even sure how long the fence had been down. There was no sign of any rogue cattle now though so, clearly, they'd eaten and gone. 'Well, I guess I'll leave you to it then, if you're sure?' She felt kind of bad that he was being sent over to do such a mundane, easy job.

'Positive. I'll get what I need from the ute and have it done in no time.'

The phone was ringing when she returned to the salon and Cash just managed to grab it before it switched to voicemail.

'The Sacred Spirit Day Spa, Cash speaking. How can I help you?'

'Umm, what happened to my greeting?' Savannah enquired.

'I never agreed to that bit,' Cash said flatly. Savannah had left a written card by the phone with the greeting she used: *Welcome to the Sacred Spirit Day Spa, where we transform your mind, body and soul.* Cash was not into the enlightening angels and tarot reading stuff that Savannah was into. 'But don't worry,' she consoled before Savannah could protest, 'everything else is done exactly the way you requested it.'

'You know, if you read those books I left out for you, you'd open yourself up to so many wonderful new experiences.'

'I think I've opened myself to more than enough experiences in one lifetime, I'm pretty sure I don't need any more. How're things over there?' she asked quickly, before her friend could continue her line of lecturing.

'It's snowing. Can you believe it? Real snow. It's beautiful.'

'It's hard to imagine, actually. It's been sweltering out here.'

'So what's the latest with Griff? Have you been out yet?'

'There is no latest,' she said dully.

'What? Already? Aww, come on, Cash, you promised you were going to give him a chance,' Savannah protested.

'I did! Against my better judgement, I might add.'

'Then what happened?'

'He kissed me and there was nothing there. Like—nothing.'

'Are you sure? Maybe you're being a little hasty. He might have been having an off night or something. You can't make a judgement call on one kiss.'

'Yes, I can, Sav. It's been leading up to this, I was trying to be positive, but the reality is, we're not compatible.'

Her friend went silent for a few moments before obviously summoning some kind of divine spiritual inspiration. 'Oh well, maybe he was sent to show you something.'

'Like what? I'm not cut out for a nice guy?'

'Of course you are, you just haven't met him yet. Sometimes people are sent into your life to teach you things. Maybe Griff was there to show you the way *towards* something. To guide you to your path. Let me get my cards and I'll do a reading.'

Cash rolled her eyes as she walked outside, 'No, Sav, I don't need your cards to tell me what I should be doing.' Cash scoffed silently, *Guide me to my* . . . The thought drifted off as she caught sight of the shirtless man tightening what looked like a winch on the fence line. His sweat-glistened back muscles flexed and rippled with each wrench of the lever. She saw him straighten and take off his hat, wiping his forearm across his brow, before bending over to retrieve a bottle from the ground. There was so much to admire about the way denim fitted his . . .

'Cash?'

Savannah's voice snapped her back to reality. 'Sorry? What?'

'Are you all right?'

Cash swallowed and dragged her gaze from Linc's distracting form. 'Yep, all good. I think my next client has arrived. I have to go. I'll call you later. Bye.' She disconnected the call quickly before her far too perceptive friend could question her further.

However, Savannah's words stayed with her the rest of the day. *Had* Griff been some kind of stepping stone? For a philosophy that spruiked love and kindness, it seemed a little harsh to be *using* people as life lessons. And if Griff had been leading her towards a path, then what the hell was the path leading to? Cash had never bought into Savannah's new age wisdom before, so she probably shouldn't start now. There was nothing in it anyway . . .

Thirteen

Linc splashed himself to wash off the morning's sweat and bit back a curse as the water stung the deep scratch across his stomach. The barbed wire had got him before he'd even started working on the stupid fence. He couldn't believe he'd ripped his favourite shirt. He bent down and scooped it from the ground and held it up to inspect the damage. With a sad shake of his head he used it to mop the water from his face and did his best to clean up the cut. The job hadn't been as simple as he'd first thought; he'd discovered the fence had snapped in two other places further along. His mood took a further plunge once he'd thrown all his gear in the back of the ute and felt the sting of sunburn starting on his back and shoulders. He climbed into the vehicle and reached for the ignition, but paused as he spotted Cash coming out onto the front verandah with her lunch.

His mood lifted slightly as she walked down the steps towards him.

'How'd it go?'

'All finished,' he said, leaning his arm out the open window. 'They really went to town on that fence. But it's sorted now.'

'You got sunburnt out there,' she said, frowning at his shoulders. 'You *have* heard of the whole sun safe campaign they've been running for the last twenty or thirty years, haven't you?' she asked with a hint of sarcasm as her eyes flickered across his bare chest, before they widened slightly. 'What happened? You're bleeding.'

He glanced down at the cut and gave a small wince. 'It's not as bad as it looks. Barbed wire scratch.'

'Have you had a tetanus shot lately?' she asked, her green eyes concerned.

'Yeah, it's all good.'

'It doesn't look good. Come inside and let me clean it up. It's the least I can do since you were doing me a favour.'

'It's not that bad,' he protested, but then heard a little voice inside his head say, *Dude, shut up and let her fix you!*

'Out,' she commanded sternly, and he couldn't help the twitch of his lips.

'You know, you're sounding just as bossy as my mum and sisters.'

'I must have been hanging around the Callahans too long then.'

He followed her up the stairs and into the house. He wasn't any kind of interiors' expert, but he'd seen enough home shows on the TV to know when someone had decorated. *This*, he thought rather smugly, was what they call 'shabby chic'. The lounge and the two armchairs were in different old-fashioned fabrics, and everywhere he looked were a variety of baskets, coloured boxes and weird ornaments. As they walked through into the small kitchen, he noticed mismatched chairs around a scrubbed, old pine dining-room table. Pots hung from a bracket over the kitchen bench, and various kitchen utensils hung from hooks attached to a wall frame beside the kitchen sink.

'They mustn't have much cupboard space,' he commented, looking around the room.

He caught her lopsided grin as she directed him to a chair while she disappeared into a small pantry at the end of the kitchen. 'Savannah likes everything she uses to be on display and within easy reach. She doesn't believe in hiding things away. Apparently it's the trend in interior decorating . . . or something,' she shrugged, carrying a box marked *First aid* and pulled out a chair across from him. 'That looks really sore.'

'Nah, I can barely feel it,' he said, leaning back as she inspected the cut, and realising that he was looking forward, with just a little bit too much anticipation, to her touching him.

She gave an unimpressed snort at his reply, which dampened his eagerness a little. 'Sorry, I forgot how tough and manly you're supposed to be.'

'I *am* tough and manly,' he protested.

'Of course you are,' she said in a voice that sounded like she was mollifying a child. She unscrewed a bottle of antiseptic and tipped it onto a cotton ball, before placing it against the open cut across his midsection. His sharp intake of breath made her bite back a smile.

'And there I was thinking how caring you were.'

'I'm caring,' she said, taking another cotton ball and repeating the action. 'This is me being caring,' she told him with an innocent smile. 'But seriously, it looks sore.'

'Okay, it might be a little sore,' he conceded, although now that she'd placed her other hand against his skin to steady the area near the wound, he wasn't feeling anything much at all—nothing above his waist anyway.

He admired the way a few small tendrils of hair hung down her neck, escaping from the messy bun she wore for work. A faint hint of coconut seemed to linger around her and he breathed in deeply, filling his head with her scent. *God, she smelled good.* As though somehow sensing he was watching her, she lifted her gaze and he saw something flare to life there before she straightened and pushed her chair back a little.

'There you go.' She sent him a bright smile that wavered slightly as he lifted his hand to close over hers, where it rested against his stomach.

'Thank you,' he said quietly, the heat of her hand branding his skin.

He leaned forward slightly in his chair, bringing their lips closer. He heard her breath catch as she gave a mumbled,

'You're welcome' and his eyes locked onto the soft fullness of her lips. Man, he wanted to taste her so bad. He saw the exact moment she surrendered and he knew she wanted him as much as he wanted her. The air between them almost sizzled with the intensity of the heat they were generating, but then something changed and in an instant the desire in her eyes melted as she lowered her lashes and eased back away from him, shaking her head firmly.

'No, I can't. Not with you.'

'Not with me?' He wasn't sure he'd heard her right. What the hell was wrong with *him*?

'You're all wrong,' she said, getting to her feet and busying herself by gathering together all the supplies she'd used and shoving them back into the first-aid kit haphazardly while Linc looked on in surprise.

'How am I all wrong?' On some level he knew this was more about her than him. He wasn't even sure she'd meant to say any of it out loud, since she was continuing to mutter under her breath as she scooped up the used cotton balls and deposited them into the bin underneath the sink.

He watched as she fussed around the kitchen, picking up a cloth to wipe the bench, picking up and putting things down again. 'Cash,' he said, approaching her and waiting until she stopped and looked up at him. 'Why am I all wrong?'

'Because you're too much like the other men I've dated. You're not the type of man I need.'

'You've known me all of five minutes,' he said, unable to distance himself from the insult.

'I can tell. I'm always attracted to the wrong kind of man.'

'So you *are* attracted to me,' he said slowly, trying to work out why she seemed so distressed by the fact.

'Of course I am,' she snapped, but before he could get his hopes up she went on to smash them. 'As much as I hate it.'

'No, really, don't hold back on account of my feelings,' he said.

'Oh please,' she scoffed at his sarcasm. 'Like you're into feelings.'

Linc frowned. Okay, this was starting to get personal. 'I don't know what kind of guy you think I am, but you're way off the mark here.'

'Really?' she said, tilting her head slightly to size him up. 'When was your last relationship?'

He opened his mouth but then shut it again. Damn it, that wasn't a fair question. How was he supposed to answer that and not have it come out sounding wrong?

'Let me guess . . . you don't *do* relationships, right?' she said smugly.

'I wouldn't say that,' he started, but stopped at her arched eyebrow. 'Well, they're just not practical in my line of work.'

'I rest my case.'

'Wait, *what*? How is that proving anything?'

'Men like you only want women for sex. They need a woman in their life, but only on their terms, and so long as it doesn't mean they have to commit to anything.'

'Now hang on,' he said, gobsmacked. *Men like him?* What the hell?

'Oh, come on, Linc. You're the classic example of the wrong kind of guy.'

'Would you *stop* saying that!' She was really annoying him with her character assassination.

'You asked. I can't help it if you don't like the answer.'

'Jesus, you must have picked some real doozies in the past.'

He saw her jaw flex slightly at the comment, and she plastered a sarcastic smile on her face. 'Hence the decision *not* to repeat the mistake.'

Well, that came back to bite him on the arse. 'For the record, I have never intentionally hurt a woman in my life. I'm always up front with what I can and can't offer.'

'I stand corrected,' she said with a large helping of sugary sweetness. 'But clearly I was not mistaken in assuming you're the wrong kind of man *for me*.'

'What exactly *is* the right kind of man *for you*?'

'Someone who isn't afraid of making a commitment. Someone who wants an equal, not a doormat or a bed warmer. Someone loyal, affectionate and reliable.'

'You forgot obedient, and I think you might be confusing a boyfriend with a dog.'

She gave a one-shouldered shrug as she turned away. 'Maybe. But I know what I *don't want* anymore and that's the main thing.'

'You wanted someone like my brother,' he said after watching her silently for a few moments. 'But that didn't work out, did it?' He moved across to stand in front of her. 'You can't pick a compatible match from an itemised list of personal traits.'

'Yes, you can,' she argued, lifting her head.

'People are not found on supermarket shelves. You don't go looking for a mate with a shopping list.'

'I know what I don't want.'

'I think you're fighting the inevitable,' he said softly, watching her eyes flicker uncertainly as he took another step closer. 'Chemistry decides who we fall for, not commonsense. You don't want quiet and docile, you want someone who makes you feel wild and alive,' he said, lowering his head slowly, their lips barely a breath apart. 'You want a man who knows what he's doing and knows all the right ways to make you feel good. You need *this*,' he said, taking her lips and feeling them tremble beneath his.

The moment he made contact with her, all the self-assured swagger left him—he was lost. He was drowning, but in a good way. The soft supple mouth beneath his was anything but compliant—it was just as demanding as his and it was unapologetic in what it wanted from him. If he thought for one moment he was proving some kind of point, he was sorely mistaken. He couldn't remember a mere kiss bringing him to his knees the way this one was doing. His hands slipped from her face down to her waist, pulling her firmly against him. A spark of satisfaction flowed through him at her sharp intake of breath, and he pushed the advantage, sliding one hand under her shirt, his hand caressing the bare skin, and feeling her shiver against him. Her soft whimper was almost his undoing. It sent a wave of longing and need through him so powerful that it made his hands shake.

When she wrenched her mouth from his, they were both breathing hard. 'I don't . . .' she started, closing her eyes to get herself under control. 'I can't . . . do this.'

'Do what?'

'This,' she said frowning. 'You.'

'You can't fight what your body wants, Cash,' he said, loosening his hold on her reluctantly.

'I can if it's only going to get me back where I started. I need to begin making changes, Linc.'

'Maybe you already have.'

She shook her head sadly. 'No. I'm still picking the wrong ones.'

'Maybe you've just got the wrong things on your list,' he said, stepping away and wishing this could be ending so very differently, but it didn't seem likely with Cash looking at him miserably, as though he was the biggest disappointment of her life. It wasn't exactly a turn-on.

He stopped at the doorway on his way out and glanced over his shoulder at her, getting momentary satisfaction from seeing she was as affected as he was. He'd done all he could do for now—he'd proven that they had the chemistry. But how to make her see she was mistaken about him being the wrong kind of man? That was going to take some thinking.

∽

Cash sagged against the back of the door and stayed there long after she heard the ute fade into the distance. If she just stayed here long enough, with her eyes closed, maybe when she opened them again she'd discover it was all just a dream and she could go on with life as she knew it.

Why had she let herself get close enough to the guy to let him kiss her like that? Although maybe her outrage would be a little more justifiable if she'd not been such a willing participant. A little flutter ran through her as she recalled the steamy kiss. She pushed away from the door. *Get a grip, Sullivan!* It was just a kiss. It wasn't *that* big a deal. Only, it was a big deal. It made the kiss with Griff seem even *more* irrelevant. She'd known there'd been no fireworks with Griff, but she'd been convincing herself that maybe it hadn't been as bad as she'd thought . . . Now she knew beyond a measure of a doubt. There was no way it compared to what had just happened with Linc. She'd been right to be wary of Lincoln Callahan. He was a temptation she needed to stay away from. Why hadn't she been stronger? *Now look at the mess you've gone and gotten yourself into,* a prim voice scolded her inside her head. *You've gone and wrecked everything.* All because she was attracted to the wrong Callahan. Damn it.

It's okay, she told herself, taking a deep cleansing breath. *This is good. It's a test, that's all.* It was like any other addiction, she had to learn how to avoid putting herself in situations where she knew she'd be tempted. She could do this. All she had to do was steer clear of the guy. She had no reason to see him again, so there was no need to panic. The situation was salvageable.

Fourteen

Cash did a double-take when she looked up to see who had walked through the front door the next day. It was *not* Hadley Callahan.

'Cash,' Linc greeted her calmly. Too calmly. Something was going on.

'Can I help you with something, Linc?' she asked pointedly when he simply smiled confidently at her as though it made complete sense for him to be standing in the reception area.

'I hope so,' he said, coming over to lean one elbow on the counter. 'I'm here for my appointment.'

'Your app—' Cash scanned the book in front of her quickly, as though she'd *not* have somehow seen Lincoln Callahan written there earlier.

'Hadley booked it.'

'She booked it for *herself*,' Cash said tightly.

'She must have forgotten to mention it was for me,' he said with a shrug.

'Funny that,' Cash said sarcastically, before the realisation hit her that the appointment was for a massage. Uh-oh. This was not good.

'Is there a problem?' he asked innocently, holding her gaze with a silent challenge.

'Not at all,' Cash said, straightening her shoulders as she stood up and led the way through to the room she'd just set up. The candles flickered gently, and a delicate scent of coconut oil and lemongrass floated through the air. Suddenly, with Linc filling up the small room, the relaxing ambiance felt dangerously seductive.

'Please take off your shirt and trousers and cover yourself with the towel, then lie face down on the table. I'll be right back,' she said, slipping out of the room and congratulating herself on sounding so normal, when inside she was a mess.

~

Linc let out a long breath as the door closed behind Cash and gave a low, self-reproaching chuckle. When Hadley had told him she'd booked him a massage, he'd thought she was crazy, but the more he'd thought about it, the harder it had been to convince himself that it was a bad idea. Having an opportunity to get Cash all alone . . . with oil? There had been pretty much nothing his head could come up with that would have overruled the rest of him. Now, though, faced with the fact he was about to lay pretty much naked on a table and have her hands running all over him, he wasn't so sure this was a great idea.

With a fatalistic shake of his head, he pulled his shirt over his head and kicked off his shoes, then unbuttoned his jeans, before climbing up on the table. *Come on, Callahan, you can do this. Just focus on something that doesn't involve being naked with the hottest woman you've seen in a long time, in a candlelit room with soft music playing.*

The door opened and he clenched his jaw as parts of him began to stir in anticipation. *For the love of God, you're not fifteen-bloody-years old,* he told himself with a measure of disgust. He could hear her moving quietly around the room preparing the things she'd need, but even though he could sense her every move, the moment she touched him, he almost jumped clear out of his skin.

'Sorry,' she murmured. 'Just relax,' she said, keeping one hand on his shoulder while he heard her reaching for something with the other, moments before he felt the sensation of warm oil and hands running across his skin. He bit back a moan. *Jesus, this was going to be torture.*

'You're very tense,' she commented, and he wondered if he was imagining the note of amusement in her tone. 'Seriously, you need to relax.'

'I'm doing my best,' he muttered.

She added some more oil and continued moving her hands over his back and shoulders, up to his neck. He couldn't stop the groan that escaped, it felt so damn good.

'I'm going to have to work out some of these knots,' she said calmly. 'You've got a lot of tension stored in your neck and shoulder area.'

'Weddings are stressful,' he said as he felt her fingers working the muscles between his neck and shoulder. He was glad he was face down because he was pretty sure his eyes were rolling back in his head as she skilfully manipulated the tightness in his muscles.

When she'd significantly warmed up the area, she began applying deeper, harder strokes and another groan broke free from his chest; however, this one was more pain than ecstasy.

'Is that too hard?' Cash asked.

'No,' his words came out sounding slurred. 'It's great. You're good at this.'

'I should be, I've been doing it long enough,' she said dryly.

'How long would that be?'

'Since I was eighteen. Now stop talking. You're supposed to relax. That's what you're paying for.'

He read the message loud and clear. This wasn't foreplay—this was a job. It was an effective mood douser. She was doing this because she got paid to do it. A rush of annoyance followed the thought and even though he knew it was stupid, he felt somehow cheapened by it, which made him scoff at himself—cheapened? He was sounding like some teenage drama queen. But try as he might, he couldn't shake the irritation. He didn't want to be a paying customer. Linc pushed himself up off the table and sat up, noticing the surprised look on her face.

'What's wrong?'

'I just remembered something I have to do,' he said, sounding gruffer than he'd intended, throwing the towel aside and reaching for his trousers.

'Are you sure?'

He felt bad about the uncertainty he heard in her voice, but he couldn't risk a glance at her face or he'd feel like an even bigger idiot. 'Yeah.'

'Okay then, I'll wait for you outside.'

If there'd been a window in the damn room he'd have climbed out that, but he knew he'd have to face her sometime. How could he tell her the reason he was acting like a spoilt brat was because he wanted her to *want* to massage him? She'd think he was nuts. Who was he kidding? He *was* nuts!

Cash stared at the closed door to the treatment room, trying to work out what had gone wrong. Had she somehow said something out loud? Oh God, she hoped not. She'd been drawing on every ounce of her professionalism to remain focused, despite the fact her fingers felt as though they were burning as they moved across his back and shoulders.

The door opened and she busied herself looking down at the appointment book as he approached the desk. 'So I can reschedule you tomorrow, or let me know a day you'd prefer and I'll tell you what times I have available.'

'Ah, no . . . thanks. I don't need to reschedule.'

'Oh.' *What?* No way was this because of any issue with her professionalism. Now she was just plain annoyed. What the hell did he mean he didn't need to reschedule?

'How much do I owe you for today?' he asked, pulling out his wallet, and Cash noticed that his shoulders were as stiff as his tone.

'Nothing,' she snapped. 'Don't worry about it.'

'I owe you for your time.'

'You weren't in there long enough to warrant an appointment.'

Linc frowned, finally looking at her. 'Look, I'm sorry I wasted your time.'

'Forget it. I'm sorry it wasn't an enjoyable experience for you.'

'Cash—'

'Linc, I said forget it. I'll just finish early today. You did me a favour.'

'It wasn't because I wasn't enjoying it,' he said.

'Then what was it? And don't say because you suddenly remembered something you had to do, cause I'm not buying that.'

He gave a low noise in his throat and ran a hand through his hair. 'It's not y—'

'You, it's me? Yeah. Okay. Fine,' Cash snapped, turning away but looking down in surprise as he reached out and took her arm.

They both seemed to freeze as Cash locked eyes with him. She didn't realise she was holding her breath until he dropped his hand and she was able to breathe once more. He didn't step away from her and she could smell a faint scent of some kind of masculine fragrance; deodorant or aftershave, she wasn't sure which, but it went straight to her head.

'Trust me, I want nothing more than to have your hands on me,' he said, and his voice had a low gravelly quality that sent a stab of longing through her. 'I've wanted it from the very first moment I laid eyes on you.'

He leaned in, the movement so slight she barely caught it, until suddenly she felt his warm breath against her cheek. The room was so quiet, all she could hear was the beating of her heart. Her breath caught, then came out in an uneven rush, making her feel light-headed. He smelled so good. She felt her body sway towards his, and before she could prepare herself, his head lowered and his lips were on hers.

She could feel the coarseness of his stubble as his mouth danced across her own. It was a slow, almost hesitant kiss, but the swell of need that it sparked inside her dulled the last of her commonsense and she slid her arms up around his neck, pulling the back of his head lower. If he'd had any thoughts of taking things slow, Cash had just ended them. To hell with safe and careful. She needed Linc and she needed him now. Ever since that first night they'd been circling around the attraction that flared between them. To hell with her bad-boy ban. She'd get back on track tomorrow. For now, she needed this—needed him. It felt like eons since she'd last felt the flame of desire touching her skin and setting her on fire. She wanted to feel alive again.

When he tried to pull back and slow it down, she pushed closer and tightened her fingers through the short hair at the base of his neck, inciting a low groan from him in surrender. There was no need to encourage him further, he took the cue and his kiss became deeper, rougher. His stubble rubbed the soft skin on her face, but the burn felt good. Still it wasn't enough. She moved her hands from his neck down the front of his shirt and gathered the bottom edges in her hands, lifting them. Without breaking their kiss, Linc manoeuvred his arms from his shirt, pulling away only briefly to pull it over his head, before gathering her back against him.

His chest was wide and there was a hardness to his body—muscular but not sculptured like the men she usually met who owed their six-packs and impressive pecs to the gym. She ran her fingers from his waistband up the centre of his chest, and felt the soft hair there.

He was like a drug. The more she tasted of him, the more she wanted. This was madness—and yet it wasn't. This was lust. Pure, unadulterated lust.

Cash squirmed her arms out of her work blouse, slipping it from her shoulders after working the buttons free of their holes, without breaking the kiss. Linc's big hands spanned her waist, holding her firmly against him, the heat of his skin against hers sending a shiver through her body. She shimmied her work pants down her legs and stepped out, kicking them to one side along with her shoes.

Linc walked her slowly backwards, back into the room they'd just came out of, their mutual sighs and moans the only communication necessary. She heard him kick the door shut behind them, moments before she was lifted onto the edge of the bed.

For the briefest of moments Linc pulled his mouth from hers to allow his eyes to roam across her body, letting out a low, guttural curse before reclaiming her lips. Impatient for more, Cash's hands went to the buttons of his jeans and unclasped them, smiling smugly beneath his kiss as she heard his rough intake of breath at the touch of her cool fingers against his hot skin.

❧

Linc bit back another low groan. Every time she touched him his minimal grip on restraint was tested. She was so damn hot. He knew she had some curves, but seeing them in the flesh, so to speak, was better than anything his imaginative mind had mustered up in the nights he'd spent thinking about her.

He ran his hands up her rib cage and along her arms, wanting to take the time to read the delicately inscribed words written around their circumference, but he was too impatient to do so now. He moved one hand up to the back of her head and found the band that secured her dark hair, watching as it fell like a curtain across her shoulders.

He swore again. He couldn't help it. She blew his mind, and she'd barely even touched him yet. God help him when she did. He liked that she wasn't shying away from her near nakedness. It was such a turn-on when a woman was confident in her own body. As his gaze reached her face once more, he realised she'd been watching him, through those sexy, lowered eyes, but there was no sign of discomfort—in fact she seemed content to simply allow him to look his fill.

As tempting as it was to explore every tantalising inch of her body, now was not the time. With a knowing, sultry look that had his pulse skyrocketing, she reached behind her and unclasped her lacy black bra without breaking eye contact. It was So. Damn. Hot.

A tiny voice tried to get his attention but he ignored it. He didn't want to think about what he was doing right now. He didn't want to examine the fact she'd turned him away once before because he was apparently the wrong kind of man for her. Clearly at the moment he was the right kind, and he wasn't going to look that gift horse in the mouth. He'd deal with all the other stuff later. Right now, he had a woman he needed to satisfy, and he was not about to back down from the mission.

Fifteen

What had she done? It was all well and good to try to justify her actions by saying she was a spineless jellyfish when in close proximity to Lincoln Callahan, but now, sitting here in the aftermath, it was a little less easy to explain it to herself. She really was a lost cause. She kept relapsing back into old habits. *He may be the wrong kind of guy, but holy mother of God, he's good.*

Stop it! That was not the point. Cash rolled her eyes and groaned out loud. Now she was arguing with herself.

After the impromptu sex—*really, really good impromptu sex,* the little voice inside her head added—Linc seemed as surprised as she was. For a long time they didn't speak. His head hung as he fought to catch his breath, his arms braced either side of her on the bed and his chest moving steadily in and out as his heart rate slowed back to normal.

She wasn't sure why she felt so nervous—she'd never been the shy type before, but now she had a sudden urge to run and hide. Hide what—she wasn't exactly sure—not so much her nakedness, it was more than that, it was her thoughts and her emotions that felt most at risk. He had an uncanny knack of making her feel as though he could see through her, and that was a very new experience. No man had ever got under her skin in quite the same way as Linc seemed able to. It was a little . . . unnerving.

'Are you all right?'

Cash's gaze flew to his, expecting to find the usual amused grin in place, but instead discovered Linc watching her with a steel-like intensity, holding her eyes firmly. 'I'm fine,' she said, clearing her throat quickly. 'Why wouldn't I be?' and she made a move to get off the table, hoping he'd take the hint and step away so she could. For a moment, she thought he didn't believe her, but then slowly he eased away enough for her to slide from the table and gather her things from the floor.

She could sense his uncertainty because it mirrored her own. She wasn't sure what he was thinking—most likely he was trying to think up a polite way to extract himself from the situation. She opened the door and followed the trail of discarded clothing out to the foyer, giving him some space to get dressed. As he came out of the room a few seconds later, she handed him his shirt and plastered a smile to her face.

She didn't feel like listening to his excuse for leaving all of a sudden, so she decided to give him an easy out. 'I better get things set up for the next client.'

'I thought you said I was the last one today?'

Damn. He was. 'I meant for tomorrow.'

'How much do I owe you?'

Cash's fake smile slipped.

Noticing her expression, he seemed to trip over his words. 'For the appointment . . . not . . . that.' He gave a swift nod back towards the room they just exited.

'Don't worry about it,' she said dully. *Just go. Please,* she begged silently.

'Cash. I'm sorry. That came out all wrong—I wasn't offering to pay you for—' He stopped at the lethal glare she gave him. 'Okay,' he said, holding up one hand in a placating gesture as she walked towards the door and opened it for him pointedly. He stared at her silently for a brief moment before letting out a small huff of frustration. 'That was—'

'A mistake,' she managed. Why wouldn't he just leave already? She wasn't holding him here with small talk, she was letting him go, free and clear, so why was he insisting on talking?

'Is that what you think it was?' he asked, searching her reluctant gaze. He was standing so close, too close. She couldn't think straight like this.

'I can assure you I do not have sex with clients. This was a huge mistake on my part, and I'm mortified that I let my professionalism slip so badly.'

'I'm not a client.'

'You came here as one.'

'Yeah, but I'd already cancelled before we . . . did anything. So technically, I wasn't a client and you were officially finished for the day.'

'That's not the point,' she said, feeling exasperated by his argument.

'Look, you can call it whatever the hell you like, but I'm calling it amazing. I'll see you around, Cash,' he said, swooping down to kiss her unexpectedly, then heading outside before she could protest.

Cash sagged against the open doorway as she listened to the sound of his engine fade into the distance, feeling as energetic as a deflated balloon. Albeit a sated, ache-in-all-the-right-places, kind of balloon. She wished she didn't have to call it a mistake, but what else could it be?

What the hell had he done?

Linc gripped the steering wheel so tightly his knuckles turned white. That had definitely not been what he'd expected when he'd called his sister's bluff about having a massage. Okay, sure, maybe the idea of Cash giving him a massage had turned into an X-rated fantasy, but he hadn't honestly *expected* it! He was a guy, of course he'd thought about having sex with Cash, but the fact that it had *actually happened* took him completely by surprise. Memories flashed through his head and when he accidentally glanced in the mirror, he caught the wide grin on his face. Probably not the most appropriate reaction to something that clearly upset Cash. A frown momentarily replaced the grin as he pondered her response. Upset was probably not the right word; she'd been pissed off. That didn't sit well with his ego at all. He'd just experienced the most incredible, mind-blowing sex he could recall in, well, way too long, and she'd waved it off as a mistake?

He instantly thought about his brother and a stab of guilt hit him in the ribs, but it soon passed. Yeah, he felt bad for Griff, who would no doubt still be feeling the effects of rejection, but in all fairness, the attraction was completely one-sided. Cash hadn't been into him. She hadn't even been on a date with him. It would be different if Cash and Griff had slept together, even though the mere thought of that was enough to send a sear of heat through his chest, but they hadn't, they'd barely kissed.

He'd been attracted to her instantly—she was sexy and sassy and smart, and he'd found himself thinking about her body way too often during the long hours of monotonous labouring work he'd been doing around the property. She'd far exceeded his expectations in the sex department, she clearly knew what she was doing there. She was almost his perfect woman—except for one thing. He'd figured once they'd set off the powder keg, so to speak, he'd be over the intense attraction he was feeling for her and he could carry on with his visit like a rational adult, but to his dismay, the craving hadn't gone away. If anything, it was even stronger. Now he'd *know* what he was missing, instead of just imagining it.

She'd called him the wrong kind of man.

Hadley had referred to him more than once as a man-whore and maybe he had been in his younger days. Now though, he'd slowed down; there weren't anywhere near the number of women his siblings imagined. He'd been too busy over the last few years to even contemplate a permanent relationship, which was probably why one-night stands had become his messed-up kind of normal. He didn't like to think of himself as a player or whatever the hell they called them nowadays. He never misled a woman, he was always upfront that there would be no texting, no 'I love you', and he was always very careful about the types of women he chose to spend time with. They knew the score. He had a select few long-term friends whose numbers he had stored in his phone—they were mostly women who travelled all the time, flight attendants mainly. It was an arrangement that had worked well for all concerned over the years, but lately he just hadn't been into it like he used to be.

Cash had flipped the switch that sent his entire being into ultra-aroused. He didn't know what the hell was going on, but she was messing with the strict order of his life. He was pretty sure he didn't like it, but she had sideswiped him so fast that he hadn't had time to realise everything inside him was shaken up.

Not that it mattered now though, he thought with a disgusted snort. Offering the woman money after they'd just had sex was probably not the smartest move. *Dumb arse.* All he could do was ride out her anger and pray to God he could fix it. It had been a case of bad timing and misunderstanding. She was pretty annoyed though, he had to concede. A smile began to tug at his lips as he remembered the flicker of reaction he'd gotten when he'd kissed her goodbye. Nope, Cash Sullivan was not as immune to him as she wanted him to believe.

Sixteen

There was a strange current running through the air when Cash woke up a few mornings later. Grey clouds had been gathering overhead. A rumble in the distance signalled an approaching storm and she wished she could spend the morning sitting on the verandah watching it.

There was nothing better than the sound of rain on an old tin roof, she decided later in the morning after her client made a dash through the gardens to her car. She'd always enjoyed storms, but she loved the ones out here. It had been a particularly hot and dry spring and everything was brown and parched. The onset of a storm had everyone excited, but for Cash it was the power and majesty of Mother Nature that she found fascinating. Here, across the wide-open plains, you could feel the deep rumble of thunder. The air vibrated. There was nothing to shield you from it—no tall buildings or neighbours built on top of you, just paddocks stretching out in all directions like a wide brown ocean.

Cash felt bad for her farming neighbours around her who were about to commence harvesting—the last thing they wanted right now was rain—but thankfully there hadn't been much in it, just enough to dampen the dust and release the pungent, sweet smell of rain into the air.

She was grateful for the little general store in Rankins Springs so she didn't have to drive all the way into Griffith to buy the basics. It boasted a takeaway and a post office as well as groceries, and although Cash wouldn't run down to the store just to buy milk, it was worth the trip into town to stock up on the essentials, like chocolate.

She pulled up outside and went in, greeting Pam behind the counter. She almost felt like a local as she commented on the rain.

Cash was perusing the selection of fruit when she heard a familiar deep voice and her heart bucked like a wild bull at a rodeo. *Crap. What is he doing here?* She glanced around to find a place to hide, but in a shop this size, that was impossible. She hadn't seen the man in two days, but his effect on her hadn't dimmed in the slightest.

She was still trying to debate her chances of slipping past him somehow when he glanced up and caught her eye. Her heart gave a flutter as she watched that slow, sexy grin form on his face. Too late.

She went back to taking a dedicated interest in coffee brands and did her best to seem unaffected by his sudden appearance.

'Hey,' he said, coming to a stop beside her.

'Hi,' Cash said with a brief glance, not quite looking him in the eye. She didn't think she was ready for such close proximity just yet.

'I'm glad I bumped into you,' he said, seemingly undeterred by her unenthusiastic greeting.

'Why? You planning on buying my groceries in lieu of payment for services rendered?' she asked, arching an eyebrow.

'I wanted to see you again and apologise. I was referring to the massage, not the s—'

'Okay!' Cash cut him off frantically, glancing up to see Pam watching their conversation with undisguised interest. 'I get it. It's fine.'

She saw Linc bite back a smile as he turned his back on Pam, shielding them from view with his rather broad shoulders. 'I was going to drop by this afternoon and apologise. We've been flat out with the start of harvesting.'

'Well, now you don't have to, do you.'

'I still want to,' he said, lowering his tone and leaning the tiniest bit closer. 'I haven't been able to stop thinking about the other day.'

Cash was suddenly aware of feeling incredibly warm and she wished someone would turn the airconditioner up higher.

'Can I come over later?' he asked, his head lowered close to hers, his body almost touching her own. *No, no, no, that's such a bad idea.* 'I have clients until four,' she heard herself saying. *What the f—*

'Perfect, I'll see you then,' he said, moving away before she could open her mouth to take it back. He'd grabbed two plastic bottles of milk and a loaf of bread and was digging out his wallet from his back pocket at the counter before she'd even come to her senses enough to move.

He must have some kind of sense-muddler device on him. There had to be a logical explanation as to why she could never think straight when he got close to her like that. *It's called hormones,* a sassy little voice told her helpfully. She tried to ignore the open curiosity written all over Pam's face as she paid for her purchases, glad that the woman wasn't pushy enough to ask any questions. Cash had a feeling the very next person who came into the store would be getting a rundown of the events that had just taken place. *Note to self, just drive the extra kilometres to Griffith for groceries next time.*

It was going to be a long morning.

∞

Cash thought that she'd be distracted all day by the impending visit, but it turned out she had more pressing matters to worry about. Her first client had driven from Griffith and decided to ask for a couple of extra treatments that hadn't been factored in. Luckily the morning hadn't been booked solid as it usually was, and Cash could fit in most of the woman's requests. However, not everything could be done and she was left with a very disgruntled customer.

'I don't have to drive all this way, you know. There are plenty of good beauticians in Griffith.'

'Yes, there are,' Cash had tried her best to remain polite and professional throughout the entire appointment—despite the fact that the woman had been more than a little rude and condescending, but now she was just plain fed up. 'And I'm fairly certain they would have done the exact same thing as I did when you added the extra treatments into your session. As I explained earlier, I can only do whatever is possible before my next appointment.'

'Well, I don't see your next appointment here, do you?'

'I still have to clean the room. I don't think it's very fair to keep someone waiting, do you?'

'I intend to let Savannah know about this, and don't think I'm not going to have a few things to say to anyone who asks which beautician I use. I have quite a lot of pull around the area, you know.' She clicked her tongue and stared down her nose at Cash. 'I'm not sure Savannah should have left her business in the hands of someone . . . like you,' she said with a dismissive glare at the red scarf Cash had worn around her hair today. Cash suspected her nose stud wasn't going over too well either—despite it being miniscule.

'Oh, Elenore, I thought that was you I could hear,' Lavinia said as she swept into the salon like a refreshing breeze.

The woman's mouth dropped open but she quickly composed herself. 'Lavinia . . . how nice to see you.'

'How's Adrian? Any word on when he'll be coming home from prison?'

Cash gasped as the woman went pale and her mouth opened and closed a few times before she snatched her handbag from the counter and hurried towards the door.

'Nice seeing you, Elenore,' Lavinia called as the front door closed.

Cash stared at Lavinia, dumbfounded.

'Don't worry about that one,' Lavinia said, waving her beautifully manicured hand in the air. 'The main reason she comes here is because every other salon in the area's banned her. I'm not sure why Savannah puts up with her.'

'Savannah believes she can help everyone. She probably thinks she can untwist her chakra or something.'

'She's a better person than I,' Lavinia said drolly.

'If you'll give me one minute, I'll just make up the room and we can get started.'

'Take your time,' she smiled wearily. 'It's lovely just sitting here, listening to this music,' Lavinia sighed. 'Oh, and I've brought along this for you,' she said, pulling out an envelope from her handbag.

Cash eyed the woman curiously before opening it and then bit the inside of her lip when she took out the glossy paper, unfolding it to find her name written on the wedding invitation. 'Oh, Lavinia, I couldn't . . . I mean, I don't even really know Hadley that well . . .'

'Hadley invited you,' Lavinia said with a smile.

'Oh.' Cash couldn't help the smile that took hold. 'I'd love to come.'

'Good. I'll add you to the RSVP'd list.'

Cash placed the envelope under the counter before getting back to business. 'I guess you'll be glad when this wedding is over,' she said over her shoulder as she went into the treatment room.

'We've still got to get through Christmas yet,' Lavinia said. Cash seriously didn't know where the woman got her energy from.

'I'm glad you've come for a massage then—I think you're due for some downtime.'

'This was Hadley's idea. I told her I didn't have time to fit in a massage—there's too much to do—but she insisted.'

Cash grinned at that. Lavinia wouldn't have been used to having too many people insist she did something. 'Well, she's right. You have to take care of yourself. Stressing yourself out by taking on too much work isn't going to help anyone.'

'Now you sound like Bob and Lincoln,' the older woman chided lightly.

Cash bumped the bottle of oil and had to quickly catch it before it fell from the trolley onto the floor. Get a grip. This was ridiculous.

'Lincoln mentioned he'd been over here fixing a fence for you the other day,' Lavinia continued. 'It's so good having him home.'

'I can imagine,' Cash murmured as she continued to set up the equipment. 'You've got a full house again.'

'Yes, it's lovely.

'Do you have any brothers and sisters?'

Cash's smile faltered at the unexpected question. 'I had a brother . . . well, half-brother. Johnny. He died a few years ago . . . in an accident.'

'Oh dear, I'm sorry, Cash. I didn't know. That must have been terrible.'

Cash managed a smile and turned away from the sympathetic look Lavinia was giving her. 'It was.' Terrible was one word for it. Devastating was probably more accurate. She hated thinking back to that time. She always felt so helpless and guilty. Johnny had been old enough to make his own choices, but she still blamed herself. She still tormented herself wondering whether she could have said anything to stop him from choosing the life he'd lived. It was a pointless and depressing mental debate. It didn't change anything. Johnny was gone and there was no way to get him back again.

'And your parents? That must have been devastating for them.'

'My mum died when I was fifteen. Johnny had a different mother, but she didn't stick around long after he was born, so Dad pretty much raised him. Dad didn't take it very well,' she said. Although Cash had rarely seen her father after she'd turned seventeen, she'd kept in touch with her younger brother and tried everything to encourage Johnny to take a different path to their father, one that involved getting a real job and avoiding the dirty money of illegal crime, but the lure of bikes and proving himself to his father had been too strong. Even though she'd always expected to hear that her brother was in trouble, she hadn't expected that he'd be killed in a drive-by shooting. He'd been nineteen years old. He'd had his whole life ahead of him. Her father's arrest a year later for a retaliation killing just made an unbearable situation worse.

Her family was nothing to be terribly proud of and thinking about them brought back a slew of insecurities. How could she tell a woman like Lavinia, who had raised her family with so much love and devotion, that her alcoholic, drug-dependent mother had died of an overdose and she'd had to live with her bikie outlaw father? The Callahans' life was so far removed from her own that she may as well be a different species.

'I'm very sorry to hear that, Cash,' Lavinia said, touching her arm gently.

A swift stab of emotion hit Cash square in the chest and she blinked hard to keep the tears at bay. Cash forced a bright smile to her lips. 'Well, if you're ready, we can get you set up in the room.'

Lavinia looked like she wanted to say more, but instead she put on a matching smile and gave a nod.

Cash took pride in all her treatments, but Lavinia Callahan was the kind of person who took care of everyone else first, and today Cash wanted to make sure she was well and truly pampered.

Seventeen

Linc pulled up outside Cash's house and turned off the engine. He hadn't been able to stop thinking about her since their last meeting. He'd been caught a few times, his mind wandering while he worked. He needed to stop doing that. His father had wanted to know what was going on, and he didn't want Griff to start asking questions. *Griff* . . . the thought of his brother was enough to snap him out of his schoolboy daydreaming. He felt like an arsehole. The last thing he wanted to do was drive the wedge any deeper between him and Griff, and even though he did feel a little bit guilty over sleeping with the woman his brother had a thing for, he wasn't doing anything technically wrong. Surely Griff had to man up and face the fact that Cash just wasn't that into him? Under normal circumstances any woman Griff would have been interested in would never had interested Linc. That was why this was so weird. Cash was not Griff's type. He had no business being interested in her. If he'd just stuck to the usual kind of women he favoured—the shy, quiet type—then they wouldn't be in this situation to start with.

Harvesting was in full swing and this year there was extra pressure to get it done. The wedding was drawing closer and there was still a lot of preparation to be done once they got the wheat in.

He'd spent the morning fuelling and degreasing the headers and blowing out the filters before going out on the chaser bin. His job was to follow the headers in order to fill up the bin with harvested seed. Every now and then Linc would swap with Griffin to drive the old header, while his brother oversaw the other workers sorting the grain, instructing them to keep what was needed, then to run it through the cleaner for next year's seed. The days were busy, and Griff and the other men worked long into the nights to keep things on track.

He'd thought about staying to help . . . briefly. The memory of Cash's skin, soft and warm against his, the way her eyes had watched him, half-closed and sleepy looking, the sound of her breath near his ear as she sighed and moaned . . . Linc reached for the door and opened it. Yeah, there was no way he was staying away.

As he walked towards the front door, he smiled at the flash of anger she'd shown him in the general store earlier today. She was even beautiful when she was angry. Although she hadn't been able to hold on to her anger for too long; maybe he was a little too cocky, but he was pretty sure he had the same kind of effect on her as she had on him. This morning he'd noticed her breathing had gotten decidedly heavier when they'd almost touched. She was not as cool, calm and collected as she'd have liked him to believe; he'd bet his life on it.

He heard footsteps approaching the door after he knocked briefly and waited. When it opened, he lost a tiny bit of his bravado. Christ, she was beautiful. He gave himself a mental shake and plastered the smile back on his face. 'Hi.'

'Hi. I wasn't sure you were still coming over.'

He wondered if she was annoyed with him, but he could see the tiny pulse fluttering at the base of her throat and he knew she was trying to hide her own nerves. 'Sorry, it took longer than I thought to finish up this afternoon.'

As she stepped back to allow him to come inside, Linc paused as he came level with her just inside the front door. He felt her go still as he lowered his head, his mouth hovering a breath away from hers for the briefest of moments before moving across her lips. It was only supposed to be the lightest of kisses, a greeting really, but the instant his mouth touched hers it started an inferno. Her arms snaked around his neck, bringing him closer, and his hands immediately went to her hips, pulling them tight against his own.

Cash couldn't feel where she ended and Linc began once they were locked together in the kind of kiss that romance books would have described as 'bone-melting'. They'd barely made it through the front door. She'd been attracted to men before—God knows she'd had her fair share of lust-induced sexual encounters—but it had never been like this. It had never been this potent. The man was like . . . she couldn't actually think of what he was like, he was doing things to her lower lip that short-circuited her brain. The tongue-and-groove wooden panels of the hallway behind her felt cool against the bare skin of her shoulders, and it was a stark contrast to the heat their bodies created pressed so firmly together.

Cash untangled her arms from her top as Linc tugged it up over her head, his big hands splaying across her midsection and his mouth doing delectable things to the side of her neck. Impatient hands tugged at his shirt, and while he lifted his head to dispose of the garment, she ran her fingers through his dark chest hair, smiling as he gave a small shudder as she traced her nails along the ridges of his rib cage, following the path of narrowing hair that dipped low beneath the waist of his jeans.

They were making out like a pair of lust-filled teenagers and she didn't care. Not one iota. He could take her right here in the hallway and she wouldn't even care. This was not what a nice boy would do. A nice boy would sit and have coffee, maybe a Tim Tam or two, before politely making out. At least that's what she assumed would happen . . . she didn't actually know for certain.

Linc slid his hands down her smooth thighs before cupping them in his hands and lifting her in his arms. The action made her gasp and forget all about good boys. Right now, with her legs wrapped around the waist of the sexiest man she'd ever known, she could barely even remember her name. It was pointless even trying to fight this. Just one more time and then she'd call this thing off . . .

❧

Linc felt like he'd just done a five-k march with a forty-kilo pack. His chest was heaving in an effort to catch his breath as he floated in the afterglow of the second most amazing sex he'd ever had. He wasn't proud of the fact he hadn't even waited until they'd left the hallway before he'd practically jumped her . . . Okay, he was a little proud. Anyone would think he'd been a monk for the last decade the way he lost control around this woman. He seriously needed to show her that he could seduce and woo with the best of them.

'This has to stop,' she said from beside him.

'What does?'

'This,' she said turning her head on the pillow to face him.

'Did I hurt you?' he asked, suddenly worried. They'd been pretty full on as they'd made their way to the bedroom. He was pretty sure he'd have the odd bruise where he'd knocked a hip on the doorway in their lust-filled hurry to get to the bed.

'What? No. It's not that . . . it's . . .'

'The bad boy thing,' he finished, realising what she was getting at. 'I don't know how many times I have to tell you, I'm not the kind of guy you think I am.'

Hearing her sigh made him a little annoyed. He'd never had a woman react to him like this. He wasn't trying to be a bad boy, or whatever she thought he was. He liked women . . . a lot. He always had; hell, he loved women. He loved everything about them: their smell, their soft skin, the sounds they made. But he didn't get off on how many hearts he could break or lying just to get a woman into bed. He'd been raised with two sisters, a mother and a dad who'd taught him to respect women. The fact that she still saw him as some kind of 'love 'em and leave 'em' bad boy really irked him.

'You're not the Tim-Tam-and-coffee type.'

'The what?'

'You know, someone you meet and invite over to have coffee. Someone you get to know first before you have sex.'

Linc looked at her silently for a few moments. Okay, so she had him there; he didn't usually go on coffee dates with women, but that didn't mean he couldn't. 'I like Tim Tams and coffee.'

The dry glance she shot him spoke volumes.

'Seriously . . . In fact, if I had Tim Tams right now I'd like to rub them all over your body and lick—'

'See! It's just not you.'

'Jeez. Okay then, fine. We can have Tim Tams and just dunk them in coffee if you want to be boring about it. But I think my idea is better,' he told her, quietly confident.

Linc let his gaze roam across her still flushed face and felt a kick in his chest. He really liked this woman . . . more than he cared to acknowledge. It should have scared the hell out of him, but it didn't. Not yet anyway. It was such a strange sensation that he allowed himself to mull it over quietly for a while. Right here, right now in this moment, he liked the way everything felt . . . except maybe the fact Cash thought he wasn't coffee-drinking-date-worthy. 'I *am* more than just a good lay, you know,' he told her, hoping to lighten the quiet reflection that seemed to be happening between them. 'I can do witty conversation.'

'Really?' she said dryly.

'What do you want to talk about? Local politics? National politics? World politics? I can tell you some of the best places to travel to and I can *definitely* tell you the places to stay clear of.'

Cash smiled a little at that and he felt the knot of apprehension that had begun to form inside him slowly begin to unwind. 'Tell me about growing up here,' she said after a brief hesitation.

Linc hadn't been expecting that, but he put one arm behind his head and held her hand with the other, linking his fingers through hers. 'Not much to tell really. I was never into farming the way Dad and Griff are. We all had to pull our weight growing up, though, so I did it, but I knew I didn't want to do it my whole life.'

'Did you always know you wanted to join the army?'

'Yep,' he said without hesitation, staring at their joined hands. 'Ever since I was a little kid.'

'Was your dad disappointed about you not wanting to be a farmer?'

'Yeah. I think for a long while he always thought I'd come around, you know?' he said, looking over at her. 'But he couldn't talk me out of joining up and I was out of here the minute I was old enough.'

'Was it so bad out here?'

'Nah,' he said, shaking his head slowly. 'I didn't hate it, not really. I think I just didn't appreciate it back then, not the way I do now anyway. I wanted adventure and excitement and there's not much of that out here. But it wasn't bad. As far as childhoods go, it was pretty cool actually. I was lucky.'

'Yes, you were,' she said softly. He wanted to ask her what she meant but he could tell from the look on her face that she'd already closed the door on any questions.

'How many girlfriends did you leave behind out here when you left?'

'None actually.' Linc chuckled at her dubious look. 'Seriously.'

'I find that extremely hard to believe.'

'Well, believe it. I could barely string two words together in front of a girl when I was a teenager.'

'So what happened?'

'The army, I guess. Once I found my niche, my confidence grew, and I suppose all the training helped fill me out a bit.'

'The uniform no doubt helped,' she added.

'I don't know—I'm told I look better out of it,' he said with a smug grin.

'And so the stud was born,' she announced sarcastically.

'What about you?'

'What about me?' she asked, but he detected the slight wariness to her tone and was curious.

'Where did you get your siren talents from?'

Her eyebrow kicked up at that. 'Siren?'

'Yeah, you know like in the old fairytales, beautiful women who lure men.'

'Oh right. Yeah, that's what I do.'

'You lured me,' he said, tugging her hand and bringing her closer.

'I guess I just have a special skill in attracting a certain type of guy . . . like bait . . . I'm like a prawn.'

'You look and smell a whole lot better than any prawn I've ever seen,' he murmured against her neck, knowing the effect it seemed to have on her and smiling against her skin at the low moan that followed.

'Maybe I should change bait,' she murmured.

'Wouldn't matter what you used, you've caught me hook, line and sinker.'

'Please tell me that line has never worked on a woman before?'

'I could, but—'

'—then you'd have to kill me.'

'It's working, isn't it?' he said between kisses.

'It wasn't the line.'

'Sure it wasn't,' he agreed, enjoying the way her heart rate picked up as he rolled and positioned himself above her. His own heart skipped a beat as he looked down at her long, dark hair spread out on the pillow around her head. She might not be a mermaid, but there was something about this woman that drew him into the depths of her bottomless, greeny-brown eyes. They acted on him like some ethereal dark forest beckoning him to lose himself in its mystery.

It was official. He'd lost his freakin' mind.

Eighteen

This was crazy. Crazy good, but still crazy. If this wasn't what she wanted, and she was so concerned that she shouldn't be doing it, then *why was she still doing it*? Linc had ended up staying the entire night, not that they'd gotten much sleep, but he'd set the alarm to leave early so he'd get home before he had to start work. There was a moment just after he'd turned the alarm off, as they lay snuggled together, that Cash had felt utter contentment. Linc hadn't said anything, but she'd known he was awake, she could feel his steady breathing against her back. Was he enjoying the warm cosy feeling too, or was he frantically trying to figure out how to chew his arm off so as not to wake her up and have to talk to her? She knew that was unfair—Linc wouldn't have stayed all night if he'd wanted to avoid the awkward morning chitchat after a casual fling. When his alarm had gone off, he'd kissed her temple before sliding from the bed, and a few moments later she'd heard the front door softly close behind him.

She may have been guilty of making bad decisions in her past, but she'd never stayed in a relationship if she hadn't wanted to be there. So *why* was this so different? *Maybe it's not as wrong as you're making out.* The little voice of reason wasn't totally lost on her. It *had* occurred to her, briefly. Maybe Linc wasn't as bad as she'd first thought, but he was still one of those guys who didn't seem likely to settle down in a cute little country cottage with a garden and a wife. Cash stopped folding the towels and frowned. Was that even what *she* wanted? When had she decided she wanted the *exact* same life Savannah had? Sure, she loved it out here, but when had the white picket fence and guy in an Akubra entered the picture?

Linc was hardly the domesticated type. He might not be in the military anymore, called away at the drop of a hat and gone for months on end, but he did have a business that would regularly take him out of the country and potentially put him in dangerous situations. At best, their relationship would be mostly long distance, with brief catch-ups when his schedule allowed. Even if he did stay exclusive to her and wanted a relationship, it was hardly a settled kind of relationship. Was that what she wanted?

Was it really worth continuing? It wasn't a one-night stand, but only barely. There wasn't likely any future in it. And yet when she was around him all her commonsense and logic flew out the window. When she was with him, she didn't care about how pointless it was—and that scared her. He was becoming a habit she didn't want to give up.

Her phone dinged a few minutes later and she gave a weary chuckle when she saw it was from Linc.

You. Me. Tonight. You supply the coffee. I'll bring the Tim Tams.

So all you want is a coffee date? she typed back.

Coffee and Tim Tams. No funny business. I hope you're not thinking of taking advantage of me?

Cash rolled her eyes at that but smiled. *Wouldn't dream of it. See you tonight.*

Yep, way to put a stop to it. After tonight. Definitely.

❧

The nights fell into a pretty regular pattern. Linc came over after work, occasionally later at night after a family meal, and stayed until his alarm clock went off, ready to head home and work with his father and brother. After the first couple of mornings, Cash broached the subject of his family, wondering if they'd asked him where he was all night.

'I don't think they know I've been out all night,' he said, easing down on the lounge next to her with his glass of bourbon, wearing only a pair of jeans he'd pulled on after they'd gotten out of bed to have a nightcap. 'They think I've been sleeping over at Griff's place. He reckons the paint fumes are worth the peace and quiet until the guests start arriving.'

'Surely they have to suspect? What do you tell them when you leave after dinner?'

'That I'm going out.'

'And they don't ask where you're going?'

'I'm not seventeen, Cash,' he grinned at her before taking a sip of his drink.

'But surely your parents want to spend time with you?'

'It's the middle of harvest, with Christmas just around the corner, and a week after that is my celebrity sister's wedding, being held at Stringybark, attended by other celebrities . . . My mother has a few more pressing matters to worry about than spending time with me and asking where I've been.'

'She loves having you home.'

'At any other time of the year, I wouldn't be able to get away for a single minute by myself, but this year it's crazytown at home and I'm doing my best to keep my head down.'

'Has Griff said anything about you disappearing?'

'Nope. He's been too busy being a damn martyr to notice anything else.'

It worried her that for such a close family, Griff and Linc clearly had some issues. 'What's going on with you two? Is it because of me? You haven't told him about . . . this, have you?'

'This?' he lifted an eyebrow.

'Us,' she amended almost grudgingly. She wasn't entirely sure what this thing they had going was supposed to be.

'So there is an "us", then?'

The slight self-satisfaction to his tone only caused her frown to deepen.

'You're trying to deflect my question.'

'The way you're trying to deflect mine?' he shot back.

'Fine, don't answer. I just want to make sure I'm not causing any problems between you and your brother.'

She heard Linc let out a long breath beside her. 'You're not the reason Griff and I have issues. I'm not sure why we always manage to rub each other the wrong way. I come home and vow we're gonna put everything behind us, but every time it just kinda gravitates back to us pissing each other off.'

'Something has to spark it off.'

'It's like he resents me. It wasn't always like this. We were fairly close after I left home and joined the army. I think it was once I got into Special Forces and wasn't getting home as much that we kind of drifted apart. I don't know what's going on with him—he's always loved farming, it was all he ever wanted to do, but lately it's like he's blaming me for the fact he's never really left here, other than his few years away at uni. It bugs the hell out of him that I come home and 'play farmer', as he calls it, then piss off again and go back to my life.'

'You'd think he'd like having an extra set of hands around the place,' Cash agreed.

'Apparently not. If I came home and did nothing, he'd bitch about that, and when I do help, that only annoys him more. So basically, I can't win either way.'

'So maybe it hasn't got anything to do with you. Maybe it's just something he's got an issue with and you're the one he takes it out on.'

'I never told him to stay here and be a bloody farmer,' Linc grumbled.

'No, but it could be that he's just reached a point in his life where he's realising that he's not where he wants to be.'

'Well, I'm done walking on eggshells around him. He needs to get the hell over it.'

Somehow Cash didn't think it was going to be as easy as that. Until Griff dealt with whatever his issue was, she doubted things would get any easier between the two men. Now was probably not the best time to be dredging up old hurts with Christmas and then a massive family wedding about to take place, but after all that was over . . . She pulled herself up. This wasn't her problem. After New Year, she wouldn't be here. She was quite sure the Callahans could sort out their family dramas on their own. So long as she wasn't part of the problem. 'I don't think it would help matters if Griff found out about you and I.'

She felt him turn his head and shift his body to look at her but didn't lift her gaze immediately.

'Let him get pissed off, I don't care.'

'You should care. I don't want to make things worse for either of you.'

'Look, I'm not gonna rub it in his face, but if he finds out, I'm not going to lie about it. It's none of his business.'

She wished that were true, but the fact was, if Griff found out about this, it was only going to cause bigger problems in an already volatile relationship. She didn't need that kind of guilt hanging over her head. Maybe she'd been listening to Savannah too long about bad karma. 'I don't want you to lie to anyone, but I think it's better that he doesn't find out.'

'I really don't want to talk about my brother while I'm sitting next to a gorgeous naked woman,' he said, reaching across her to slide her on top of him with unexpected skill and speed.

'I'm not naked, and I'm serious, Linc,' she said, trying to keep her voice firm despite the heady sensations swirling through her as his hands roamed lightly up her thighs.

'There's the problem then. You need to get naked and stop talking, Cash,' he mimicked her serious tone before lifting his head to kiss her.

~

The next day Linc opened the door to the spa and found Cash talking on the phone at the front counter. She looked up and smiled when she saw him and mouthed that she would only be a minute. Inwardly he cursed himself when his stomach flip-flopped as though he was a love-struck teenager.

'I know for a fact you're not booked in today for a massage, so what are you doing here, Lincoln Callahan?' she asked in that sexy damn voice he thought about all day long.

'I'm playing delivery boy,' he said, wiggling his eyebrows at her and gave a disappointed sigh when she informed him she had a client due any minute. 'Fine. Your loss. Pam gave me this to give to you. She said she forgot to tell you when you were in yesterday.'

Linc handed the parcel to Cash and saw her frown slightly as she turned it over, seemingly searching for a return address before cautiously opening it.

He watched as she ripped the outer paper off to reveal a cardboard gift box and carefully removed its lid. Inside was a wad of fifty-dollar notes, secured with rubber bands and stacked neatly. He caught only a brief glance, and he had no idea how much money was in there, but Cash quickly slammed the lid back on the box and placed it under the counter.

'Everything okay?' he asked, watching her stilted movements.

'Yeah, all good. I'll check it out later,' she smiled, before coming out from behind the counter to slide into his arms and kiss him. 'How's the harvest going?'

He knew she was trying to distract him, and damned if it wasn't working: he could hardly recall his own name when she kissed him like that. 'Almost done, thank God,' he said. Now he remembered why he'd never gone into farming. The work was bloody relentless. The sound of a car engine pulling up outside made him groan.

'I'll make it up to you tonight,' she promised.

'I'll be looking forward to it,' he told her, kissing her one last time before reluctantly allowing her to slip from his embrace to prepare for her client.

It wasn't until he was up inside the cabin of the harvester, sitting in for his old man for a while, that his thoughts drifted to the mysterious package. Who would have sent Cash a shitload of money? What was it for? And more importantly, why had he detected a brief moment of panic before she'd hidden it?

⁂

Cash tried not to think about the box out under the front counter. Damn it, just when she thought she had her life on track, he always managed to find her. Why the hell wouldn't the man just take no for an answer?

Wes Sullivan wasn't a man people refused. No one, that was, except his daughter. After Johnny's death, Cash cut any ties with her father that still remained, but even after he'd been put in prison, he continued to have her tracked down so he could send her money. The first few times it happened, she'd bundled it up and sent it back to her father's trusted club treasurer with a note telling him she didn't want any of her father's money or anything more to do with him. The next year she had a package delivered to her front door with no postmark and the club had moved underground to avoid being raided by the police. With nowhere to return it to, Cash had done the next best thing and donated it to charity. It had been a while since she'd received a delivery and she had hoped her father had given up on her. Today's package only proved that Wes Sullivan never gave up and that he could find her whenever he wanted to—even from behind bars.

She knew he was only trying in his misguided way to be a good father. He was providing for her by sending her his cut of the club's profits from the illegal enterprises they had scattered all around the country. The fact that she'd left him and his life behind when she was seventeen didn't deter him. She'd despised the violence of his world—the world that had killed her mother, after she'd given up even trying to be a mother and wife, and then her brother. She was so tired of the messed-up childhood she'd endured. She'd wanted so much more for Johnny, but her father had never known any other kind of life. She knew cutting him from her life after Johnny's death had hurt him, and that in his own warped way he'd really tried his best to be a father to her, but it wasn't enough. She refused to end up like her mother.

Opening that box earlier had made her feel dirty. Maybe it was a sign. Maybe it was the universe's way of reminding her where she'd come from and that all the big plans she had to mould herself into something better were just a waste of time. Who was she to think she could possibly ever fit into the Callahan's world when she'd grown up the way she had?

Her heart was heavy for the remainder of the day, and for the first time, Cash texted Linc to call off their plans for the evening. She couldn't face him. She couldn't find the energy to pretend she was fine when all she wanted to do was curl up in a ball and cry.

Linc frowned at his phone as he pulled it out of his pocket. She was cancelling on him? He had a strange feeling that it was connected to that damn box he'd delivered this morning. What had she gotten herself into? A million things raced through his mind—none of them very comforting. Could she be caught up in dealing drugs? He immediately dismissed it. No, not Cash. That couldn't be it, but he couldn't shake the gut instinct that something was not right.

He lay awake late into the night. More than anything he wanted to go to Cash and find out what the hell was going on, but something held him back. What if she was caught up in something bad? Were they at a point in whatever this thing was where he had a right to know what was going on? What was he to her? A boyfriend? A friend with benefits? Did that give him any say in how much he should know about her past? All he did know was that for the first night in weeks he was sleeping alone, and he missed having that warm body curved around his more than he liked to admit.

Nineteen

Linc wiped the sweat from his forehead with his sleeve before banging in the last nail to secure the loose timber floorboard of the old shearing shed. It had been years since the Callahans had used it for its original purpose. It had been built during the height of Stringybark's heyday when wool ruled the market. His great-granddad had returned from the war with grand plans for Stringybark, determined to create his legacy by doubling the number of sheep they ran and increasing the size of the shearing shed to make it one of the biggest in the district. His gamble had paid off and the property had gone from strength to strength with each new generation. While the sheep had been replaced by crops after a devastating drought that had gone on for almost ten years back in the 1990s, Stringybark still dabbled in sheep, but the emphasis was now on meat rather than wool.

As with most things around the place, the shearing shed wasn't wasted, it was used for storage. Linc's father came from an era when you didn't replace something if it could be fixed. There was no flogging things off just because a new model had come out. That was all well and good, except that when something broke down, as older machinery had a tendency to do, there was always a long delay to source spare parts and replace them. And that's why Linc was spending the day starting on the renovations in the shearing shed, instead of driving a chaser bin around the paddock filling up with grain. A broken cutter bar had put one of the headers out of action, and while it was never great timing for a breakdown, on this occasion it was even more frustrating because there was so much work to get to after harvesting in order to have the place ready for the wedding.

'It's looking good in here.' Hadley came into the shed carrying an insulated bag that she set down on the ground beside him. 'Mum sent lunch,' she said as an afterthought, while she surveyed the shed.

'I'm starving.' Linc wiped his hands on his pants before unzipping the bag to pull out a stack of cling-wrapped sandwiches and a thermos of coffee. 'There's no cake today,' Linc said, searching the bag.

'You're lucky you got what you did. Mum's been on the phone all morning.'

'Why? What's going on?' It was not like his mother to skimp on the goodies in his lunchbox. He was getting used to being spoilt with a homemade lunch every day.

'The hall committee just had a donation of over thirty grand to put towards their fundraiser for the Holm family. You know, Larry and Katie's little girl who needs that operation?' she added when Linc frowned slightly. 'Some anonymous good Samaritan donated it.'

This piqued Linc's interest immediately. 'Anonymous?'

'Yep. Everyone's trying to figure out who it was. The phone's been ringing off the damn hook all day.'

An image of bundles of fifty-dollar notes in a box flashed though his mind and his eyes narrowed slightly. 'Sounds like a bit of a mystery.'

Linc refocused his attention on finishing the floor repairs after a short break for lunch. He had a strong suspicion he knew where the donation had come from and he needed to find out what the hell was going on. Right or no right—he was determined to get to the bottom of it.

She knew she wasn't going to be able to fob off Linc for too much longer. It had already been two days since her father had barged his way into her life once again. She'd spent a sleepless night trying to come to terms with the jumble of emotions the package's arrival had created. She missed Linc. When she was around him she felt alive. He awakened things inside her that she hadn't felt in a long time. She was happy. She hated that the arrival of her father's money had intruded on all of that like a rude reminder of her past and where she'd come from.

There was no way she was keeping it—she didn't need any help from him, she never had.

Her father had disappointed her too many times as a child to take the risk of letting him back into her life. Her parents' volatile relationship hadn't been easy on her as she grew up. As much as she'd often wished she had her father in her life, the reality was that every time he did come back, it only ended in her mother spiralling into a pit of depression when he left again. Even at a young age, Cash had known she'd never become her mother. She would never be that dependent on anyone—her father, other men, kind-hearted friends—but herself. She remembered the indignity of watching her mother asking people for money to buy food when she'd sobered up and realised she'd spent everything they had on alcohol. She'd hated that look of pity on the faces of her mother's friends.

Cash paid her own way through life. She never once had to accept anyone's money, and she was not planning on starting now.

The answer to her problem had come to her while she was in town waiting to be served at the store. Pam had been talking with another woman about the hall committee wanting to raise funds for a local family with a sick child who needed urgent treatment, but they weren't sure if they could raise the necessary money in the short time they had.

Cash had asked for some postage stamps before heading to her car and withdrawing the box she'd placed under the front passenger seat. Taking out the money, she had quickly transferred it into a large yellow envelope, scribbling a note about using it to help towards the little girl's treatment; then, addressing it to the hall committee treasurer, she had placed it in the bright red postbox out the front of the post office.

It had been as though a weight had lifted from her shoulders. The heavy cloud of depression that had seemed to hover above her had cleared and for the first time since the parcel had arrived she had felt the sunshine on her face. It felt good to help someone. Maybe the money had come from illegal business dealings, maybe not, she didn't know and she didn't care. Regardless of how it was earned, it was now going towards helping someone who desperately needed it.

She heard the familiar sound of a vehicle approaching and braced herself for the questions that were sure to come. Linc was not a man easily fobbed off.

He came to a stop with one foot propped on the bottom step as she waited on the verandah. 'Hi,' she said, watching him for an indication of his mood. He didn't seem particularly annoyed, but there was something about his demeanour that made her wary.

'Everything okay?' he asked.

'Yep,' she answered.

'I didn't get a brush-off today, so I figured it was safe to come over.'

'I wasn't giving you the brush-off,' she said softly.

'Really?'

'Seriously. I just needed some time alone.'

'That sounds like a brush-off to me.'

'I just had some things to sort out. It wasn't about you and me.' This was getting off track, she needed to avoid any questions that related to the damn package. 'I missed you.'

'Are you in some kind of trouble, Cash?' As she narrowed her eyes slightly he went on to add in a don't-bother-to-deny-it tone, 'I saw the money in the box.'

'It's really none of your business, Linc.'

'I'm making it my business.'

'Are you serious? You're really going to stand there and do the whole macho thing?'

'I'm worried about you.'

'There's no need. I've got it all under control.'

'Cash, who sends that much money in the mail?'

God, this man was relentless. Fine. He wanted to know, she'd tell him. Maybe this would be the thing that woke him up to what he was getting into. 'My father. Okay? The package was from my dad.'

'Why wouldn't he just deposit it in the bank?'

'Because that's a little hard to do from behind bars.'

'Your father's in prison?'

'Yep.' Great. *Well, that certainly makes the break-up scene a lot easier,* she thought, feeling her buoyant mood plummet once again.

'For what?'

'Murder.' Technically it was discharging a firearm with intent to murder, and a few other bits and pieces, but it was basically murder.

She was pretty certain not much managed to stun Lincoln Callahan, but this had.

'So you see, sometimes it's best to leave things alone.' She turned to walk away, angry at having to reveal the dirty truth about her past and frustrated that it hurt so much to feel so exposed.

'Cash, wait. I'm sorry. I didn't mean to get pushy, I was just worried about you.'

'I've been taking care of myself for a long time. I don't need anyone's help.'

'Too bad,' he said quietly, making her stop and glance back at him. 'I'm here and I care,' he shrugged, taking the remaining steps to stand in front of her. 'I want to know everything about you, Cash. The good and the bad. Will you tell me about your dad?'

He had no idea what he was asking of her. The only person who knew about her childhood was Savannah. This wasn't something she told just anyone. But suddenly she realised that Linc wasn't *just anyone*. 'What do you want to know?'

'Everything,' he said simply.

Oh right, so just *everything* then! 'We're going to need something stronger than beer,' she warned him, turning to lead the way inside. She wasn't sure they made anything strong enough to make her family history sound palatable, but she found some bourbon in the cupboard and took down two glasses. This would do for starters.

'I guess you've figured out my family life wasn't like yours,' she started. 'Actually, it couldn't have been any more different. I lived with my mum mostly. Dad used to come and go—my parents had a love-hate relationship. Mum had a lot of emotional issues, mostly brought on by long-term drinking and drug use. I used to cook for us. We had help from my dad and the club, people would bring groceries over and sometimes cook us a few meals.'

'The club?'

'Motorcycle club . . . not the Ulysses kind,' she added dryly. 'My parents had this weird relationship. It was like they couldn't ever really end it. They couldn't stand each other, but they couldn't stay away either.' She'd struggled to work it out most of her life. It wasn't until her adult years that she realised it was something to do with animal magnetism. They were drawn to each other, but her mother's emotional issues and dependencies made it almost impossible to have any kind of normal relationship. Maybe if her father hadn't had his own demons to fight—his drinking was almost as bad—he could have gotten her the help she needed and they could have worked it out.

'Anyway,' she said, shaking off her melancholy, 'he lived part of the time with another woman, Janice, and they had my half-brother, Johnny.'

'Johnny and *Cash*?' he said doubtfully.

Cash closed her eyes wearily, 'Yep, you heard correctly.'

'Wow.'

'He had his heart set on me being a boy and naming me Cash, after his hero. When I turned out to be a girl, it must have taken the wind out of his sails, but he was determined to stick with the plan. A few years later he got his son.'

'What happened to your mum?'

'She overdosed when I was fifteen. That's when I went to live with Dad, Janice and Johnny.'

'Were you and your brother close?'

'Yeah, we were. I mean I lived with Mum, but we spent a lot of time together as kids. He worshipped the ground Dad walked on. When I got older I could see how messed up our life was, but Johnny didn't care. All he wanted was Dad's approval. He couldn't wait to follow in his footsteps. I couldn't wait to leave. I tried to convince Johnny to come with me, but it was like talking to a brick wall. I wish I'd tried harder.'

'I think that would have been pretty hard to do. Speaking from experience, teenage boys never listen to their sisters,' he told her, taking a sip of his drink. 'You were just a kid.'

'Yeah, I know. But part of me still feels guilty for leaving him behind. I could see he was headed for trouble. Dad was in and out of prison all his life and that's exactly where Johnny was headed when I left. Then a few years later there was this huge war between rival clubs and Johnny was killed one night outside our house. The club retaliated and Dad killed the guy who killed his son.'

'That's pretty full on.'

'Yep.'

'So how does the money come into it?'

'After I left he used to keep tabs on me. Then once he went to prison, he had his mates do it for him. Now and again money turns up when they track me down.'

'Where does the money come from?'

'No idea,' she shrugged, looking into her drink. 'Probably from nothing legal, but who knows, I haven't had anything to do with my father in years.' She'd had nowhere else to go after her mother died but it had been a miracle she'd lasted twelve months living with Janice who'd pointedly ignored her. She'd overheard enough arguments between Janice and her father to realise she was an unwelcome guest. She'd left at the first opportunity. 'Maybe he has legitimate investments but, either way, I don't want anything from him so I don't keep it. Never have.'

'So what do you do with it?'

Cash gave a nonchalant shrug. 'Find somewhere it can do some good.'

'Not many people would do that. No one would blame you if you decided to keep it and set yourself up.'

'I would.'

She took a sip of her drink, enjoying the sudden quiet between them.

'So I guess you wouldn't know anything about the anonymous donation made to the Holms, then?' he asked, eyeing her with a slightly lifted eyebrow.

'I don't know what you're talking about,' she answered calmly.

Hearing about the little girl who needed that operation had just about broken her heart.

'That was a pretty awesome thing to do,' he said quietly.

'I was in a position to do something. I guess in this case, I can be grateful for my father's reappearance in my life,' she said dryly. 'Please don't tell anyone, Linc,' she said, looking up at him. 'You're the only person other than Savannah who knows about my father. I've worked hard to distance myself from that life and I don't want to have it dug up for everyone to hear about now.'

'People aren't going to judge you because of who your father is, Cash.'

'Just promise me, okay?'

'Okay.'

Cash was glad that the rest of the day was relatively normal. They cooked dinner together and Linc entertained her with stories about his time in the army. It took her mind off the unpleasantness of having told him about her less than ideal childhood, but a lingering sadness remained. Yes, she was angry at her parents for not stepping up and doing what parents were supposed to do, and yes, she felt cheated of a childhood that most people took for granted, but mostly she was just sad. Sad for the woman who couldn't be happy, even with a child who adored her; and sad for the father who led his son down such a destructive path when he should have been trying to save him.

Twenty

It was hard to believe it was only a few days shy of Christmas. Last night she'd opened the front door to find a huge pine tree leaning against the frame and Linc, looking very proud of himself, standing next to it.

'What's this?'

'It's a Christmas tree,' he had said slowly.

'I know it's a Christmas tree, but what's it doing *here*?'

'I cut it down, just for you.'

Cash leaned her shoulder against the doorjamb and raised an eyebrow. 'How very manly of you.'

'Exactly. And I expect a manly reward in thanks after we set this big guy up inside.'

'You want to be rewarded for chopping down a perfectly happy tree living in the wild to shove it in a bucket in my living room to wilt and drop pine needles all over the place?'

'Where's your Christmas spirit, woman?' he asked, shaking his head.

'I have plenty of Christmas spirit, I just don't usually do the whole tree thing.'

'You have to have a Christmas tree . . . even in Afghanistan we had a Christmas tree,' he protested. 'It's not Christmas without one.'

It did smell good, though, and seeing as he was already carrying it inside, there had seemed little point in arguing with him about it. Apparently this year she was having a tree!

The past weeks had flown, with Cash kept busy with back-to-back appointments through the day and intoxicating nights of sex with one extremely hot commando.

Cash couldn't get enough of him. She'd expected the novelty to have worn off by now—he was rugged and charming in a God's-gift-to-women kinda way. There was nothing romantic about the man—he was pure, unadulterated sex on legs, and sparks seemed to ignite the moment they were within touching distance of each other. He could be cocky and brash, yet when they were together he made her feel as though she were the most exquisite thing he'd ever seen. She'd never felt as though she were the centre of someone's universe the way Linc made her feel when they were together. He always put her needs before his own, and as small a thing as that might be, when you'd never experienced it before, it meant a lot. Of course, she knew she wasn't really the centre of his universe, but for the time they were together he made her feel like she was. She'd stupidly believed that when the time came she'd be capable of switching off this whole holiday fling thing, but with each passing day it was becoming harder to remind herself of the rules she'd set for herself.

The hall in the centre of town was the pride of the community. Lavinia and Bob were part of the committee responsible for its care. They'd raised money for renovations over the years and it boasted an enviable kitchen, a necessity for the amount of time volunteers spent in there cooking and cleaning, or making endless cups of teas when hosting the multitude of events held at the hall.

Tonight they were hosting a carols by candlelight and Christmas party for the town. Each Christmas for as long as Cash could remember, she'd watched the Christmas Eve carols by candlelight on TV. It was her one guilty pleasure for the season, but she'd never actually been to a carols by candlelight event in person and she was possibly a little more excited by it than she should be.

As she parked her car, she noticed that each side of the street was lined with vehicles and already the park was crowded with people seated on fold-out chairs and blankets. Colourful fairy lights had been hung on the many beautiful trees the park boasted, and tinsel and Merry Christmas signs had been draped on every other available wall or post.

As she drew closer to the crowd the hum of happy voices in conversation flooded around her. She nodded at semi-familiar faces as she passed, exchanging Merry Christmases as she moved towards the hall. She wasn't sure where she was supposed to set up her chair, and as she searched the sea of faces for someone she recognised, she heard someone call her name.

Lavinia came towards her wearing a bright red apron with *Santa's helper* written across the front and carrying a tray of meat. 'I'm so glad you decided to come along,' she beamed.

'Wouldn't miss it,' Cash grinned back. 'Can I help?'

Lavinia smiled. 'If you'd like to? I don't want to put you to work when this is your first Christmas here.'

'I'd like to help out, if I'm not in the way.' She'd feel less conspicuous doing something rather than sitting on a chair by herself like a Nigel-no-friends.

'Well, all right then, come this way. I'll just drop off this meat to the men.'

Lavinia introduced her to a number of ladies in the hall who were performing various jobs inside the spacious kitchen area. Everything seemed to be working with military precision. Women up one end buttered bread, while others chopped onions and were arranging various salad components on the bench. Cash spotted Harmony stacking the dishwasher and smiled, getting a hesitant nod in return. It seemed there was one Callahan she was never going to win over. While everyone else seemed to be dressed in as much tinsel as humanly possible and wearing a variety of Christmas-themed T-shirts in red or green, Harmony looked as stylish as always in a white top and matching long, flowy lace skirt. The only colour she wore came from the chunky emerald abalone-shell bracelet edged in gold on her wrist. The woman knew how to throw things together to look classy.

At the other end of the hall was a large Christmas tree with wrapped gifts beneath and a few tables set up selling raffle tickets. To say it was a hive of activity would be an understatement, and yet despite the hustle and bustle, everyone was happy and there was a definite festive vibe filtering through the air.

Outside a band was playing a number of country Christmas carols, and various acts from the local primary school were performing on a makeshift stage.

Cash was given the job of running out anything needed by the food stalls. She kept up a steady stream of paper plates and napkins, emptied overflowing rubbish bins and helped out wherever she was needed. She couldn't remember a time when she'd smiled so much. Everyone was pitching in and the most mundane of chores were suddenly enjoyable. She chatted to a few women who lived out of town on properties, discovered a few common interests and generally enjoyed herself passing the time in easy conversation. She admired the strength of character a small place like Rankins Springs built in the people who lived out here. There was nothing close by when you lived so far from a major regional town. Even simple things like needing a doctor or a dentist involved fairly substantial travel time. And yet the children out here didn't seem to be suffering from lack of amenities. They were involved in sports and after-school events just like any kid in a larger town, only they had to drive a lot longer to get there, and the dedication of their parents to make time for these things was quite remarkable.

Once it got darker and the dinner rush had subsided, Cash and quite a few of the other helpers were ushered out of the hall to go and enjoy the carols.

'Go along with Harmony,' Lavinia said when Cash picked up her chair from where she'd left it earlier. 'I'll be over shortly. She'll show you where we're all sitting.'

Cash tried to engage Harmony in conversation, but her curt answers were not encouraging. She didn't know what she'd done to the woman, but she was getting sick of her frosty attitude. 'Do you come out to this every year?'

'Yep.'

'It must be nice to have something like this . . . a tradition.'

'Not that there's much choice when your parents are Lavinia and Bob Callahan,' she said dryly.

'I think it's great that they're so involved with their community.'

'Of course it is. They're the backbone of this town.'

'Are the kids here?' Cash asked as they drew closer to a group of people she recognised, among them Hadley and the Dawsons.

'No. They had previous engagements with friends in Griffith.'

'Oh.' She didn't want to ask about Don. Something told her that this was not Don's thing.

Hadley greeted Cash with a bright welcome, reintroducing her to Olivia and her mother, Sue, before rattling off another few names of people she hadn't met before who were clearly part of the Callahan social group. 'Where have you been?'

'Helping in the kitchen,' Cash said as she set her chair up, her protest as everyone shuffled their positions so she could fit in falling on deaf ears.

'I would have come over and rescued you earlier if I'd known,' Hadley said with a small grimace.

'It's okay, there were plenty of helpers,' Harmony put in briskly, and Cash regretted being seated between the two sisters.

'I knew you'd have everything under control, Mon,' Hadley threw back lightly. 'Between Mum and Mon, there's never any room for anyone else in a kitchen anyway.'

'Well, it's easier if everything's just left to those who can do it.'

What was it with this family? Cash wondered. Even the sisters had some feud brewing under the surface. For a picture-perfect family, they sure did seem to have some unresolved issues.

'How are the wedding preparations going? Or are you sick of everyone asking that?'

'Everything's under control,' she said. 'Mitch arrived this morning. It's starting to feel a bit real now.'

'At least you can take your mind off it for a while with Christmas,' Cash said, 'and it must be nice to see your fiancé again.' She caught sight of the man in question holding court nearby in the centre of a small group of men.

'Oh, we're used to being separated,' she said, waving off the question, 'but it'll be nice to show him around the place.'

'He hasn't been out here before?' Cash hadn't meant to sound surprised, but from the small grimace on Hadley's face, she guessed she had.

'Yeah, I know, but our schedules have been a major headache. We've just never seemed to be able to coordinate a time when we're both in the same country and have holidays at the same time.'

'Let's all keep our fingers crossed the wedding actually happens this time,' Harmony murmured.

'Don working again, is he?' Hadley asked, sipping her glass of wine while she watched her sister.

Harmony's mouth straightened into a tight line and Cash was grateful that Lavinia arrived with a couple in tow to save the sniping from escalating.

'Cash, have you met Bev and Kel yet? Bev's one of our local councillors.'

'No, I don't think so,' Cash said, greeting the couple warmly.

'I don't suppose you know anything about reading cards, do you?' Bev asked Cash. 'Savannah was going to do a night of angel card readings and we've never really gotten it organised.'

'Ah, no. I'm afraid the only cards I know anything about are poker and blackjack,' Cash said. At Harmony and Hadley's surprised glances, she quickly added, 'I worked in a casino for a while.' Which she had, but her father had taught her how to play poker when she was eight, although that probably wasn't a polite conversation topic to be broaching right now.

'You're a regular Jill of all trades,' Harmony commented.

'You have to be if you want to work and travel.' Bev and Kel moved on to find their seats and Cash noticed for the first time that it was finally dark enough for the candles to be lit and a hum of excitement ran through her. Maybe it wasn't as big and extravagant as the carols on TV, but what it lacked in size, the locals more than made up for in enthusiasm. Cash belted out the carols with gusto—Mariah Carey she wasn't, but she didn't let that stop her from enjoying the experience. There was just something about Christmas carols that made you feel happy.

When the last carol was sung and Santa had been and gone in the back of a ute, having thrown out lollies to the kids and handed out presents from under the tree, everyone began to disperse. Chairs were folded, blankets shaken, handshakes swapped and hugs given, and within minutes the crowded park was deserted.

The group said their farewells and Lavinia gave her a hug. 'You *are* coming over on Christmas Eve, aren't you?' she said, although it sounded more like a statement to Cash, who smiled and nodded. 'Lovely! I'll see you then, and thank you for all your help tonight. You know, this community suits you.'

Cash experienced one brief moment of elation at the words, before swallowing it back. She wasn't staying here forever. Very soon she'd be moving on. It was important to remember that before she let this fantasy that had been forming in her head take root. As much as she adored this little town, she didn't belong here. The thought made her sad. She'd been fooling herself to think that she could find some nice wholesome boy and reset her life. She'd tried but look where she'd ended up. With Lincoln Bad Boy Callahan.

'So, are you coming to the pub?' Hadley asked as they headed towards their cars.

'I wasn't planning on it,' Cash said honestly. She was on a Christmas carol high and wasn't sure she was in the mood to handle drunken farmhands and loud pub music.

'Come on, it'll be fun,' Hadley urged. 'Linc's there.'

Cash had assumed carols weren't Linc's thing, or his brother's for that matter . . . Actually, come to think of it, there'd been very few males under the age of thirty at all there tonight. Of course, they'd all be across at the pub. The night before, Linc and Cash had agreed to do their own thing tonight. She didn't really want to be seen by the entire town with Linc at the carols, and although she felt a little bad, she still believed it had been the right decision not to tell anyone about their fling. It was bound to cause drama and that was something this family seriously had enough of at the moment. What would it prove? It wasn't going to last, so why create problems if there was no need to.

However, knowing he was at the pub only a few hundred metres away made it very hard to say no. Damn it, she missed him.

'I suppose I could stop in for one drink.'

'Great! Let's go.'

Cash put her chair in the back of her car and locked the door, hoping her mouth didn't drop open when she saw Harmony had joined her younger sister and Olivia by the time she caught up to them.

The pub was crowded. Clearly this was a general meeting place and on a night like this, when everyone was in town for the carols, it was a good time to catch up with people you hadn't seen in a while. Everywhere she looked people sat in groups laughing and smiling. The roar of conversation outdid the music from the jukebox and it was almost impossible to hear anything without shouting. Within moments of coming through the door, Hadley was swept into a nearby group of people about the same age, and Cash gathered they were all old schoolfriends. She didn't want to gatecrash the reunion so she continued walking towards the bar. She glanced around to see where Harmony was but couldn't see her anywhere. Great, ditched as soon as possible. As Cash debated whether she should bother ordering a drink or just go home instead, a hand slid around her waist and she jumped as a slurred voice greeted her.

'Cash! You're here. This is Cash,' Griffin said, turning her to face a small group of men who'd been standing behind her. She recognised Oliver Dawson, who gave her a friendly enough smile, but she didn't know either of the other two men who weren't bothering to hide their leers. Cash instantly recoiled. Griffin still had his hand on her waist and while she wasn't repulsed by the action, she was getting an uncomfortable feeling that it was a little too intimate and was about to move away when Hadley and Olivia joined the group.

Over the last few times they'd met, Olivia had begun to warm to her, or so she'd thought. The look she was sending her right now was cold enough to rival even Harmony. *Now what?* She couldn't possibly have done anything within the short space of time from the park to here. However, when Olivia's gaze shifted to Griff, she looked wounded and suddenly it became clear. Olivia had feelings for Griff.

In an instant the moment was gone and Olivia had turned to join another group. Griff dropped his hand from her waist and announced that it was his shout and headed for the bar.

'How were the carols?' Linc's question startled her and she turned around to the slightly dishevelled but undeniably hot man who now stood beside her. How did a man in a wrinkled shirt and cargo pants manage to look this damn good? God help her, she swallowed past the sudden dryness of her throat as her gaze fell onto the tuft of dark chest hair that poked out from the undone top button of his shirt. She wanted to tear off his clothes right here and now. 'Sorry? What?'

His lopsided smile told her that, somehow, he'd managed to read her thoughts. 'The carols? How were they?'

'They were great. I had a good time,' she said, raising her voice over the noise, although with him standing this close, she was surprised she had the strength. The warm smell of his body made her legs go weak.

'That's good,' he said, nodding. His eyes held hers with an intensity that anyone nearby who hadn't been drinking most of the night would have recognised as lust-fuelled. They had to knock this off now, before someone *did* see.

'I think I'll head home.'

'I don't think I'll be hanging around either,' he said, holding her gaze just a little longer than was acceptable for polite strangers. She was pretty sure the message was clear: he'd follow her home shortly. The prospect made her stomach do flip-flops.

'It was nice to see you,' she smiled and nodded before turning away from his knowing grin. The others were all deep in conversation, or nowhere to be found in Harmony's case, so she decided to leave without interrupting.

Outside she could still hear the noise, but it was muted and her ears had to adjust to the quiet. The wide empty road through town stretched off into a black abyss in both directions. The evening air was warm, but much cooler than it had been through the day, and Cash breathed in deeply, filling her lungs with the sweet scent of blossoms and gum trees that surrounded the area in a green oasis. A movement and sound drew Cash's attention across into the relative shadows where a bench sat, mostly hidden from the glare of the streetlights. She could make out the silhouette of a couple deep in conversation; the larger, a man she assumed, was comforting the smaller figure of a woman.

Cash trod carefully, hoping her footsteps wouldn't disturb the intimate moment, but it was obvious that the couple were too absorbed in each other to hear anything other than their own low murmuring. As Cash drew level with them, a beam of moonlight hit the woman's arm and Cash caught the flash of something green and gold before the light shifted and she passed by, unnoticed.

She hurried the remainder of the way to the car and unlocked her door, feeling ridiculous at how stealthy she was being. As she reversed and headed onto the road towards home, she glanced across at the park bench, but no one was there. An uncomfortable feeling settled in her stomach. She could, of course, be mistaken, but that flash of colour on the woman's wrist had looked remarkably like the emerald and gold bracelet Harmony had been wearing tonight. And she was pretty sure the man sitting on that bench had not been Don.

Twenty-one

'Your mum's invited me over for Christmas Eve drinks,' Cash told Linc as they lay quietly listening to the night sounds outside her bedroom window.

'Pretty sure you've wrapped both my parents around your little finger.'

'Your parents are great.'

'Yeah, they are. I don't know how they've made time for everything they've done over the years. Dad's worked the farm and is in the rural fire brigade,' he said. 'They're both involved in the Farming Federation, the hall committee and the race day committee.' He shook his head. 'Mum's always been on school and sports committees, plus raising us four kids. They've always been there for us.'

Cash couldn't even imagine how they managed. 'It blows my mind how many roles they take on around here.'

'In small places like this, you have to if you want to keep things like sports groups and events going. As kids grow up and leave, the parents who volunteer also drop out, so there has to be a constant handing down of the reins to keep things going. There's been a lot of changes over the years and people just don't want the responsibility, so the committee members feel like they need to stay on longer and longer. I think Mum and Dad just can't bear to see all their years of hard work lost if things close due to lack of volunteers. It's a shame, because they should be able to retire and take it a bit easier.'

'Maybe they'd be lost if they didn't stay busy. It'd be hard for them to suddenly find themselves with nothing to do.'

'Yeah, that's a part of it too. Mum in particular—she's only happy when she's busy. I think she thrives on stress myself.'

'Some people are like that,' Cash agreed. 'Harmony reminds me a lot of your mother.'

'Yeah, she's grown up around the whole community thing, I guess.'

'She doesn't like me very much.'

'Don't take it personally. I don't know what's going on with Mon lately. She wasn't always this . . .'

'Bitchy?'

'Yes,' he conceded. 'I've tried to talk to her, but she's not exactly opening up. I guess I haven't really been around enough to figure out what's been going on. I'm pretty sure

Griff knows more than he's letting on. But then he's not exactly into having any kind of meaningful conversation with me either.'

'I think you need to try again. You guys have to get this sorted.' She really wasn't sure why this upset her so much—it wasn't any of her business. There was just something sad about watching a family that contained so much love fall to pieces like this. If only they realised how precious a gift it was, to be born into a family like theirs.

She'd debated about telling Linc what she'd seen on her way home but decided not to say anything. She didn't want to start anything—particularly if she'd made a mistake. But she had a sinking feeling that whatever was going on with Linc's eldest sister, it couldn't keep going the way it was. Eventually something was going to snap, and it wasn't going to be pretty when it did.

Cash pulled up in her usual spot at Stringybark Creek and noticed there were a lot of cars already here. She ticked off the Dawsons' vehicle, and Harmony's expensive Land Rover, a few bulky farm utes and Oliver Dawson's flashier sports ute, which had probably cost almost as much as Harmony's imported monstrosity.

She bought only a box of chocolates this time, after getting in trouble for bringing anything last time and then feeling more than a little intimidated by the quality and quantity of Lavinia's cooking. She knew there would already be a ton of food.

As she approached the foot of the stairs a hand shot out of the darkness and dragged her into the shadowy well beneath the staircase. Her stifled gasp was lost as a warm mouth closed against her own, and fear instantly turned into fire at the familiar touch.

Linc buried his face in Cash's neck and she let out a shaky breath, her body liquefying. Behind her the timber boards of the closed-in understorey of the large house pressed into her back, and the cool touch on her skin contrasted the heat from his body which pressed against her from the other side. His roughly whispered coarse words would have earned anyone else a slap across the face, but somehow his deep, gravel-like tone softened the words and sent a shiver of need through her.

The sound of voices coming out onto the deck above them froze Cash to the spot and had her clutching Linc's arms in warning. He lifted his head to listen and another low expletive left his mouth—this time a soft mutter aimed at bad timing and interruptions. When he didn't move away, Cash gave him a glare and tossed her head in the direction of the voices pointedly.

'Stuff 'em,' he said quietly. 'I'm over this, Cash. I don't care if they know about us. I'm pretty sure they already suspect anyway.'

'*Griff* doesn't know, and you can't let him find out like this,' she said urgently, genuinely worried about how such an announcement would affect the rest of the evening's festivities. 'You know how much your mum's been looking forward to Christmas, we can't risk ruining it if Griff gets angry.'

'Bugger Griff. He's a grown man, he can take it. He's invited a date tonight, so I'm pretty sure he's moved on. In fact, the more I think about it, the stupider I feel that we didn't just tell him from the beginning.'

'It's not about whether he's moved on or not. He's going to think you were the reason he and I didn't work out.' Confrontation had always made her anxious and somehow she knew that Griff wasn't going to take the news of their dating, or whatever this was, too well.

'Okay, fine,' he sighed wearily. 'But I'm not pandering to Griff forever. He's going to have to find out sooner or later. I'm getting too old for this shit.'

A slow smile spread across Cash's mouth as she took in his angled eyebrows and fierce expression. 'Has anyone told you how sexy you look when you pout?' she teased quietly.

'I don't pout,' he growled, dipping his head back down to nuzzle at her neck, wiping the smile from her face in an instant.

'My mistake,' she sighed, before reluctantly sidestepping from his embrace and straightening her outfit. 'If you behave yourself for the rest of the night, I might let you explain what you were doing,' she told him.

'You like it more when I *don't* behave,' he said, flashing her the cocky grin that seriously made her knees buckle—not that she'd ever tell him that, though.

'Oh, there you two are,' Hadley said with a wiggle of her eyebrows as they reached the top of the steps. 'Gran's serving the eggnog.'

'I don't think I've ever had eggnog before,' Cash said.

'For real?' Hadley said, giving her a double-take.

Cash shook her head. 'Christmas wasn't quite the same as this in my house.'

'This family does Christmas to the max,' she said dryly, swapping a look with her older brother. 'Oh well, at least your first eggnog will be memorable. A word to the wise,' she said, dropping her voice a little. 'Go steady. At first they seem harmless, but they have a nasty habit of sneaking up on you and, before you know it, you find yourself half-naked in the back of Tezza Ashcroft's ute singing "Six White Boomers" as you do circle work around the paddock at three in the morning.'

Cash swapped an amused glance with Linc before following Hadley back towards the house.

'So where have you three been hiding out?' Harmony asked as they walked into the living room where everyone seemed to be gathered.

Cash was conscious of Griff looking up at their entrance, watching them closely. Thankfully Hadley stepped in calmly and saved the day. 'We were outside admiring Mum's decorations.'

'Here you go, dear,' Gran said, handing over a glass of creamy eggnog from the tray she held. 'Take a seat, it's present time.'

Cash snapped her head around to look at Linc in a panic. 'Presents? What presents? I didn't bring any!' Who the hell did presents on Christmas Eve?

'It's all right, it's just a tradition Mum likes to do, it'll be fine,' he reassured her, reaching around her to take his own glass.

Cash looked on in bemusement as a commotion erupted outside, and moments later Lavinia stepped into the room dressed in a short red Mrs Claus outfit, with a fluffy hemline over fishnet stockings, red boots and a red stocking cap on her head. Santa Claus followed, ho-ho-ho-ing into the room and carrying a large red sack.

'Santa!' Lavinia gasped as the jolly man in the red suit planted a smack on her bottom as he walked past.

'Let me check who's been naughty and nice,' Bob's deep, after a few too many Scotches, voice boomed through the room as he pulled out a piece of paper and tried to focus on the writing, holding it at arm's length. 'I can't read the bloody thing,' he complained. 'Never mind! I'm pretty sure you're all on the naughty list anyway. Let's see who we have here,' he went on, pulling out the first parcel.

'Holder, where's Holder?' he called in a Santa voice, looking around the room. The reluctant teen put his hand up, looking as though he'd rather be anywhere else but here with his crazy grandparents playing Santa and Mrs Claus in the middle of the room.

'Here you go, Merry Christmas Eve.'

'Thanks, Granddad.'

'No, no young man, it's *Santa Claus*,' Bob insisted with a wink, before turning away to dig back in the bag and missing the young boy's roll of the eyes as he headed back to his seat to open his gift.

'Do we have a Harmony here?' Santa Bob asked, before spotting his eldest daughter and handing over the brightly wrapped parcel.

Cash noticed with interest that Harmony wore a real smile; it was only a small one, but it was the first time she'd seen the woman relaxed. Clearly this family tradition must have held some special memories, if the ice woman's softening was any indication.

Cash noticed that Linc had found a seat, perched on the arm of the lounge beside Harmony and his niece. She wasn't sure if it was to maintain distance, or just because seating was limited. She caught his look and felt a lick of heat caress her skin at the message she read there: *Later, we're going to pick up from where we left off.* She dragged her gaze back to the entertainment in the centre of the room and tried to calm her frantic pulse.

'Where's Cash?' Santa said, scanning the room until he came to rest on her, his white moustache slipping slightly. 'Ah, there she is,' he grinned, handing the gift to his wife.

'Merry Christmas,' Lavinia said, placing a kiss on her cheek.

'Thank you,' Cash stammered, looking up from the red-wrapped square-shaped object. 'You shouldn't have—'

'Rubbish,' she said, waving off her protest as she moved back to assist Santa in giving out the next present.

Cash stared at the gift a moment, before gingerly placing it on her lap, fighting a barrage of unexpected emotions. Christmas had never been like this for her. Growing up she hadn't had the luxury of believing in Santa and waking up to presents under the tree. Her father had tried one year, when she'd been about seven or so. There'd been a tree and tinsel and even presents. Looking back, it had been her parents' final attempt to resurrect their marriage. Things had started well; her dad was home and her mum had seemed happy, the happiest she'd been in a long time. Cash had lain in bed on Christmas Eve, asking Santa to please, please make it last. She missed her dad when he wasn't there, and Mum didn't cry as much when he was around. She didn't sleep all day on the lounge either.

On Christmas morning, Cash had woken up early and run out to the tree, only to find it knocked over and the presents scattered around the room, crushed and broken. Her mum was asleep, draped across the lounge, an empty bottle tipped over on the floor beneath her outstretched hand. Her makeup was smudged and marked with tear tracks, and her left eye was swollen and red. It always ended the same way.

Cash carefully picked through the debris on the floor, managing to save a few of the presents. There was no sign of the Pound Puppy she'd been hoping for, but there was a My Little Pony, lying under some ripped wrapping paper, one side of the box crushed. It wasn't the purple one she'd wanted but that was okay, it was still pretty. It was an apricot colour with a pale pink mane. She'd lifted it to her nose and breathed in the plastic, sweet smell and gently touched the flowing mane. It was beautiful.

There were a few board games, all of which had been smashed in drunken rage, her mother's or father's, she couldn't tell. Not that it mattered—who was she supposed to play board games with anyway? She never had any friends from school come to her house to play; how could she when she never knew what kind of mood her mother would be in from one day to the next?

Now looking up from the parcel on her lap, she found herself smiling at the obvious love in the room. Christmas had never been a big event in her life even as an adult. She usually avoided it. What a different life she would have lived if she'd had functioning parents instead of the two she'd been given. Cash blinked away the memories and swallowed past a tightening throat.

She hadn't thought about that Christmas in years. She did her best not to think about the past—what was the point? She couldn't change anything, and all it did was make her feel sad. If there was one thing she couldn't stand, it was feeling sorry for herself. She'd witnessed first-hand the damage that kind of habit could do. Her mother had blamed everyone else for the life she had. It wasn't until Cash was older that she realised there were a lot of people who had terrible lives, but complaining about it never helped. You either picked yourself up and found a way around your problems, or you laid down and stayed where you were and never got up again. She was never going to be in the same situation as her mother. She didn't want success in a monetary sense, she just wanted to make a life for herself that was better than the one she'd had growing up. She'd learned early on that the only person she could count on was herself, and that lesson had served her well.

It made her self-sufficient, and if she stuffed up, there was only herself to blame and only she got hurt.

'You can open it, dear,' Gran said, coming around with the tray of eggnog and handing Cash another one. 'Santa always brings us one gift on Christmas Eve to open.'

Cash took a sip of the eggnog and placed it on the table beside her, before turning the package over and lifting the sticky tape from the neatly folded corners. As she peeled back the paper, a wooden sign was revealed, the kind that Savannah had dotted through her house. This one had *Friends are the family you find along the way* painted on it in an elegant script and Cash found herself blinking back the sting of tears as she read the words.

She quickly wrapped the paper back around the gift and slipped it into her handbag. She needed time to digest the thoughtful present, something she couldn't do here. Mr and Mrs Claus continued their way around the room, handing out brightly wrapped gifts, and Cash took in the smiles and laughter from around the room. Christmas carols played in the background and there was an overwhelming feeling of happiness and cheer in the room. It felt almost magical. She'd always scoffed at the Hallmark-type Christmas movies that played each year, depicting smiling faces and Christmas-card perfect scenes, figuring they were all fantasy, but being part of this tonight made her question that idea. Maybe it wasn't as fake as she'd thought. Maybe people really did have these kinds of perfect Christmases after all.

Twenty-two

Hadley came to sit down beside her, opening her parcel and lifting out a T-shirt with *Mrs Elf* scrawled across it in bright red letters. 'My mother kills me,' Hadley said, shaking her head and pointing to her fiancé seated across the room, who held up a matching *Mr Elf* T-shirt.

'Do your parents do this every year?' Cash asked after she picked up her drink and took a large sip.

'Yep,' Hadley said with a tolerant smile. 'Bless their cotton socks.'

'I feel really bad that I didn't bring them anything. I didn't know they'd get me something.'

'Don't feel bad, Mum shops all year to find these silly presents. They're only supposed to be a bit of fun. She gets a kick out of it.'

Cash noticed Linc wearing a baseball hat with a long straw attached to the side, and *Beer hat* scrawled across it.

After all the presents had been delivered, Mr and Mrs Claus left the building and everyone was free to mingle once more.

Hadley dragged her fiancé across and introduced him, and Cash had a brief moment of gaping silence. She knew Hadley was a celebrity of sorts, being that she regularly featured on the news, and she knew her husband-to-be hosted his own nightly current affairs program, but she hadn't been prepared to actually meet someone famous face to face. Thankfully she shook herself and snapped out of it; after all, it was a little hard to take someone seriously when they were wearing a *Mr Elf* T-shirt, even if they looked less amused by it than everyone else was.

'Please tell me I don't have to wear this tomorrow?' he whispered in a low voice to Hadley.

'Just humour them. You only have to wear it in the morning.'

'It's nice to meet you, Mitch,' Cash said, hoping this wasn't going to turn into a mini domestic with her stuck in the middle.

'Yes, you too. Cash, was it?'

'Yes. I'm the fill-in neighbour . . . sort of . . .'

'I see.'

'Cash's the beautician we're using for the wedding.'

'Oh,' he said as something obviously registered. 'Great. I guess I'll be seeing you soon then,' he said with a quick grin as his mobile went off and he excused himself to answer it.

'He's a little distracted,' Hadley apologised with a dismissive hand as he disappeared from the room without a backward glance. 'Work.'

'I imagine it's hard to escape it when you're so well known.'

'Anyway,' Hadley smiled brightly, 'I've been meaning to ask where you went to the other night. I looked everywhere for you at the pub and couldn't find you . . . or my brother, oddly enough.'

Cash flashed a warning glance at the other woman as she discreetly looked around to make sure no one else was listening. 'I saw you were busy so I decided to go home early. I was pretty tired.'

'Oh, of course,' Hadley gushed with a wink. 'I can only imagine how *tired* you were.'

'I think I might head outside, it's a bit warm in here,' Cash said, ignoring the devilish chuckle from the woman beside her.

It was cooler outside, not by much but at least there was fresh air. Cash headed towards the railing and jumped slightly as a low voice greeted her from nearby.

'How you been?' Griff asked, leaning forward as he cradled his beer in his hand and watched her through slightly hooded eyes.

'Busy. I've been booked out.'

'That's good.'

Cash nodded, looking anywhere but at Griff. *Stop acting guilty. You've done nothing wrong.* 'How've *you* been?'

'Yeah. Busy. Been flat out tryin' to get the last of the wheat harvested. And the wedding stuff,' he added with a pained expression. 'That's pretty full on.'

'I can imagine,' she smiled at him, but it wavered slightly when she saw his eyes dart away from hers to look down at his beer. 'Is that the woman from the pub that you were sitting with earlier?'

He glanced up at that and she saw a flicker of irritation cross his face. 'Yeah. Ashley.'

'She seems nice,' Cash said, wishing this wasn't so awkward.

'She is. What about you? Seein' anyone?'

'What?' She felt jumpy all of a sudden, surprised by his question.

'Haven't seen you around much lately.'

'Like I said, it's been crazy with pre-Christmas bookings.'

'Apparently you've been having affairs with just about everyone in town,' he said drolly.

'What?'

'Every time I go into town I hear a different version of who you've been seen out with.'

'Sorry to disappoint you, but I'm pretty sure they've got the wrong person.'

'I heard you were flirting with Benny Rogerson the other day.'

'Who on earth is Benny Rogerson?' Cash asked, bewildered.

'The guy who works at the petrol station.'

'The petrol . . . oh, please,' she scoffed. 'We talked about the weather!'

Griff gave a half-grin and shrugged. 'That counts as chattin' someone up out here.'

Cash felt the previous tension slip away and was relieved to see him smile. 'Well, in that case, I guess I have been flirting with pretty much everyone in town,' she told him dryly. 'Seriously? Do people not have anything better to do than create gossip?'

'Nope. That counts as most of our entertainment.' Griff gave a choked kind of laugh at her shocked look, before taking a hurried sip of his beer, making her eyes narrow suspiciously.

'Please tell me you didn't believe any of that?'

'What? Nah, of course not,' he said but didn't look her in the eye.

'I'd like to know how I've found the time to go through every man in town when I can barely find enough time to go shopping and buy food.'

'That's what happens around here. You're a pretty big deal, being new and all. People talk.'

Cash winced. 'Yeah, well, I wish they'd find something else to talk about.'

'You just have to wait until the next big scandal breaks out.'

'Or the wedding of the century,' Hadley put in as she came over, having clearly been eavesdropping. 'Don't worry, they'll forget all about you once the wedding gets closer. They'll be no doubt expecting me to do a runner at the altar.'

'They couldn't just be happy that you're getting married?' Cash still couldn't get used to strangers finding her life so fascinating that they enjoyed talking about it to one another.

'Where's the fun in that?' Hadley said, sending her a sarcastic look. 'Don't worry about it, it'll pass.'

Another tray of eggnog came around and Cash reached for one with a smile. It really was the most delicious drink she'd ever tasted.

'Go steady on those things, they have a tendency to sneak up on you,' Griff warned as he eyed her downing the drink.

'They're delicious,' she said, waving off his concern. If he knew how much she and the other resort workers used to drink on the islands, he'd be horrified. Linc wouldn't. Linc would probably have been right there beside her, back in the day, but poor Griff wouldn't be too amused with a girlfriend who held the record for the most shots drunk in a night. It really was a shame there was no spark between them, she mused as she studied Griff now. She just couldn't understand it. He was a good-looking guy. He was kind and polite. He was perfect . . . *perfectly wrong for her,* she thought with a silent sigh. Then again, she corrected as her eyes fell upon his brother, Linc was *perfectly wrong* for her too, but in completely opposite ways. Everything was so damn confusing. Why couldn't it be simple just this once?

'More eggnog anyone?' Gran asked.

'Yes, please!'

'Ah, maybe you should ease up on those, Cash,' Griff cautioned, lifting an eyebrow at her as she frowned across at him.

'I've had,' her frown deepened as she tried to remember how many glasses she'd already had, before shaking her head and having to stop when everything kept moving a little. 'I haven't had that many,' she finally said, giving up trying to count. There was no way she could be drunk on the handful she'd already had. She gave Griff a sharp eyebrow lift just to drive home her point, but from the dubious look on his face, she wasn't altogether sure her eyebrows were cooperating the way they were supposed to.

'Griff, you still okay to drive me home? I'm actually not feeling well. I think it was something in that eggnog.'

Cash turned to look at the newcomer to the conversation, noting it was Ashley.

'Ah, sure,' Griff said. 'You want to leave now?'

'Yes,' she said curtly as she forced a smile at Cash.

'I can drop you off at home on the way, Cash, if you like,' Griff suggested, looking unamused as Cash tossed back another glass of eggnog.

'No, that's all right, Griff. You two go ahead.' She was surprised by Griff's offer of a lift, and as tempting as it would be to flirt a little with him just to mess with the other woman, Cash couldn't do that to Griff. She couldn't send out mixed signals to him and risk hurting him. It wasn't fair. She may be inexplicably tipsy, but she could still read the flashing warning signs from Ashley, who had slipped an arm around his waist.

She watched them walk across to say goodnight to everyone, and Cash inwardly shook her head. Everything would have been so much easier if she'd been the kind of girl who could fall in love with Griffin Callahan and live out here forever, happily ever after.

Twenty-three

Linc knew Griff was probably pretty ticked off that he had to take Ashley home just when he'd been settling in for a long cosy chat with Cash. He told himself not to be childish, but he couldn't deny he was getting more than a little annoyed that he'd agreed to keep this thing he had with Cash quiet. Earlier, under the front steps, he couldn't have cared less who came around the corner and sprung them. He just didn't care. He liked her—a lot. She made him crazy and he couldn't stop thinking about her. He felt like a damn teenager again, getting all sweaty and excited when he saw her. Jesus Christ, imagine if the boys in his unit could hear what he was thinking, they'd never let him live it down.

As Cash reached for yet another top-up of his gran's potent eggnog, he got to his feet. Someone had to put a stop to the train wreck that would follow tomorrow morning if she didn't stop drinking those things right now.

'Having fun?' he asked, taking the seat his brother had just vacated. He watched her eyes widen slightly as she looked up at him. 'Are you ready to head home?'

She looked around nervously, checking that no one was watching them, he supposed, before giving a nod of her head. 'I'll just go and say goodbye to your parents.' She stood up abruptly and caught him off guard as she swayed on her feet.

'Whoah. You right?' He stood up, his hand shooting out to steady her.

'I'm fine! Why does everyone keep asking that? I haven't even had that much to drink,' she told him, but spoilt her outrage by taking a step and clasping onto his arm for support again. 'Stupid high heels,' she muttered under her breath.

'Come on, Cinderella, let's get you home before you lose your shoe.'

He watched her as she made her way around the remaining guests, saying her goodbyes. When she reached his mother, his amusement slipped as he saw her say something, before his mother pulled her in close for a tight hug. When she finally released Cash, he saw her wiping her eyes. When he reached Cash's side, he swapped a glance with his mother and had the uncomfortable sensation that he was being assessed. 'Everything all right?' he asked, uncertainly.

His mother smiled as she gave Cash's shoulders a reassuring squeeze. 'Everything's going to be just fine,' she said, holding Linc's gaze steadily in a silent message that he wasn't completely sure he understood. She put Cash at arm's length and ducked her head to catch her eye. 'Linc will take good care of you. And we'll see you over here tomorrow for Christmas lunch.'

'Oh no, Lavinia. I can't do that. I've already imposed on your family time too much over the last few weeks.'

'Rubbish. I'm not having you all alone for Christmas. And you are not imposing. We love having you here.'

'I don't know . . .' Cash hedged, clearly uncomfortable with the invitation.

'It's no use arguing, once Mum's decided something, there's no way you're going to get out of it. Just say you'll come and let's go,' Linc suggested bluntly, even though his spirits had lifted at the thought of spending Christmas Day with her. He'd been trying to figure out how he'd manage to slip away with everyone here.

'Thank you, Lavinia,' she said softly, but Linc detected the slightest quiver in her tone and a sharp stab hit him in the centre of his chest.

They didn't speak as they left the house and walked towards his car. The gravel sounded loud beneath their feet and the air was heavy with the threat of an evening thunderstorm, although none had been forecast.

'Did you have a good time?' he finally asked as they drove home.

'I did. Your family's the best,' she said on a sigh.

'They have their moments,' he smiled without taking his eyes from the road.

'I didn't really believe people did Christmas like this . . . I guess I've been out of touch with it for too long.'

'What do you usually do for Christmas?'

'Work,' she said simply. 'The hospitality industry is great when you have nowhere else but work to go to for Christmas.'

'Yeah, I guess,' he said, feeling bad for her. He'd spent his fair share of Christmases away. While he'd rather have been home on holidays celebrating like everyone else, he'd felt worse for the guys and girls who had wives, husbands and kids at home missing them. The thought of Cash having nowhere to go saddened him. 'I'm glad you're coming over tomorrow.'

'I still feel like I'm intruding. Your mother makes it hard to say no, though.'

'She wouldn't have asked you if she didn't want you there.'

'But Christmas is for family.'

'And you haven't got any nearby, so you'll be part of ours,' he said, frowning a little.

As soon as the words were spoken out loud, a warmth began to spread through his chest. The rightness of it stunned him into silence. *She belonged.* He wanted her to be part of his family—part of him. *What the hell?* It was as though once he'd acknowledged it to himself, the emotions were free to spread through his veins. He could feel them: hope, trepidation, fear. Was he ready for a life-changing event like falling in love? He had to admit, he hadn't had a nightmare since before things got serious with Cash. Maybe she was good for him. Maybe he just needed some stability in his life before to make everything settle down.

But what if everything hadn't settled down? Would she have seen through him? At the moment, he managed to keep everyone else at a distance but letting someone into his life would mean he'd have to come clean. Would she still want to be with him if she found out he was . . . what? Frustration washed through him. *He wasn't anything.* He felt sweat begin to prickle along his forehead. There was nothing wrong with him. It was just leftover shit from a different time. He'd come good. He had to.

Cash had been feeling more than a little tipsy as she'd gotten into the car but the conversation about Christmas had sobered her up faster than a black coffee and a cold shower. '*You'll be part of ours.*' Linc's words had stolen the air from her lungs. The words had caught her off guard and brought a rush of tears to her eyes. It was almost too good to be true. For the last few weeks, every time she'd been over to the Callahans' she'd fitted in so easily and they'd accepted her so graciously that if she closed her eyes for a minute she could almost imagine she really was part of the family. But that would be stupid. They were just very friendly, kind people who wouldn't think twice about welcoming a next-door neighbour into their lives. It didn't mean they thought of her as part of their family. That would be crazy . . . She swallowed hard over the tightening of her throat and blinked away the sheen of hot tears that threatened to fall. They weren't her family. She didn't have a family.

They pulled up in front of her house and Linc turned off the engine, the quiet cocooning them. Cash risked a glance across at Linc, unsure what to make of the serious look on his face. Maybe he was realising what an imposition she was on his family. Maybe he was trying to think of a way to politely ease out of this affair they had going on.

'I don't have to come, if it bothers you. I don't want to make things awkward.'

He snapped his head around and stared at her, his expression guarded. 'It doesn't bother me. I want you there.'

'Okay,' she said quietly. She wasn't altogether convinced. Something was definitely going on with him. 'Well, thanks for the lift home.'

'Cash wait,' he said when she went to open the door. 'Can I come in?' he asked, holding her gaze steadily.

'If you want,' she said, trying to sound a lot more offhand about it than she was feeling. She felt him behind her as she unlocked the front door and walked inside, the hallway lamp casting a gentle glow and the Christmas tree lights in the loungeroom twinkling in merry greeting. 'Coffee?' she asked over her shoulder without pausing on her way to the kitchen. She needed something to clear her head of whatever the hell was in that eggnog.

'That'd be great.'

'Are you okay?' she asked as she calmly measured out the ground coffee.

'Yeah.' His face cleared and she was relieved when he smiled, but she sensed that he was having a deep internal struggle about something.

'Linc, if something's bothering you, just come out and tell me. I don't do the whole nervous hand-wringing thing very well.'

He gave a half-chuckle, half-groan before rubbing his hands across his face briskly.

Cash's spirits dropped. This was not good. 'Just do it, Linc,' she said wearily, turning away from the coffee, bracing her hands behind her on the kitchen bench as she faced him. 'Here, let me help. You've had enough of this thing, whatever it is between us.'

'Yes, I have had enough of this,' he said, and she was surprised at the speed with which the pain hit her chest. 'The sneaking around and the few stolen hours here and there. I don't want to do *this,'* he stressed, waving a finger between them.

Cash blinked at him uncertainly as he swore and pushed away from the kitchen counter to come to a stop in front of her. 'I want it to be real. I want people to know that we're together. I want people to know you're with me, Cash.'

She'd assumed this was a holiday fling. This was sounding like a whole lot more than that. A faint stirring of hope unfurled inside her along with a hearty dose of trepidation. 'I've never worried about what people thought before, Linc. But that was before I came out here and met your family.' She searched his eyes, wishing she could make him understand. 'I really care about them and I'd hate for them to remember me as *that woman,'* she made quotation marks in the air, 'who caused all the trouble between Linc and Griff at the wedding.'

'It's not your fault.'

'But that's what it would stem back to. And even if it didn't cause a big scene, it would still cause grief between you two, and I just don't see how it's worth taking the chance when neither of us are even going to be here for much longer.'

Maybe it was the alcohol fuzzing her mind, but she could swear she saw his eyes dim a little. He was confusing her; how could he forget that within a matter of weeks he'd be leaving and she'd never see him again? And why did it bother her so much that his parents might only think of her as the girl their son had had a brief fling with that Christmas he came home?

'Maybe you're right,' he said eventually, and that cocky roguish face was firmly back in place.

All of a sudden, she didn't want to be right. She wanted to take the words back and forget that one day it was going to end. If she didn't think about the day she'd have to say goodbye to him, then it didn't hurt . . . the way it was suddenly hurting now.

'Hey,' he said, stepping closer and tilting her chin up gently. 'I'm sorry, I didn't mean to upset you.'

'You didn't,' she told him, hoping she sounded convincing. There was no way she was strong enough to resist this much Linc up close. God, that sexy, knowing look he gave her was her undoing every damn time. She loved how he smelled, a mix of cologne, leather and a salty musky maleness that she couldn't get enough of. She loved everything about him. She loved . . . Cash froze, her eyes widening as she pulled back just enough to stare into his bemused face. *Holy crap.* She *loved* him.

'What?' he asked, searching her eyes, clearly aware that something was wrong.

'I—' *Don't tell him, you idiot! He'll think you're insane.* She had to be insane. Was it possible to suddenly realise you were in love with someone like this? She had no idea, she'd never experienced it before. What if she wasn't? What if it were something weird in the eggnog making her *think* she was in love with him? No, she couldn't tell him. She'd leave it till there were no other possible variables—or she was completely sober, whichever came first.

'You okay?'

'I'm fine, I think it's just your gran's eggnog.'

'I tried to tell you,' he said.

'Yeah, I know. I'm just really tired all of a sudden. I think I need to go to bed and get some sleep,' she said. 'Do you mind?' She felt bad, but she needed to get things straight in her head and she really was tired.

'Nah, I don't mind. Come on and I'll tuck you in before I leave.'

When she raised an eyebrow at him, he chuckled and drew a line across his chest. 'Cross my heart, I'll restrain myself from molesting you tonight.'

She was actually more worried about *her* doing the molesting, but she didn't tell him that. 'Fine.'

'You go get into bed and I'll make you some tea.'

'You don't have to do that.' But it was too late, he'd already tipped out the coffee and started boiling the jug.

Cash gave up protesting. When would she learn? Bossiness ran in their veins.

She washed her face in the bathroom and changed into her pyjamas, smothering a yawn as she pulled back the covers and slid down in between the sheets. She turned her head a little and her nose buried into the pillow, and she smiled as she breathed in Linc's smell. Yes, she could get used to this, she thought dreamily as she gave in to the temptation to float away on the soft cloud that picked her up and took her off.

Linc realised he'd been stirring the tea for a long time, lost in his thoughts. What had he'd been thinking earlier? He hadn't been thinking—he'd just blurted out what he'd been going over in his head for the last few days. Tonight had driven it home even harder. He wanted Cash. He wanted everyone to know she was his. But she was right. After the wedding he'd be heading back to Brisbane, back to his life, and she'd be leaving here to go . . . wherever the hell she was planning to go next. The thought depressed him. He silently shook his head. When had this started becoming more than just a perk to a visit home?

He gave a rueful snort as he recalled the surprised look on her face when he'd spilled his guts about wanting everyone to know about them. She was reacting the way he would have reacted. Well, she'd sure as hell brought him back to earth in a hurry. In a few weeks they'd probably never see each other again. He stopped stirring and stared into the cup. It didn't have to be the end. A glimmer of hope reignited. He still had a week or so to convince her that this didn't have to be a holiday fling. She could come to Brisbane with him . . . What was stopping her? She had no plan—she'd said so herself. She could stay at his place until she figured out what she wanted to do. Maybe she'd decide to stay . . . A smile touched his lips as the ideas began to click together. He had a week to convince her that this was doable, and damned if he wasn't going to play every last one of his cards to make it happen.

Linc carried the cup of herbal tea down the hall towards her bedroom. After all the time he'd been spending here over the last few weeks, he could find his way blindfolded. In her bedroom he found her tucked into bed, fast asleep. He placed the tea on the bedside table and pulled the blanket over her. *Christ, she was beautiful.* Lying on her side like this, hands tucked beneath her cheek, she looked younger, almost like a child. He thought back over the night and how happy she'd been to be part of his mum's crazy Santa visit. He wanted to give her that—this Christmas and every other one after. He wanted to make her smile like that every day. She had had a crap upbringing and there was nothing anyone could do about that, but he could make sure from now on she was surrounded by people who loved her and didn't need to find ways to avoid Christmas.

A powerful surge of protectiveness washed through him as he watched her sleeping so peacefully. It still staggered him the way these feelings had snuck up on him so quickly.

Why now? He gave a quick shake of his head; he couldn't wrap his head around it and there was no point struggling, he was just going to have to accept it. He was in love with Cash Sullivan and there was nothing he could do about it.

Twenty-four

Cash woke up early, feeling slightly disorientated, until she remembered how she had got to bed last night. She looked over her shoulder and saw that the other side of the bed hadn't been slept in and a quick scan of the room showed no signs of Linc's clothing. That was odd. He'd driven her home and then they'd been in the kitchen and . . . It all came flooding back in crystal-clear detail. She was in love with Lincoln Callahan.

Cash groaned as she sat up and touched her hand to her forehead. What the hell was in that eggnog? She sat up carefully so as not to jostle her throbbing head and noticed a glass of water on the bedside table, with a note that said *Drink me* propped up against the glass. She smiled and then grimaced when her head throbbed with the movement.

The Callahans obviously knew what to expect from a night on Granny's eggnog.

She made her way to the kitchen and placed the empty glass in the sink, resting against the bench as she looked at the Christmas tree she and Linc had put up . . . then she remembered it was Christmas. She noticed there was a second present next to the one she'd placed there yesterday before heading off to the party. She picked it up to inspect it and saw her name written on the card. She hadn't noticed Linc putting it under the tree, but then again, she hadn't been at her most perceptive, thanks to the bloody eggnog.

Her phone beeped and she walked across to her bag to dig it out.

A smile broke across her face. *Merry Christmas, beautiful. See you soon. P.S. Don't even think about opening that present yet.*

She looked across at the presents and blinked quickly. She wasn't sure why she had a sudden urge to cry. She went over to touch the branches of the tree. A sharp waft of pine and the smell of rain filled her nostrils. The red glittered baubles reflected the morning sun that beamed through the window and sparkled merrily. A sharp pang of regret hit her chest as she thought about her brother and her mum, both gone, and her father locked away in a cell. So much pain and so much wasted life.

She pushed the CD button and the room filled with Michael Bublé crooning 'Jingle Bells' and the atmosphere immediately brightened. It was Christmas Day and she was going to start a new tradition of enjoying it instead of running away from it. Starting with a huge breakfast celebration of bacon, eggs, hash browns and toast. As she pulled out the ingredients for the feast, her stomach gave a grumble of protest, and she decided that toast with Vegemite and a strong cup of coffee might be the safest option for now.

❦

The morning started out as hectic as the rest of the day was destined to be, with the traditional barbecued breakfast and enough food for an army. And, as usual, Linc could not restrain himself in preparation for the lunchtime feast to come.

All night he'd lain awake thinking about Cash. Linc's gaze fell on his brother as he helped himself to a second helping of bacon. He understood Cash's reservations over telling Griff about their relationship, but it had to be done. The longer they let it drag on, the worse it was going to be. In his experience, it was better to deal with problems and move on.

Move on. He gave a soft snort. He was an expert at moving on. That's just what you did in the army. You packed up your shit and moved on to the next place without dwelling on what you were leaving behind. The only problem was, some of the things you left behind had a way of catching up with you. Something stirred in the back of his mind but he pushed it away quickly. *Not yet. Not today . . .*

'You need help, mate,' his partner Tommo had said simply, but in a voice that was done being delicate. 'You're a liability to the company at the moment.'

'A liability? Are you fucking kidding me? I started this company. I was the one who brought you and Richie into it, you remember that? And what? You're tryin' to push me out?'

'Linc, calm down. No one's pushing you out, but Tommo and I are both concerned that you're not dealing with your shit, man. What happened on that last assignment could have happened to any one of us,' Richie said, opening his hands in a gesture of acceptance. 'But the thing is, Linc, our reputation is on the line and we can't afford any more stuff-ups. It's our futures that are riding on this thing too, mate.'

'Get some help, Linc,' Tommo added. 'For your sake as well as for ours.'

The bottom line was, his mates, who were also his businesses partners, weren't going to let him put the company at risk. Either he took some time off and sorted himself out, or they'd have to reconsider their role in the business. He understood where they were coming from—they were worried about their own investment in the company—but it'd been one careless moment, that was all it was. It wouldn't happen again. He just needed a break. He didn't need some psychologist telling him what his problem was. He didn't do therapy.

Besides, coming home had always been *like* therapy, for him and since he'd been here and getting his hands in the dirt, he'd felt a thousand times better. He knew some of that credit belonged to Cash. She was the distraction he'd needed. He frowned slightly at that. She'd become more than a distraction and he had a feeling a shrink would probably pounce on that and tell him distractions weren't exactly the same as dealing with things. His hand tightened on his glass. No. He'd just needed a break from being cooped up in an office building and stuck in traffic every day. He'd told Tommo and Richie he'd be okay after a trip home and he'd been right, he felt better. They just needed to stop acting like a pair of over-protective mother hens and let him do his job.

Later as Linc finished setting up another fold-out table along the verandah to fit all the guests, Griff walked past him. 'Mum needs us to bring up the ice and eskies.'

Linc clicked the table leg into place and followed his younger brother down the stairs and under the house to the elaborate man cave his father had created there. They dragged two old cold boxes up onto the verandah and began filling them with drinks from the cool room.

'What's the story with you and Ashley?' Linc asked, hoping to lead into the announcement after testing the waters.

'There's no story,' Griff answered in a clipped tone.

'Must be *some* kind of story. I've seen her leaving your place pretty early in the morning a few times.'

'It is what it is.'

'Then what about Olivia? Any chance of that goin' anywhere? She's single at the moment.'

'You thinking about a career in online dating or something?' Griff asked, giving him a sideways glance.

'No, I'm just saying that you've got all these single women hanging around, you probably should think about makin' a move on one sometime soon. You and Olivia had a pretty intense thing in high school. Maybe you should see if it goes anywhere.'

'You and Hadley seem to have the same idea. Like I told her—that ship sailed a long time ago. Olivia's out of my league, she's a lawyer.'

'So?'

'So? Look around, bro. I'm a farmer. Not exactly the kind of guy she's been dating since she left town.' He continued unpacking the drinks into the esky.

'Maybe things with Ashley will change?'

'Nah. Ashley's not into relationships. She's just looking for a bit of fun. I dunno, I guess maybe I hoped that Cash might get jealous or something if she saw another woman hanging around,' he shrugged and gave a twist of his lips. 'Hasn't worked out too well though.'

'I thought you two had decided that wasn't going anywhere?' Linc asked, feeling a sharp kick to his gut at the mention of Cash's name.

'I dunno. There's just something about her. We were hitting it off really well. I've been trying to get her alone but that's bloody near impossible in this madhouse. Dad's been keepin' me so busy I don't have time to even scratch myself, let alone get over there to visit her, but after things settle down, I'm gonna give it another go.'

Linc fought to keep his face neutral. This wasn't exactly how he'd thought the conversation was going to go. 'I don't know, mate, maybe she's just not interested?' His brother glanced up at him sharply and Linc reconsidered the rest of what he was going to say. 'But I'm no expert on women.'

'If she wasn't interested, then why does she keep coming over?'

'Well, it's not like she's had much choice. Between Mum and Hadley, it's kind of hard to say no.'

Griff shook his head briskly. 'We talked last night, for a bit,' he said without looking at Linc. 'I felt something. I can't give up without a fight. I've gotta try again.'

Linc swore long and hard inside his head. What the hell was he supposed to say to that? His gut was telling him to just do it. Rip it off like a bandaid. But this was his brother, and seeing the hope and determination shining in his eyes as it was now, there was no way he could bring himself to do it.

So much for his good intentions. Maybe Cash was right to worry about how Griff was going to take the news. Maybe it would be better to wait until after the wedding. He already felt bad about hurting his brother; he'd hate to ruin his sister's wedding on top of that.

Twenty-five

Cash could hear the Christmas music blaring from the Callahan house as she pulled up. Today she'd come prepared. Cash took out the bag of gifts from the back seat she'd been saving for Christmas Day, and shut the door, before turning around and letting out a start of surprise as she almost colliding with a wide chest.

'Sorry, I didn't mean to scare you,' Griff said, reaching to carry the bag of presents for her.

Cash did her best to hide her disappointment at discovering the chest didn't belong to the Callahan she'd been expecting. 'I didn't hear you over the music.'

'Yeah, it's festive in there, all right,' he agreed with a slight grimace. 'Merry Christmas,' he said, before surprising her as he lowered his head and kissed her, briefly, but definitely *not* in a neighbourly kind of way.

Cash was too stunned to do more than blink as he pulled away, then turned towards the house before she could say anything. As she shook herself from her stupor, Cash glanced up at the verandah and caught sight of Linc, his hands braced against the railing, looking down with a thunderous scowl. *Great. The day was off to an awesome start.*

Cash's mind was racing as she climbed the steps. What on earth was Griffin doing? She'd figured they'd already laid that particular idea to rest. He had seemed happy enough with Ashley the few previous occasions she'd seen him, so why would he suddenly try to reignite this thing between them now?

'Cash! Merry Christmas!' Lavinia's happy welcome momentarily distracted her and she smiled widely as the older woman hugged her. It was something Cash hadn't gotten used to yet—the physically demonstrative side of the Callahans. There was always a hug and a kiss on the cheek in greeting and farewell. Hadley came out of the house and hugged her too, before she was passed into Bob's arms for a welcome. The greeting from Harmony was a little more restrained; Don, on the other hand, seemed more than happy to give her a hug that felt slightly invasive.

There was always such a crowd at these gatherings. Everything was big, from the amount of food to the number of people who made up this extended family. As usual the Dawsons were there, as were various cousins, uncles and aunties who'd arrived early for the wedding. Cash counted thirty people and even then she wasn't sure she'd counted everyone.

She tried to catch Linc's eye, but he was deep in conversation with two uncles. Cash watched as he leaned closer to listen intently to something one of them was telling him, beer can in one hand resting casually on his knee. God, he was sexy.

'Come on, everyone, take a plate and serve yourselves,' Lavinia called out.

The food was laid out on a long trestle table, as impressive as any smorgasbord Cash had ever seen in the many fancy resorts she'd worked in over the years. There was so much food, she wondered how on earth they were ever going to get through it all.

'Come on, love,' Bob urged from beside her. 'Get in there and dig in.'

She gave a chuckle as he gently prodded her in front of him and helped add things to her plate when she was obviously being too modest. Her protests were useless, he simply ignored her and continued piling on the food.

Cash stared at the huge plate before her and shook her head. There was no way she was going to get through it all, but her mouth was watering despite herself. There were roasts and every kind of salad known to mankind; she'd only briefly glimpsed the desserts lined up inside, but she knew this was the beginnings of the massive food coma that was sure to follow this afternoon.

Lavinia settled Gran at the table and put her plate in front of her. Cash took a seat next to Payton and noticed she had only a small helping of salad on her plate.

'Are you a vegetarian?' Cash asked.

'I'm a vegan.'

'I knew a vegan once. Odd chap,' Gran piped up.

'Oh, for goodness sake, Payton, you can eat more than that,' Harmony snapped.

'I could,' Payton said, eyeing Cash's plate disdainfully before looking back at her mother, 'but I don't want to end up the size of a house. You're the one who told me I need to watch what I eat.'

'That was when you were fussy and only liked dessert and wouldn't eat your dinner.'

'You were saying I was getting fat.'

'I said if you didn't start eating healthier food, you'd have problems. That doesn't mean you just exist on lettuce.'

'Leave her alone, Harmony,' Don muttered from the other side of the table. 'There's nothing wrong with caring about your weight. If she wants to catch a bloke, she doesn't want to be a heifer. Something maybe a few others could learn from,' he added snidely, glancing up at his wife, and Cash's mouth dropped open in disbelief.

Surely he did not just imply that his wife needed to lose weight in front of the entire table? A quick glance around indicated that other people were just as shocked. Cash saw Olivia drop her eyes to her plate uncomfortably. Beside her, Griff lowered his cutlery and his fingers tightened on the handles. Linc also wore a glacial glare as he stared at his brother-in-law.

'I think,' Cash said, battling to control her own fury, but determined to jump in before the situation got worse, 'any potential *bloke* who was only concerned about how much a woman weighed wouldn't be much of a catch and you'd be better off without him anyway,' she said, holding Don's gaze steadily before turning to his daughter. 'There's no perfect size you're supposed to be, and your mother's right, your body needs more than just salad. Eating sensibly is not the same as starving yourself. If you really want to be a vegan, I know Savannah has a lot of books about it. I'm sure she'd be okay with lending you some so you can read up on how to make sure you stay healthy.'

'Thank you,' Harmony said with strained politeness, 'but I'm sure it's just a fad she's going through.'

'It isn't!' the girl protested, glaring at her mother.

'I'd like to make a toast,' Linc said suddenly, his voice cutting across the mother-daughter drama unfolding before them. 'I think we all need to give Mum a big thank you for putting on such a huge spread and working her butt off to make it all happen. To Mum,' he said, lifting his beer bottle.

With everyone busy toasting, the potential disaster had been averted. Cash exchanged a look with Linc as he took his seat once again and smiled.

'How's business going, Cash?' Sue Dawson asked from a few seats down.

'It's been pretty hectic. Savannah's built up quite a following.'

'She's a real credit to the town,' Sue agreed. 'And I'm only hearing good things about you as well.'

'That's a relief,' Cash smiled. 'I'll miss the place when I leave.'

Next to her, Griff shifted and she did her best not to glance in his direction.

'When will that be? We'll be sad to see you go.'

'I'm not sure about Savannah's exact return date yet, but the agreed time frame was six weeks and that'll be up just after New Year.'

'Well, I think you should speak to Savannah and stay on. You've gained quite a few fans out here and there's more than enough work for two therapists,' Lavinia put in. 'Savannah would be crazy to let you go.'

'I don't know what her plans are for the spa,' Cash said, trying to dampen the growing enthusiasm. Her glance briefly brushed Linc's and she saw his set jaw.

'You should give Savannah a call, Mum,' Griff told his mother.

'Really, I'm not sure Savannah wants to grow the business that much.'

'You won't know till you ask. You said you'll miss it here. Why go if you can stay?' Sue added.

'I don't know where I want to go after this . . . This was only ever supposed to be temporary.'

'Would you all just back off? The woman clearly doesn't want to be pressured.'

'No one asked you, Linc,' Griffin snapped at his brother.

'Maybe not, but if you could actually hear yourselves, you're backing her into a corner. Ease up.'

'Mind your own business.'

'I'll ask Savannah,' Cash said quickly, placing a hand on Griff's arm, then regretting it as she saw Linc's eyes narrow. 'I'll give her a call and see what she thinks.'

It seemed to satisfy everyone; everyone, that was, except for Linc, who continued to scowl on the other side of the table all through dessert and through to coffee and tea.

'Can I get you a drink?' Griff asked, coming up to her as she finished helping clear away the dishes.

'Ah, no, thanks. I'm taking it easy after last night.'

'Told you to go easy on the eggnog,' he said, leaning against the railing beside her.

'Yes, you did, and next time I'll make sure I stop at one.'

His smile settled into a satisfied grin as he watched her closely. 'Next time. That means you're thinking about next year. I think it's great that you're going to ask Savannah about keeping you on.'

'I said I'd ask her about it. I'm not sure she'll want to do that.' It was a lie; Savannah would jump at the chance to keep her on. She was her best friend and she knew there was nothing Savannah would like more than for Cash to stay out here. The business was more than able to support two therapists—they were turning appointments away. Maybe had this come up before last night she'd have seriously considered it, but last night she'd realised she was in love with Linc Callahan and that had changed everything.

He'd avoided her all day.

All. Day. What was with that? Yes, she'd told him she wanted to keep everything quiet, but he could at least make polite conversation with her, for goodness sake. She'd tried to approach him earlier, but he'd been called away to help and she hadn't had another chance. He was clearly not impressed about something, and she had a feeling it was more than just the run-in with Griff about her staying on.

'I hope you stay. I hope you'll give . . . this place a chance.'

'Griff,' Cash started to protest, but he pushed away from the railing and raised his beer bottle at her in silent farewell before she could finish.

'I better go see if Dad needs a hand.'

The afternoon wound down, everyone seeking out a place to stretch and relax, and Cash decided to say her goodbyes. She hugged Lavinia and thanked her. She'd never know how special today and last night had been for her—to be included in a real family Christmas.

She thanked Hadley, having to wait until Mitch finished enthralling his small audience with another war story. 'Not long now,' Cash said with a grin.

'I know. Now that Christmas is over, the days are going to fly.'

The next week was going to be full of wedding preparation appointments. There was the spa day for Hadley, the multiple appointments for all those bridesmaids, and even Mitch was coming in for a manicure, facial and wax. Added to that were the various other family members arriving en masse for the big day. She was going to be spending pretty much every day leading up to New Year's Eve with at least one member of the Callahan family.

Twenty-six

'Cash,' Griff called as she finally headed down the front steps towards her car. She bit back a frustrated sigh and smiled as she turned to face him. 'You're going home already?'

'I'm so full and I'm really tired after last night. I think I'll head home for a sleep.'

'Oh. I was kind of hoping we could . . . talk.'

Cash bit the inside of her cheek. Part of her hated dashing whatever hopes he seemed to have about the two of them, but another, smaller part was angry that he was making her do this again. She didn't want to upset him, but as far as she knew, she hadn't given him any signals that her feelings for him had changed. 'Griff . . .'

'Look, I know you said you didn't feel that way about me,' he cut her off quickly, 'but when you're stuck in a cab, driving back and forth harvesting all day, you have a lot of time to think. The thing is,' he said, holding her gaze levelly, 'I don't think that was the best I could do.'

'The best . . .' she murmured, feeling a little confused until she saw him lean closer and realised, too late, that he was referring to their kiss. This time the kiss wasn't gentle and hesitant, and for the briefest of moments Cash, stunned into surprised reaction, kissed him back. As soon as she realised, she pulled away, but not before she caught the triumphant light in Griff's eyes as he stared down at her expectantly.

'Griff, no,' she said, shaking her head. 'I'm sorry. I just can't.'

As soon as the words were out she saw the satisfaction fade from his face.

'You kissed me back,' he said harshly.

'I . . . Griff.'

'I don't get it,' he said angrily.

Cash was still shocked by the sudden kiss. It had been the very last thing she'd expected and all she could do was shake her head as coherent words refused to come out of her mouth. 'I'm . . . I have . . . There's someone else, Griff. I'm sorry. I thought you understood last time.'

'Someone else? Who?' he demanded, and his temper was not something Cash had ever witnessed before.

Cash shook her head and turned away to open her car door. 'Just leave it, Griff. Please.'

He pushed the door shut and Cash snapped her gaze upwards in alarm.

'I want to know who it is,' he said in a low, angry tone.

Hurt feelings were one thing, but men who demanded were an entirely different kettle of fish. Linc's brother or not, she was not putting up with this crap from anyone. 'It's none of your business,' Cash said tightly. 'And what's more, I don't owe you an explanation for anything I do. I'm sorry things between us can't work out, but I have done nothing to make you think that they could. I tried to break it to you gently but you're the one who overstepped the mark, buddy, not me.'

She reefed open the car door and saw his shoulders slump in defeat as he stepped away. If this was how Christmases ended, she was glad she'd stayed away from them for so long.

~

Linc saw Cash saying goodbye to everyone and tried to catch her before she left, jogging down the front staircase and coming to a halt at the sight that greeted him: the woman he loved kissing his brother. *What the fuck.* His first instinct was to run across and drag Griff off her. Rage pumped through his veins and his fists clutched by his side, but then the red fog cleared slightly as Cash pulled away. Everything inside him screamed for him to get over there and demand answers, but somehow through all the testosterone and wounded ego, a small voice of reason held him back.

He couldn't hear what they were saying, but he could see from Griff's body language that he wasn't happy with whatever Cash was telling him. He wondered briefly if she'd told him the truth, but in the next instant he saw Cash turn on his brother and slam the door shut before revving the engine and driving away.

There wasn't time to leave before Griff saw him, not that he seemed inclined to stop and talk, so clearly she hadn't told him then. He opened his mouth to speak as Griff approached, but all he got was a snarl from his brother as he pushed past and headed back towards his own house.

Linc took the keys out of his pocket and climbed into his car. A mixture of delayed shock, anger and the need to track down Cash to find out what the hell had just happened propelled him into action.

Pulling up in front of her house, he took a moment to compose himself before climbing out of his car. He knocked on the front door and waited, listening for her footsteps up the hallway and frowning when none came. Linc turned and walked around the house, opening the side gate that led to the salon, and found her sitting on the bench beside a small water feature, staring into the water as flashes of orange and gold carp swam just below the surface.

'You left in a hurry,' he said, coming to a stop beside her.

She didn't immediately look up at him, but when she did he saw her eyes were clouded with emotion. 'I need to tell you something,' she said quietly.

'You made out with my brother,' he said dryly.

He would have laughed at the speed with which her eyes widened and her mouth dropped open had the situation not been so damn serious. The image of her kissing Griff was still too raw to laugh at just yet.

'I did *not* make out with your brother.'

'Kinda looked like you were into it a little bit,' he said, striving for a casualness he was far from feeling.

'He caught me off guard. I had no idea he was going to kiss me.'

'He still has a thing for you,' Linc said after a moment of silence.

'Apparently,' Cash confirmed, sounding bitter. 'However, I think he has a clearer understanding of how things stand now, though.'

'Did you tell him? About us?' He was fairly sure he wouldn't still have his head attached to his shoulders if she had.

'I told him there was someone else. He wanted to know who. I told him it was none of his business.'

'I see.'

'Do you, Linc?' she snapped, sending him a narrowed glare.

'What's that supposed to mean?'

'What's going on with you? You've been avoiding me all day.'

'You were the one who insisted on keeping us a secret.'

'This was different. You knew something was up with Griff today, didn't you?' she demanded.

He made a small grunt deep in his throat but couldn't very well deny it. 'I tried to feel him out on how he'd handle you and I getting together and he told me he wanted to try with you again.'

'And you just stepped aside and let him?' she asked, sounding horrified.

'What was I supposed to do? You didn't want me to tell him before the wedding, remember?'

'So you were okay with allowing your brother to make a move on me? I can't believe you.'

'I didn't *allow* him to make a move on you,' he growled. 'How was I supposed to know he'd kiss you . . . or that you'd let him,' he added, then regretted it the moment he saw the wounded on her face. 'I'm sorry,' he said, rubbing his eyes briskly. 'Forget it.'

'Did you even mean what you said last night?'

'What?' He dropped his hands and stared at her. 'Of course I meant it.'

'You stepped aside for your brother,' she pointed out in a tone that held a note of betrayal.

'I didn't step aside . . . I . . .' He sure as hell hadn't spoken up and said anything either. He felt like a bastard caught in the middle of a hopeless situation. 'What did you want me to do exactly, Cash?'

He saw her shoulders lose some of their stiffness as she eased back against the bench and let out a long, frustrated sigh. 'I guess we should have told him.'

'Yeah, well, maybe in hindsight earlier would have been better. I don't think we can though, not this close to the wedding. It's not about us now,' he said. And it wasn't—it was about Hadley and making sure her wedding wasn't ruined by her two brothers glaring at each other all day.

The gentle trickle of the water fountain and hum of insects hung in the air around them. 'Hey,' he said, holding out a hand to her. He saw her look up at him before taking it. 'Let's put today behind us. It's Christmas and we still have some celebrating to do.'

He tugged her upwards and into his arms and suddenly all the negativity that had hung over him through the day was gone. She felt so good in his arms, pressed up tightly against him, her head resting perfectly against his chest. Everything he'd felt last night flooded back through him. That was all that mattered. He would never stand back and allow anyone to come between them again.

Cash closed her eyes and breathed in the scent of the man whose chest felt so solid and safe beneath her cheek. Her arms tightened around his waist as a wave of longing and love washed over her. She'd been hurt by Lincoln's refusal to step in earlier, and yet, standing here like this, it no longer mattered.

'I think we should go inside and open our presents,' she said, pulling away slightly to look up at him.

'I can think of a present I'd like to unwrap,' he told her with a wiggle of his eyebrows that made her laugh.

'Come on, I was so good not unwrapping it this morning.'

'Fine. Let's go unwrap presents then,' he said, trying to sound hard done by, but allowing her to pull him along the garden path towards the house. She couldn't wait till he unwrapped his. She'd had to arrange for one of the clients to pick it up and bring it out for her only the day before and had been worried it might not turn up on time.

Kneeling in front of the tree that she secretly loved, despite its delicate pine needles that drove her batty each day as she swept them up, Cash waited impatiently for Linc to hand her the wrapped gift. Buying your own presents wasn't the same as someone else buying them for you. Almost reverently she began unwrapping the delicate tissue paper until she came to a flat, square box inside. She opened it slowly and her breath caught as she stared at the shimmer of gold that lay in the centre of the satin-lined box. 'Linc,' she breathed, unable to drag her eyes from the beautiful bracelet.

'I was thinking more of sexy lingerie, but Hadley reckoned jewellery was the way to go.'

'Linc, this is . . . too much. It must have cost a fortune.' The diamond-set belcher bracelet twinkled up at her in all its golden glory.

'I can swap it for a skimpy nurse costume,' he offered.

'Hmm, let me think . . . slutty nurse outfit or classy gold bracelet?'

'Whatever. Your loss,' he shrugged, although he looked rather pleased with himself.

'What if I *only* wear the bracelet?' she offered.

'That could work.' His eyes darkened and Cash shook her head helplessly at him, before reaching across to hand him his gift.

'If this isn't a skimpy pool boy costume, I'm gonna be really disappointed,' he warned.

'I don't have a pool,' she shrugged.

'And apparently I don't have a pool boy costume,' he said, tearing open the wrapping paper.

She watched him take out the photo frame and stare at it silently. Cash bit her lip. *He hated it.* 'It was probably a dumb idea,' she said feeling awkward.

'No, it's . . .' He looked up at her with an almost stunned expression. 'It's perfect. Thank you,' he said softly, his voice sounding huskier than usual.

Cash breathed a small sigh of relief. She'd been trying to think of something special to get him and had almost given up until she remembered him telling her that driving through the front gates of Stringybark always made him realise he was home, and how he'd sometimes dreamed of it when he'd been away on deployment. Early one morning she'd driven over to Stringybark and taken a photo of the front gates and had it blown up and framed so he could always have it with him always.

'Thank you,' he said, reaching out to slide a hand around the back of her head as he kissed her gently. 'And now for your real Christmas present,' he said, turning towards the bedroom.

'There's more?' she said, opening her eyes wide in mock surprise.

'I've saved the best for last,' he promised confidently.

'I don't know, Callahan,' she said, holding her wrist up to admire her bracelet, 'it's gonna have to be pretty impressive to outdo this.'

'Oh, it's impressive,' he assured her as he kicked the door shut behind them.

Twenty-seven

Cash reached out a hand early the next morning, groping for the source of the insistent ringing that had woken her from a very deep, relaxing sleep. Locating the phone, she brought it to her ear with an irritated, 'Hello?'

'Oh. Sorry. What time is it?' Savannah's voice sounded far too bright and chirpy for whatever obscene time of the morning it was.

'I don't know, I can't focus my eyes,' Cash muttered.

'Sorry, but I needed to call you.'

'It couldn't have waited just a few more hours till the sun came up?'

'No. Listen. George has been offered an amazing job.'

Cash scrunched her eyes and rubbed her nose, trying to concentrate on what Savannah was saying. 'What kind of job?'

'Well, it's not a job so much as an opportunity. He's been invited to design a garden for a big gardening show coming up over here. The guy he's been talking to has seen some of George's work and thinks he has a shot at making a real name for himself.'

'Wow, Sav,' Cash said, her eyes finally open and her mind registering what was being said, 'That's really exciting.'

'I know. I'm so proud of him. This could be huge.'

'So what would that mean . . . for you? Would you be staying over there?'

'That's what I was calling about. How would you feel about staying on longer?'

'How much longer?' Cash asked slowly.

'Maybe another three or four months.'

Three or four months!

'Cash?'

'I'm here,' she said quickly.

'I thought you'd fallen back to sleep or something.'

'No, no, I'm here.'

'I know you were supposed to be leaving in a few weeks, but this has come up unexpectedly and it's really too good an opportunity for him to pass up.'

'Of course it is. He should totally go for it,' Cash said, but her mind was still fixed on Savannah's offer to stay on longer. A couple of weeks ago she wouldn't have even hesitated about extending her stay—she had no real plans in place and she loved it here—but Linc would be leaving soon. It wasn't like that should have any bearing on her decision, though, but it was the first time she'd really allowed herself to think about what would happen when Linc left. It was a depressing thought. She tried to shake off the gloom—their relationship wasn't supposed to be long-term, and Linc had made no mention of them continuing after he returned to Brisbane. It was time to start facing reality. She needed to make plans.

'Look, I know it's come out of the blue, so you think about it for a bit and let me know. It's not going to change our decision to stay—I'd just like to keep the spa running for as long as possible, that's all.'

'Yeah—of course, that's important. I'll let you know, okay?' She couldn't think about it now, she needed to clear her mind of all the distractions, namely the drop-dead gorgeous man who had not long ago got out of bed to start his day.

Cash rolled her eyes as she turned away to get the hot towels that had been heating. Mitch hadn't stopped talking the entire time he'd been here, and Cash was just about ready to shove a sock in his mouth to shut him up. The man sure liked the sound of his own voice. She got that he was obviously a big deal in the news world—she was even somewhat impressed that she'd occasionally seen him on TV but, try as she might, she could not warm to the guy. The only conversation he seemed to bother taking part in were the ones that involved him talking about . . . well, *him*. Cash wasn't sure there was actually room in the marriage for Hadley, Mitch *and* his massive ego. While Hadley often brought up funny stories about her work in the field, she rarely mentioned anything grisly. Mitch, on the other hand, seemed to take great pride in reliving every gruesome detail about each story he'd covered, complete with sound effects and re-enactments. It was exhausting to watch.

Her thoughts had been drifting back to Savannah's offer all morning. It made sense. She'd built up a clientele and she knew they'd be happy for her to stay on in Savannah's absence. So what was holding her back from saying yes?

Linc. She let out a long sigh. He'd be leaving soon. She pressed the hot towels onto Mitch's face a little harder than she meant to and mumbled an apology. She'd always known their relationship wasn't going to go anywhere; unfortunately, her heart hadn't been listening to her head and had gone and fallen in love.

She unwrapped the towel and replaced it with another.

'So there I was, unable to walk on my injured leg, all alone in the dark. The Taliban out there somewhere, watching and waiting,' Mitch continued his theatrical monologue, breaking into her troubled thoughts. 'I had no idea if I'd survive the night.'

And yet here you are, so I guess there was a miracle. 'If you'd both survive the night, you mean?' She had to admit, though, the guy had amazing skin. Despite his harrowing time reporting from overseas battle zones, he clearly took time out for a skin-care routine—skin like this didn't stay hydrated and undamaged without some pretty regular maintenance, especially if it was exposed the harsh elements of the Middle East.

'Pardon?'

'Well, you said this was the story that won your award, so it wasn't just you out there. You had a camera man with you, right?' Cash explained.

Mitch looked at her blankly.

'So there were two of you there, and you couldn't walk because of your leg being injured. Why couldn't the cameraman help you walk?'

'Well, he was . . . there was nothing he could do . . . besides, he was busy filming. That's not the point. The point is, in my line of work, there's great risk and that night I came very close to staring death in the eye.'

'Oh. I see.' *Tosser.* The longer Cash spent around this guy, the more concerned she was that Hadley was making a very big mistake.

❧

'Seriously, what is your sister doing marrying this guy?' Cash asked, exasperated after telling Linc about their encounter.

Linc gave a slow shake of his head and exhaled loudly, 'Buggered if I know. She loves him. I guess he must have some redeemable qualities the rest of us can't see.'

Hadley was such an intelligent, independent woman, how could she not see what an egotistical, self-centred twit this guy was?

'There's no point trying to tell her, she's a Callahan woman—once they make their mind up about something . . .' he shrugged.

'I hate to break it to you, but I don't think it's only a female Callahan trait.'

He flashed a grin at her. 'Yeah, but on me it's called perseverance.'

'Hmmm,' she said doubtfully. 'So, can I interest you in a facial, Mr Callahan?'

'Yeah, no,' he said backing away from the table slightly, 'I wouldn't be caught dead with cucumber on my eyes.'

'Hey, Mitch Samuals is man enough to do it . . .'

'Yeah, well, he's a bigger man than me,' Linc said sarcastically. 'However, if you were offering a massage . . . the full-body *naked* kind, I might just be tempted.'

'So, sex, in other words?' she said, lifting an eyebrow at him.

'Pretty much,' he agreed with the half-smile that played havoc with Cash's resistance.

'Sorry, you're out of luck, cowboy. I've got two more clients due in shortly, and I believe they're your cousins . . . so unless you want them reporting back to your mother that their beauty therapist was running late because she was having sex with their cousin . . .'

'Like that's never happened before,' he scoffed and caught the bunched-up hand towel she threw at him.

'Haven't you got something more constructive to do than bother me?'

Linc dropped the towel on the bed and moved closer to her. '*Do* I bother you?' he asked, lowering his tone as he leaned forward to nuzzle the side of her neck.

Cash couldn't suppress the shiver that ran along her arm and produced a trail of goose bumps. How was she supposed to resist the guy when he did that? A reluctant moan escaped her lips as she tipped her head back, allowing him better access to the sensitive skin of her throat. Oh damn. 'Forget the massage,' she said, turning and working the buckle of his belt. His grin widened appreciatively as she made quick work of the buttons on his jeans and took charge of the situation.

Linc put his hat back on his head and opened the door, greeting his cousins as they walked up the path. He turned round and winked at Cash, holding up his watch as proof that they'd managed to beat the clock with time to spare.

His grin widened as he saw Cash shake her head helplessly at him, before leading the women into the treatment rooms to get started, a smug grin on her face. Man, she was perfect.

The phone beeped before it automatically switched to message bank as it did whenever Cash was with a client. Linc stopped in the doorway as he heard the caller's message.

'*Cash, it's just Sav. I know I said to take your time and think it over, but I'm just wondering if you've thought anymore about the offer to stay on? Give me a call when you get a sec. Bye.*'

Linc's cocky grin faded as he slid into the ute and stared out the front windscreen. He was so far gone it would be funny if it weren't so pathetic. He braced his hands on the steering wheel and dropped his head in defeat. He thumped the wheel and swore out loud. Everything was falling apart. If she stayed here, he'd lose her.

He should have asked her to move with him earlier.

This was crazy. He knew she couldn't get enough of him, just like he couldn't get enough of her. They were perfect together. How could she possibly be considering staying on here after everything they'd shared over the last few weeks? He frowned and muttered another curse. Okay, so he knew they hadn't known each other long, but it felt like they had. He didn't want to see the blaringly obvious reason why his asking her to move to Brisbane could be considered a risk. In his gut, he knew it was the right decision. They'd have the time and space to get to know each other like regular couples did. But how could he ask her to move now, when she was clearly considering Savannah's offer to stay?

There was nothing for her here. *Except Griff*, a small voice reminded him. No, he didn't believe that. Griff had had his shot. Cash wouldn't go through that again when she knew there was no spark between them. Not to toot his own horn, but there was no way she'd be able to go back to that after the chemistry she'd had with him. Unless she forgot about him once he left and headed back to Brisbane and decided she *could* settle.

It was eating him up inside. This wasn't like him—he never allowed uncertainty to mess with his head. Then again, he'd never been head over heels in love with Cash Sullivan before. He needed pull one huge-arse rabbit out of the hat or he was going to lose the only shot he had at a future with Cash.

Cash slowed down as she reached the main street of town and gaped at the sight that greeted her. This was *not* Rankins Springs. Everywhere she looked there were cars and people. Two news vans were set up in the park and she noticed a cameraman and reporter interviewing two women across the street.

The circus has well and truly arrived, she thought with a grin. Hadley had been right when she'd warned of the media interest in their wedding. Cash supposed it was only natural, considering there would be celebrity guests arriving in town and the bride and groom were celebrities themselves. She wondered how Hadley was feeling about being on the other end of the camera for a change.

Inside the grocery store people were gathered in twos and threes, animated faces clearly discussing the excitement that had taken over their tiny town. Cash couldn't help the smile on her face as she left the shop with her purchases, hopefully enough to keep her out of town for the next few days—if the traffic and lack of parking was anything to go by, it would be a good place to avoid.

'Excuse me, can we just ask you a few questions?'

Cash stopped abruptly as a young guy in a suit held a microphone in front of her face.

'Are you a local?' he asked without waiting for her to agree.

'Ah, no, not really,' Cash said hesitantly, looking at the man warily.

'So you're here for the wedding?'

'Ah . . .' *Oh my God, woman!*

'Are you invited?' The young reporter's eyes were beginning to light up. Clearly not many of the locals he'd managed to ambush so far had been invited guests.

'Well, sort of . . . I mean, I'm doing the makeup.' *Stop talking!*

'Can you give us any details about the wedding? Do you know what the bride will be wearing?'

She did *not* have time for this today. 'No. Sorry, I don't. Excuse me, I need to get back.'

'Get back? To wedding preparations? Will you be seeing Hadley and Mitch today?' he persisted.

Cash closed her eyes on a moan and pushed past the reporter to head for her car. Hadley would *not* want her blabbing to everyone about her wedding preparations.

'Excuse me, miss?' he called, jogging to keep up with her. 'You can understand that Mitch has a huge following and viewers are very interested in his upcoming wedding. Is there anything you can share with them?'

'No, sorry. No comment,' she said, slamming her door shut. *No comment? What the hell was that?*

'Does that mean you've signed some kind of privacy clause? Have you been told not to comment to the media?'

Cash turned the key and reversed, hoping the guy had the good sense to get out of the way. This was crazy. Who would have thought a wedding in a small country town could cause so much fuss? Once the town was in her rear-view mirror, Cash let out a long sigh. She would definitely *not* be making any more trips into town until after the wedding.

Twenty-eight

If Cash thought the last few days were hectic, she hadn't seen anything until she arrived at the Callahan house just before lunchtime on New Year's Eve. It was D-day and all hands were on deck. Vanessa, the beautician from Griffith, had arrived yesterday evening and stayed at the farmhouse, so Cash hadn't seen Linc since the day before yesterday. More than once she found herself shaking her head in dismay at finding herself pining over him. Yesterday he'd gone to a local cricket match and caught up with mates he hadn't seen in a while, and while she was happy that he was having a good time, she was secretly counting up how many more days they had left together and doing her best to hold off the sadness.

The hairdresser had finished with Hadley and passed her along to Cash. There was no more time to dwell on anything other than making sure she did her bit to make this wedding day memorable.

Hadley was quieter than usual and Cash eyed her carefully as she applied foundation. 'Everything okay?' she asked quietly.

'Yep,' Hadley said brightly—too brightly, and Cash's eyes narrowed slightly as she searched the other woman's face.

'It's okay to be nervous if it's just pre-wedding jitters.'

'Of course that's what it is,' Hadley said, looking Cash in the eye briefly. 'What else would it be?'

'I don't know,' Cash said, dabbing the foundation on her wrist as she blended it carefully before applying it. 'But if it's something else, you can talk to someone about it.'

'It's my wedding day . . . finally. I've been planning it forever. It's just the normal jitters everyone gets. I'll be fine.'

That sounded a lot like a self-pep talk to Cash, but she let it go—there was no point stressing the woman out more than she already was. Cash had done a lot of weddings in her time, and while most brides had a few nerves, there was also an underlying excitement. Cash didn't detect any of the eagerness that usually went with the shaking hands and shallow breathing, and that concerned her a little. Still, it wasn't her place to say anything. Maybe she could find Linc and ask him to have a talk to his sister.

It became something of a production line after that, with various bridesmaids and relatives slipping into the seat for Vanessa and Cash to work their magic. By the time Cash had finished, she only had twenty minutes to spare to get ready herself.

She'd brought along her clothes, anticipating she wasn't going to have enough time to race home and get changed, and Lavinia had placed her things in one of the spare rooms at the rear of the house.

Cash smiled to herself as she made her way through the usually spotless house, now looking like a mini tornado had hit it. Clothing was draped over kitchen chairs, tulle seemed to be scattered throughout the huge open-plan family room. Suit coats hung on doorknobs along the hallway, and there was a general air of controlled chaos. It was contagious; Cash felt the excitement and nervous tension humming through her own body and it wasn't even her wedding. She was still a little worried about Hadley, but surely someone else—Lavinia, Harmony, Olivia—would have picked up on it if it was a problem.

Cash hadn't exactly been expecting to be invited to a wedding when she'd packed her bags to come out here, and she hadn't had time to travel to Griffith to go clothes shopping, so after a quick call to Savannah the previous evening, she'd asked if she could borrow something from her friend's wardrobe. She'd settled on a deep turquoise scoop-neck sleeveless cocktail dress, keeping it simple. She slipped her feet into her strappy heels, did a quick touch-up of her makeup and she was ready.

A low whistle from the doorway caught her unawares and she jumped at the sound, her heart thudding at the sight of Linc dressed in a suit.

'You look . . .' He paused, shaking his head a little. 'Beautiful.'

'You scrub up all right too,' she managed, feeling ridiculously shy and tongue-tied. Denim was one thing . . . but in a suit his roguish, hard edge was only emphasised. *Dear Lord*. 'Shouldn't you already be down at the service?'

He stepped closer and slipped his hands onto her waist. 'I haven't been able to see you all day—I just wanted to make sure you were okay.'

'It was pretty hectic, but we got through it,' she told him wearily, allowing herself a moment to lean against him and breathe in his scent, which was, if she wasn't mistaken, a very expensive brand of cologne. 'You smell good,' she said, grinning as she felt a slight shiver run through his body as she nuzzled her nose into his neck, enjoying the payback.

'Groomsman gift,' he said with a dry edge to his tone. 'Old Mitch has good taste and clearly more money than he knows what to do with.'

'Well, it's certainly worth it. It's making me want to do very bad things,' she said, lowering her tone.

'In that case, I better thank him then.'

'But,' she said, pulling away and smiling cheerfully, 'we have a wedding to get to, so we better get moving.'

Linc gave a reluctant groan and hung his head. 'They won't miss us,' he argued.

'You're the bride's brother and a member of the bridal party . . . I'm pretty sure an odd number of groomsmen to bridemaids is going to stand out.'

'Fine,' he growled, 'but the minute all this groomsman crap is done, we're leaving the party, got it?' He tugged her closer for a swift, commonsense-erasing, kiss, before setting her away from him again. 'We've got some bad things that need to be done.'

Cash watched Linc as he headed down the hallway with his sure, purposeful stride and couldn't help the grin she felt spreading wide across her face. Once outside, she walked down the red carpet that led towards the rows of seating placed in front of a raised platform. A beautifully decorated arch spanned the small stage, with gum leaves and native flowers woven into it to form a breathtaking centrepiece. Banksia, protea and flowering gum in deep shades of crimson decorated the aisles, and the sweeping landscape beyond them provided a stunning backdrop.

Her gaze swept over the men lined up in their black suits, making a rather impressive sight. She felt for them dressed in their heavy clothing, though; it was hot and although it was later in the afternoon, the sun still had a sting to it. Her eyes held Linc's just a moment longer than was polite, and she bit back a smile at his knowing grin as it sent a wave of heat through her.

Lavinia looked her usual serene self, dressed in a soft musk lace dress and matching hat. Watching her now, you'd never suspect she'd been running about doing all the cooking and organising for Christmas and a wedding. Gran sat beside her, a contented smile hovering on her lips as she looked around at her clan. The rest of the Callahans took up the majority of the next few rows and Cash glanced across at the groom's side to get a look at Mitch's parents. His mother was a professor at the University of Sydney and his father was a doctor—Mitch, apparently, came from a very academic gene pool.

She looked around curiously searching for the famous guests everyone had been talking about and spotted a few familiar faces. You knew you were at a celebrity wedding when you could count at least one Stefanovic brother in the crowd. She noticed some prime-time celebrities, journalists who featured on prominent news programs and the odd TV presenter, most of them seated on Hadley's side. A little buzz of excitement ran through her, despite herself.

As Cash found a seat on the bride's side, towards the back, she glanced across at her neighbour, doing a double-take before gathering her wits and manners to smile politely and say a friendly hello. She was sitting next to Talitha Cummins. Thankfully she seemed used to having people react like idiots and graciously ignored Cash's dumbfounded expression. They swapped small talk and within minutes Talitha had put Cash completely at ease. Cash wasn't sure what she'd been expecting, but she felt stupid for assuming she'd be anything but a normal, down-to-earth person.

Music broke the gentle murmur of conversation between the waiting guests and all eyes turned to the procession of bridesmaids gliding elegantly down the aisle in dresses of varying shades of pink through to red. It made a stunning image as they lined up across from the men at the front of the platform.

Olivia stopped, taking her position as maid of honour, looking beautiful in a deep ruby dress that flowed about her legs and hugged her curves. She looked tiny compared to Harmony, who came to a stop beside her, looking tall and graceful in crimson. Cash saw her send a glance across at the men, smiling serenely before dropping her glance down to her bouquet as the music changed, announcing the arrival of the bride.

For a moment Cash continued to watch Harmony curiously. She saw her lift her gaze, but not to watch the bride coming down the aisle, as everyone else was doing, but to look at the groom. Maybe she was one of those people who liked to watch the groom's expression as he watched the woman of his dream floating towards him. But Cash couldn't quite interpret the look on Harmony's face. Was she remembering her own wedding to Don? Her face held an almost wistful look, maybe even sad.

Cash's attention was dragged from Harmony as Hadley neared and she felt her breath catch. She was stunning. Cash had never quite understood why people cried at weddings, but to her horror she discovered her eyes were beginning to prickle with tears. Hadley was an absolute vision. She wore a misty tulle strapless gown with a sweetheart neckline that was decorated with beads and flared into a soft swirl of skirt with a dropped waist. The way the material draped across her torso and hips made her look like a Hollywood starlet from the 1940s. Cash had seen Hadley's hair earlier after the hairdresser had finished with her, but now, seeing everything come together, she couldn't believe how perfectly the loose waves and curls suited the dress. She looked as through she'd stepped straight out of another place and time.

Robert was every ounce the chuffed father of the bride as he walked his daughter down the aisle, kissing her cheek tenderly before placing her hand in Mitch's and heading back to sit beside his wife. Cash swallowed over the lump in her throat that came after watching Lavinia slip her hand through her husband's arm and lean close, dabbing delicately at her eyes with a handkerchief.

The ceremony was brief and went off flawlessly. Within minutes, the vows had been read, rings exchanged, and the bride had been kissed. The Callahans beamed from the front row as they hugged their daughter and new son-in-law. The Samualses were a little more stand-offish but seemed happy nonetheless.

The groomsmen escorted the bridesmaids down the aisle. Cash noticed Griffin was paired with Olivia Dawson, while Harmony seemed a little flustered to be partnered with the rather handsome brother of the groom. She looked around for a glimpse of Don to gauge his reaction but couldn't see him anywhere. No doubt he was taking an important business call somewhere. But it was Linc she feasted her eyes on. He had his head tilted slightly to listen to whatever the woman on his arm was saying, and Cash couldn't drag her gaze away. She knew the bridesmaid was a cousin of Hadley's, she'd had a brief conversation with her while doing her makeup earlier, and they made a striking couple. If she hadn't known they were related, maybe she would have felt a little threatened by the sight of their heads close together. Then Linc lifted his gaze and found her, and she felt it touch her as though he were standing right there beside her. She could read the message loud and clear in his eyes. 'I want you,' it said, as clearly as if he'd spoken the words in her ear.

This was going to be the longest evening she'd ever had to endure.

After the ceremony, Cash followed the other guests as they moved towards the large shearing shed the Callahans had spent months readying for the occasion. She knew Lavinia had her doubts about holding the reception in the old building—it had been abandoned for years. However, Hadley had been determined. She saw a beauty in it that no one else could see . . . until now. Late evening sunshine streamed through missing timber planks in the walls of the shed, casting a bright golden glow across the now-gleaming floor. Fairy lights had been stapled around the large posts that supported the roof, and big decorative lanterns hung from the beams above. Tables were scattered throughout the shed, set with crisp white linen and gleaming cutlery. Candles graced each table, and the flicker of the flames, dancing in their tiny glass jars, gave the space a warm ambience. A table out the front held the modest, yet gorgeous, wedding cake, and timber crates artfully arranged made the perfect display case for an assortment of cupcakes in shades of champagne, cream and ivy.

Waiters came around with tall flutes of champagne and large trays of hors d'oeuvres. Everything was breathtakingly perfect, and uniquely Hadley. If the woman ever wanted to hang up her flak jacket, she could have an awesome career in wedding planning.

Cash had found her seat—next to her new best friend, Talitha, the two had been admiring each other's shoes and just discovered a mutual love of sneakers—when the wedding party arrived, making a grand entrance after their photo shoot.

Cash studied Hadley, searching for any sign of her earlier apprehension, but saw only a bright flawless smile as she and Mitch greeted family and friends. After they'd taken their seats, the reception took on more of a party atmosphere, and Cash noted that everyone relaxed considerably, except perhaps the Samualses, although it was a little hard to tell with them.

As the evening wore on, the drinks began to flow more freely and people mingled. She jumped slightly when a deep voice sounded close behind her, and she turned to find Lincoln smiling down at her. 'Dance with me?' he asked quietly.

Cash glanced around and noticed the dance floor area was fairly crowded.

'Come on, Cash, just this once? No one's gonna care,' he said.

'Okay.' Why not? Soon he'd be leaving. Tonight was probably one of the few remaining nights they had left together. The wedding was over, she hadn't even spoken to Griff since their argument and, quite frankly, she'd been desperate to be in this man's arms all day.

He took her hand in his and led her through the crowd, turning to draw her in close as they moved slowly in time to the music. It was hard to remember she shouldn't really be melting against him, despite the urge her body had to do so.

'I can't wait to get you out of here tonight,' he murmured low enough for her to hear, while keeping a polite, friendly smile on his face.

'You won't have to ask twice,' she smiled back. Anyone looking on would never suspect the tone of their conversation; at least Cash hoped they wouldn't.

'Do you know the first thing I'm gonna do when I get you alone?'

Cash supressed a faint shiver of anticipation and widened her eyes innocently, 'No, do tell.'

'I'm gonna rip off your—'

'Linc,' a slightly slurred feminine voice cut in. 'They're about to do the speeches and they need you back at the table,' Olivia said, swinging her gaze across to Cash. 'Sorry to steal him away from you,' she added, and ran a hand up and down the lapels of his tux jacket as she held Cash's gaze.

Cash lifted an eyebrow at Linc as he gave the woman a tolerant smile, stepping away from her busy hands and giving Cash an apologetic glance. 'I'll be right back,' he promised.

Cash watched them move away, surprised by Olivia's uncharacteristic behaviour. Had she really just stared Cash down while she pawed at Linc? Granted, she hadn't spent a great deal of time with Olivia, but she'd never got the impression she was this . . . predatory.

After the song ended, the best man took the microphone and asked everyone to take their seats. As expected with journalists, the speeches were funny and well written, the toasts heartfelt and the stories about Hadley and Mitch highly entertaining. Then Bob Callahan got up to talk and afterwards there wasn't a dry eye in the room.

Lincoln and Griff stood up next and gave a speech about their baby sister and read out a compiled list of their many combined talents, ranging from cattle castrating to close combat training, to remind their new brother-in-law who he was dealing with now that he had the welfare of their little sister in his hands. She almost felt sorry for the guy—something told her they hadn't been altogether joking.

Throughout the speeches, Cash's attention was repeatedly drawn back to Olivia, who seemed uncharacteristically animated. When she got up to respond to the best man's speech, she stumbled a little and had to be righted by Mitch and Hadley as she passed behind their chairs. She saw Hadley whisper something to Olivia, who shook her head and continued to make her way to the microphone. A low murmur of voices trickled around the tables and Cash held her breath, hoping this wasn't going to be as bad as she feared.

'Well! What a wedding, huh?' she started. An ear-piercing squeal came from the speakers and Olivia took a step back, teetering on her high heels a little before clutching the podium for support. The best man jumped up and adjusted the microphone, handing it back to Olivia after a hesitant glance towards the bride and groom.

'My best friend in the entire world got married,' Olivia said, pausing with a somewhat dejected face. 'I'm happy for you, Hads,' she said, turning her head to look at Hadley, 'I really am. It's just that I always thought we'd be getting married together, you know? Remember when we were like, ten, and we planned our double wedding?' She chuckled into the mic, but the laughter seemed to go on for an uncomfortably long time and, to Hadley's horror, turned into a full-blown sob. 'Where did my life go so wrong, Hads?'

Hadley stood and crossed to her friend, putting her arm around her shoulder and leading her outside away from prying eyes.

An awkward buzz of conversation followed the departure, but the best man was used to handling crises like this, thanks to his years as a news host. He smoothed over the hiccup and wrapped up the speeches to announce that cake, tea and coffee were now being served.

Cash spotted Hadley coming back inside and, to her surprise, Olivia also returned moments later, seeming to be over her mini breakdown as she let loose on the dance floor. Tomorrow she was going to be dealing with a world of regret, but tonight, apparently, she was partying like there *was* no tomorrow.

She noticed Hadley speaking to Griffin off to one side, the two of them glancing across at Olivia now and again. Eventually Griff made his way through the other revellers to Olivia, who had managed to climb up on one of the tables and start dancing. Cash was impressed she was managing to keep her balance so well in those lethal-looking heels.

At Griff's arrival, Olivia broke out in a wide smile and waved him to come up and join her. She seemed oblivious to the set expression on Griff's face, which, even from this distance, Cash could tell was bordering on furious. Seeming to have no luck in talking her down, Griff took another step closer, swooping the drunken woman into his arms amid cheers from the guests and carrying her through the crowd and out of the shearing shed.

'Is it just me or does that remind you of a scene from *An Officer and a Gentleman*?' Harmony asked from beside her.

Cash bit back her surprise at the almost friendly tone and laughed. 'It's very Richard Gere-like,' she agreed. If you ignored the fact that Griff looked like he'd rather strangle Olivia than make mad passionate love to her. 'I don't think she's going to live this down for a while,' Cash added.

'Nope. It's going to make for some juicy gossip over the next few days.'

'I wouldn't have picked Olivia as the type to party hard,' Cash said doubtfully.

'She's not . . . usually,' Harmony said dryly before taking a sip of her wine, 'but, then, nobody's perfect.'

'Harmony,' Cash started hesitantly. 'Is everything okay?'

The woman sent her a swift, sideways glance, before taking another sip. 'Of course. Why wouldn't it be?'

'No reason.' *It's none of your business,* the little voice tried to warn her once more. 'I know we don't know each other that well, but if you ever need to talk to someone . . .'

'Thanks,' she said briskly, straightening. 'I need to find the kids. It's getting late.'

Cash watched her walk away and pushed aside the lingering disappointment that followed their exchange. For the briefest of moments she'd thought they'd actually made a breakthrough. It was like trying to win over a skittish animal, only she'd run out of time and it looked like it was never going to happen before she had to leave.

Twenty-nine

Linc had to draw on every ounce of his patience to see out the day. Other than a few brief moments, he hadn't been able to get Cash to himself. He'd thought dancing with her would help ease the frustration, but all it had done was remind him of how badly he wanted her.

Thank Christ the party was finally winding down—well, at least for most; some of the younger guests looked like they were only just getting started. Jesus, he must be getting old. He even *sounded* like an old man. He stood up and managed to catch Cash's eye, discreetly nodding his head in the direction of the door. He saw a ghost of a smile dance across her lips as she picked up her bag and said goodnight to the few people remaining at her table.

He followed her with his eyes, loving the way her hips moved as she walked. He loved everything about her. A surge of pride flowed through him; she was with *him*. He wanted to tell the whole damn world—but the shearing shed would do in a jam, only he was pretty sure no one would really care right now. It didn't matter, tonight was the last time they needed to be careful—the wedding was all but over, the bride and groom having already departed for their honeymoon, and that only left his brother to worry about. Tomorrow he'd take Griff aside and he'd tell him. Man to man, brother to brother, he'd just tell him and get it over with so they could all move on. Griff would handle it—he didn't have any choice. Cash was his and there was no way he was going to give up the chance at a life with her just so his little brother's nose didn't get put out of joint.

Outside, a row of torches had been set up to light a path towards the paddock where guests had parked. Linc detoured off the path and crossed to the house, figuring Cash would have headed there to collect her things before going home.

Linc saw light spilling from beneath the door of the spare room and softly rapped his knuckles against the timber before opening it.

Cash stood with her back to the doorway, the soft fabric of her dress falling away to reveal a long, smooth back as she undid the zipper. She glanced over her shoulder at his arrival and smiled, holding his gaze as he moved toward her.

There was no hesitation as he reached for her. She turned, wrapping her arms around his neck as he pulled her tightly against him and kissed her. She tasted of champagne. He'd wanted to do this all night. He ran his hands up through her hair and cupped the sides of her face as their kiss became almost feverish in its intensity. He felt her hands tugging at the shirt tucked into the waistband of his trousers moments before the cool softness of her hands touched the hot skin of his abdomen. His harsh intake of breath made her smile, until he lowered his face and sucked gently on the soft skin of her neck, dragging a long, deep moan from her in response.

'What the hell?'

Linc swore violently under his breath as he looked up and saw his younger brother staring at him, a mix of anger and disbelief written across his face. 'Griff—'

'You didn't waste any time, did ya,' he snarled, his eyes narrowing dangerously and his mouth a straight, angry line.

'It isn't like that,' Cash said, quickly wriggling her arms back into her dress while trying to calm the potentially volatile situation. 'Linc was just—'

'Yeah, I know what he was *just* doing,' Griff said with a harsh laugh. 'He was doing what he always does. Whatever the hell he likes.'

'Mate,' Linc said wearily, positioning himself in front of Cash as she finished dressing. *Damn it.* This was not how he wanted it to happen.

'If I was one of your *mates*,' he almost spat the word and Linc's gaze snapped up, 'you'd never do this. You and your bloody army mates with your codes and your brothers-in-arms shit. Don't worry about the real brother you have—clearly that's not worth anything. I didn't fight alongside you in a freakin' war somewhere, so I'm not good enough to worry about stabbing in the back, am I?'

'That's not true.'

'Bullshit. You don't give a rat's arse about anyone or anything other than yourself—you never have.'

'What the hell?' Linc started to protest.

'You took off from here without a backward glance. You stayed away for years on end without bothering to visit. You put Mum and Dad though hell riskin' your damn life. You only ever come home when you've got nothing better to do, or when it suits you. Lincoln Callahan,' Griff said dropping his tone scathingly, 'the big war hero. You can fight for your country but you couldn't give a toss about your own family.'

'You don't know what the hell you're talking about.'

'Course not. I'm just a dumb farmer. What would I know about anything? Do whatever you want. You will anyway,' he said and stalked off, the angry strike of his boots echoing along behind him in the sudden stillness.

'I knew this was going to be an issue,' Cash said.

'There's nothing we can do about it. At least it's out now.'

'I'm not talking about him finding out about us, I mean causing a problem between you two,' Cash said miserably.

'He was just striking out. He'll calm down.'

'He might have been saying things to hurt you,' Cash said, suddenly feeling overcome by weariness, 'but I think there was a lot of truth behind it, at least in his mind. You need to talk to him.'

~

In the distance the last of the partygoers were saying good-night. Linc's jaw clenched as he replayed Griff's scathing words over and over in his mind. What a bloody mess, but Cash was right—he had to set the record straight. Griff was way off the mark if he thought Linc didn't have his brother's back. He did—always had. They may have drifted apart over the last few years, but Griff was his kid brother. He'd just explain, rationally and calmly, about Cash. She wasn't just some chick he'd hooked up with. She was important.

Linc's footsteps slowed as he heard a rhythmic sound and rounded the corner of the huge machinery shed, yellow light spilling out into the darkness, to find Griff pounding a tyre rim out of a tractor tyre with a large mallet. He'd wanted to wait till tomorrow, let Griff cool down a bit, but Cash had been so upset about coming between the two of them and he couldn't stand the torment he saw in her eyes. It had to be done tonight.

He saw Griff glance up as he approached and pause mid-stroke before hitting the tyre with even more force. His chest was bare but he still wore his dress pants from the wedding. Jumping down, holding the handle of the long mallet with one hand, he wiped his brow with the other and gave Linc a steely-eyed glare. 'Here to gloat?'

'Don't be a dick,' Linc started, then regretted it when he saw the fury mount in his younger brother's eyes.

'Me be a dick?' he yelled. 'I'm not the one who swooped in on his own brother's girlfriend.'

'She wasn't your girlfriend,' Linc protested.

'It doesn't matter. You knew I liked her.'

'Yeah, I did. And I'm sorry, all right? I swear, I wasn't planning on going anywhere near her. It just . . . happened.'

'You accidentally tripped over and fell into her bed?'

'It wasn't like that.'

'It was exactly like that. How long has it been going on for?'

'It doesn't make any difference.'

'How long, Linc?' Griff demanded, squaring his body towards him.

'A few weeks.'

'Weeks! Are you shitting me?'

'Look, we didn't want to cause a problem with the wedding coming up.'

'You two have been sneakin' around behind my back for weeks!' He gaped at Linc, fury in his eyes. 'You stood there and listened to me tell you how I thought I still had a shot with her at Christmas. Guess that must have given you a laugh.'

'Not really, no. But I couldn't do it. I couldn't tell you.'

'Why the hell not?'

'Because you're my brother and I didn't want to hurt you!'

'So you just let me make a fool of myself instead. Thanks a lot.'

'Aw, come on, Griff, how would it have been any better if I'd said anything? We'd be doing this exact thing on Christmas Day and Dad would have skinned us both alive for getting Mum upset.'

'I'm so sick of your shit, Linc.'

'My shit? What about yours?' Linc shot back. 'You've been moping around the place, takin' out your bad mood on everyone for weeks and giving me nothing but a hard time. I've been bustin' my arse around here trying to help.'

'No one asked you to come home and work.'

'No one had to. Last time I checked I was part of this family too.'

'When it suits, right?'

'What's that supposed to mean?'

'When was the last time you gave a shit about this place?'

'What are you talkin' about? I've always cared about Stringybark.'

'Bullshit. You couldn't wait to leave. When was the last time you stayed up all night harvesting? Or mustered sheep in the rain to get them to higher ground during a flood? Or watched Mum and Dad stress over paying bills? You think spending a few days out there fixin' a bloody fence makes you part of this place?' he asked disdainfully.

'I never claimed farming was in my blood the way it is with you and Dad,' Linc growled. Griff might as well have kicked him in the guts, he felt such a dull, aching pain deep in his stomach.

'Do you have any idea how sick and tired I am of hearing how great you are from everyone?' Griff continued, his fury simmering down to just plain pissed off. 'Mum and Dad think the sun shines out of your arse. It doesn't matter what I do around here, how I hold the bloody place together, the minute Linc walks through the door, everything's fine again. They're happy. The bills suddenly don't matter. "The prodigal son has returned",' Griff said, using his free hand to throw the words, like a newspaper heading, in the air.

'I never asked to be treated any different, Griff. You can't blame *me* for the fact Mum and Dad are happy to see me. Jesus, how old are you? Four?'

Griff threw down the mallet and came towards him.

'You're going to fight me?' Linc asked incredulously.

'Someone needs to bring you down a peg or two,' Griff said, and the punch landed surprisingly quickly across Linc's jaw, snapping his head back with unexpected force.

Linc instantly saw red. Brother or no brother, he wasn't going to be anyone's punching bag.

'You couldn't leave her alone, could you?' Griff circled him and his fist struck out, lightning fast, clipping the side of Linc's head. He let loose a torrent of expletives as the sting of contact to his ear burned.

'Just this once, you couldn't walk away. You couldn't find *any other* woman in the district to hit on—it had to be *her,* didn't it.'

This time Linc was ready and he dodged the next sharp jab, blocking a second one and landing one of his own in his brother's stomach.

There was a flurry of fists and swearing, grunts and groans as the two brothers fought their way through years of pent-up frustration. It felt good to hit something, Linc thought as he felt another punch make contact. Then he forgot who he was fighting—there was just pain and fear and anger, so much anger he'd kept tightly under wraps for so long. Anger at himself. Anger at that one, brief moment in time that had changed his life forever—that had ended any misconceptions he'd had of being a hero. It was the moment he'd found out he was a coward.

'I said enough!'

His father's roaring voice finally managed to cut through the red veil of pain and fury long enough for Linc's vision to clear. He saw his brother lying beneath him, bloodied and beaten on the ground.

'What have you done?' His mother's voice, sobbing and fearful, floated somewhere in the mist that surrounded him. He saw faces staring down at him and briefly thought he saw Cash as he felt himself being pushed aside onto the floor. The smell of dirt, diesel and blood filled his nose and flooded his senses. Blood. So much blood. The air smelled of explosives and burnt flesh. The heat rolled across him in waves as everything around him burned. And the face of the men he'd served with stared back at him, sightlessly, as they lay dead, scattered around him in the street.

Thirty

Cash took the cup offered to her, sending a numb 'Thank you' to Sue Dawson, who patted her gently on the shoulder. The waiting room at the hospital wasn't so much a room as a corridor with seating for the shell-shocked few who'd witnessed the aftermath of the Callahan brothers' fight.

Bob and Lavinia sat close together at the end of the row, their faces etched with worry and shock. Bill stood, leaning against the door, beside his son, Oliver, who'd sobered up remarkably quickly after having stumbled from the reception hall to the machinery shed to investigate the screaming and yelling.

Cash had been relieved when Linc had gone to find Griff to sort things out, but the longer she'd sat alone in the Callahan's spare room, the more anxious she'd become. Eventually she'd decided to track down the men. If they were deep in conversation, she'd just back away and leave them to it.

There was no sign of them on the verandah, and they hadn't gone back to the reception. Lavinia and Bob, as well as Sue and Bill Dawson, along with the catering staff, were packing away some of the mess, but there was no sign of the brothers.

She was backtracking, making a slight detour, when she heard muffled swearing somewhere in the dark, only to round the corner of the machinery shed to find the two men beating the hell out of each other. She'd tried to break them up, but they were both too fuelled by rage to hear her protests. Cash had witnessed her fair share of drunken fights, but this was more than a pub brawl. She ran from the shed to get help, returning to see Linc relentlessly pounding his brother's face and body with iron-like fists.

They all froze at the sight for a moment, then pandemonium broke out as men raced to pull the two brothers apart. She heard Lavinia cry out, her hand covering her mouth in horror.

But it wasn't the blood or the swelling flesh that terrified Cash. It was the image of Linc after the fight had been broken up—her tough, handsome, heroic Linc, lying on the ground, crying and muttering incoherently—that haunted her.

Something had happened. Something terrible, and it had broken the man she loved.

Linc tried to work out what the strange noise was. But every time he tried to concentrate on the sound, he fell back to sleep, until the noise woke him again. Eventually he roused himself enough to keep his eyes open, and when he did he wondered if he were still dreaming.

'It's all right, son. You're in hospital,' Bob said calmly. A little too calmly for his father.

Linc forced himself to shake off the remaining cobwebs of sleep and focus. *Hospital?* The last thing he remembered was . . . What the hell *was* the last thing he remembered?

Griff.

The thought came like a rush of white hot liquid and he tried to sit up, the movement sending a ripple of pain through his entire body.

'Just relax.'

'Griff,' he managed to get out. His voice came out as little more than a croak. His father handed him a glass with a straw and helped him lean up to take a sip. His lip stung like a son of a bitch and he could barely manage more than a few sips before his head started feeling light. As he lay back against the pillows he stared at his dad, waiting for an answer.

'Your brother's going to be okay.'

The whole nightmare came back to him in vivid detail and he felt a wave of nausea wash over him. His skin felt clammy and he closed his eyes. What had he done? 'Dad,' he started to speak but heard his voice crack as emotion welled up and flooded out.

Bob roughly patted his shoulder, but Linc felt only grief and overwhelming shame and remorse.

'You just rest up and get back on your feet. We'll get you sorted,' Bob said in his gruff, no-fuss way.

If only it were that easy. He'd ignored the signs he wasn't coping. He'd declined any help while he was still enlisted in the army—he thought he'd be fine. He'd been a combat veteran for too many years to count. He'd done three tours of the Middle East. He was a soldier, for God's sake—he could handle his shit. It was only bad dreams and sleepless nights and a few flashbacks. He hadn't lost his legs or had his head blown off like so many others he'd worked alongside over the years. There was nothing wrong with him . . . and, yet, clearly there was. He'd almost killed his brother in a fit of rage. He hadn't even realised he was doing it.

The nausea came back and he turned his head away from his father's concerned face. He couldn't look at him. He couldn't bear to see that look of pity . . . or the disappointment. He was messed up, and now everyone would know.

~

He wouldn't look at his mother when she came in to see him later that day. He couldn't. He refused to talk to any of them. They tried their best to act as though everything was fine, but he heard the fear and uncertainty in their voices. Nothing was fine about this. The only person he spoke to was the doctor when she came to check on him.

He couldn't ask his family about the details, but he asked her. He wanted to know how bad Griff was. He needed to know. His family wouldn't tell him because they were trying to make him feel better—as though his beating the living shit out of his own brother somehow entitled him to feel better. They were all sure he was one eggshell-step away from losing his mind.

His brother had been unconscious when he was brought into the emergency room in Griffith, and had a broken nose, lacerations to the face and swelling. Luckily there'd been no internal bleeding and he was being kept for observation before being allowed to go home. *I could have killed him.* The thought continued to run through his head.

Linc had copped a concussion and his own fair share of cuts and bruises, but they'd sedated him because he had been so distressed on his arrival at hospital. A mental health worker would assess him before they decided whether transferring him to a hospital with a psychiatric ward was warranted. He didn't even care anymore. Once he would have fought them—argued and bulldozed his way out of the hospital. Mental health worker? Psychiatric ward? He wasn't a nutcase. But now, after the fight, he couldn't hold on to the anger that'd been fuelled by fear for so long. There was something wrong with him. He was dangerous; he'd almost killed his brother.

Later, he wasn't sure when as he'd been dozing on and off, Linc heard someone enter his room, but he didn't turn his head. They all knew he wasn't in the mood to talk. When he heard the chair beside his bed move, he frowned.

He tried to ignore whoever it was, but they refused to leave. After a while, it got the better of him. Who the hell was so stubborn that they'd just sit there in silence and wait him out? He turned his head and felt his eyes widen slightly before he slammed them shut again. Oh. Hell no. He was not doing this. Not here, not now, not ever.

'You can ignore me like you've ignored everyone else, but don't think for a minute you're fooling me with this act,' Cash said, and the words washed over him like a smooth, aged port, warming him from the inside out.

Then her words actual registered. 'Act?' he croaked.

'You may have your family bluffed into accepting this bullcrap silent treatment you're giving them, but that's not going to work with me.'

'What are you doing here?'

'Trying to work out what I ever saw in you,' she said calmly, and her words stabbed at the already bruised and raw emotions inside him.

'Jesus, don't hold back, will ya,' he managed through gritted teeth.

'I don't plan to.'

'You're wasting your time. Go home.'

'The thing is. While you're lying here feeling sorry for yourself, you don't get to tell me what to do.'

Linc stared at her, dumbstruck. *What the hell?* 'I almost killed my brother,' he snarled at her, furious that she was goading him like this.

'I know. I was there. And it seems to me you're refusing to take responsibility for it,' she said.

'Refusing to take responsibility?' He watched her sitting there with her arms crossed, looking at him with those knowing green eyes. Christ, she looked so smug . . . and freakin' sexy. He closed his eyes briefly and gave a silent groan. *Get a grip, Callahan.* 'Of course I take responsibility for it! I did it. I hit him so many times, he lost consciousness, and I would have kept hitting him if Dad hadn't pulled me off him,' he said, raising his voice. *What was wrong with this woman?*

'Why?' she asked, leaning forward in her chair.

'Why what?'

'Why were you hitting him? Why would you have kept going until you killed him? Why were you doing that to your brother?' She shot the questions at him. 'What made you hate him so much you were willing to beat him to death?' she demanded, her voice rising.

'I didn't know it was him!' he yelled back. The words tore from him like a razor, slicing him apart. 'I didn't know . . . I thought it was . . . that I was back . . . there,' he said, almost whispering now. 'I didn't mean to hurt him.'

'I know you didn't,' she said softly, moving from the chair to the side of his bed to cup his face gently in her hands, forcing him to look at her. 'We all know you didn't,' she said pointedly, and held him firmly when he went to turn his face away from her in shame. 'Look at me, Linc,' she said, her voice as sure and commanding as any drill instructor. 'Your family loves you. They want to help. You have to stop shutting everyone out.'

'I can't,' he jerked his head out of her hold, and winced. 'I'm not who they think I am,' he practically spat the words, filling them with all the self-loathing and disgust he felt inside.

'Tell me,' she said, refusing to budge from beside him.

Through the thin hospital blanket he could feel the heat of her body.

'Tell me,' she said again.

What did it matter what she thought of him after this? She was already lost to him. There was no way after all this he could ever have a future with Cash, not after all the pain he'd inflicted on Griff. If nothing else, he'd step up and be the brother he should have been in the first place.

'We did a lot of close-contact work in Afghanistan, moving through villages and towns, clearing buildings and searching houses. It was always hard to tell the good guys from the bad ones—half the time they were the same people. You learned to trust your gut after a while. If something felt wrong, you stopped and listened.' He paused, more to organise his thoughts than to catch his breath, although as he spoke he felt almost light-headed. It was a weird sensation, saying the words in his head out loud. He had never told anyone about his time over there—not like this anyway.

'We were clearing this apartment building when a kid comes out of nowhere. He was carrying a rifle and had a vest strapped to him. He was running straight at us.' He dropped his gaze, he couldn't watch that disgusted look enter her eyes when she heard the truth. 'I should have shot him.' Her hands squeezed his tightly. 'But I couldn't . . . he was just a little kid. It happened so fast and I screwed up. He took out most of my unit. I'm responsible for the death of those men.'

'No,' she shook her head, 'the people who sent that child out to kill you are responsible for their death.'

'I failed them.'

'It wasn't your fault.'

He'd heard the words a hundred times, but it *was* his fault. He failed to do what he'd been trained to do—Christ, he'd done it a thousand times during training over the years. It was instinct, the instantaneous decision to shoot or not to shoot. He saw the weapon. He saw the vest full of explosives, he saw a hand holding the trigger . . . but then . . . he saw the kid and he froze. His nephew was around the same age, for Christ's sake. That fraction of a second was all it took for everything to go to shit. If he'd just squeezed the trigger, if he'd not hesitated for that one heartbeat, maybe he could have saved his men.

'Is that the reason you left the army?' she asked quietly.

'Partly,' he said. 'I'd been thinking about it for a while, that was just the tipping point.'

In truth, there'd been so many other things that he'd forced to the back of his mind in order to get on with it the job. Everywhere you looked in the places he'd been there was so much that was incomprehensible to him. The loss of humanity, the abuse, the total disregard for life . . . He couldn't understand how any of it could be made acceptable in the name of religion. How could someone strap explosives to a child, knowing they would be blown up in the process of taking out the infidels? How could the life of a woman be worth so much less than a man? How could it be lawful to punish a victim of rape?

He had seen things and been forced to look the other way unless it became a direct threat to him, but so much of it had worn away at his morale. After a while he had become numb inside. He'd lived with an empty, dirty, helpless feeling in the pit of his stomach for too many years to count. Even coming home, leaving the army far behind, hadn't erased the emptiness. He carried it with him, no matter how hard he tried to scrub himself clean—it was imprinted on him, branded into his soul.

'Just go, Cash. You were right before. I'm not good for you. You should stay away from me.'

'Oh, now you tell me?' she said in an attempt to lighten the mood, but he was too empty to respond.

'Please just go. It's over.'

'Linc, we'll get through this—'

'There is no "we",' he said, raising his voice more in panic than anger. He couldn't do this. He didn't have the strength to fight her on this. He'd hurt his brother. He didn't deserve to be happy with Cash, or anyone for that matter. 'There never was. It was just a bit of fun on the side and now it's over. You were right, I'm not the kind of guy who does relationships, and you're kidding yourself if you think you're going to change me.'

'I wasn't trying to change you,' she said softly, and he steeled himself against the hurt he detected in her voice.

'It was fun.' He forced himself to hold her wounded look, relieved when she stood up and turned away. He closed his eyes when he heard her footsteps fade and only then allowed himself to open them, taking in the empty spot where she'd been sitting and knowing that being alone was the only way he could guarantee not to disappoint anyone ever again.

❧

Three days later Linc stopped in the open doorway of his brother's bedroom and knocked briefly.

The mental health assessment had been everything he'd imagined it would be—invasive, brutal and a waste of time. He didn't need some kid fresh out of university telling him what he already knew, but hadn't wanted to acknowledge. He'd spent the last few days convincing doctors he'd get treatment, but he'd be buggered if he'd do it out here. Nope, he needed to get as far away from this place as he could.

He didn't wait for Griff to answer before walking into the room. Even though he'd been preparing himself for this all morning, nothing could soften the shock of coming face to face with the result of his actions. Inside, his resolve crumpled to a heap, but at least the army had prepared him in one sense—outwardly he remained composed.

There was a large gash under Griff's eye that had been stitched, and tape was strapped across his nose. The hospital doctor had realigned it under local anaesthetic, but thankfully she didn't think it would need any further surgery. The bruising spread from his nose around his eyes and along his lower jaw, although apparently the swelling around his eyes had gone down a little and at least he could now open them.

It was hard to tell what Griff's reaction was, his face was so swollen, but Linc didn't need to see an expression to feel the tension in the room. He opened his mouth to speak and then had to clear his throat when his voice cracked a little. 'I know I'm the last person you want to see. I won't stay long,' he said quickly, lowering his gaze. It was too painful to look at the damage he'd caused, but then he forced himself to. This was his punishment—he had to face up to the consequences.

'I just came to say sorry. It's not enough . . .' he said, shaking his head slightly. 'There's nothing I can say to make this right, I just wanted to let you know that I'm going to get some help . . . so it doesn't happen again. It should never have happened to you. If I'd just gone and . . .' He searched for the words to make things right, to explain how sorry he was, but nothing seemed adequate. If he'd stopped trying to be some tough guy, stopped worrying about what people would think of him and spoken up when he'd first noticed something wasn't right, none of this would have happened. 'I'm sorry, Griff, about this, and about . . . Cash. It's over. Me and her, I mean. I'm leaving. I just wanted to see you . . . before I left,' he ended, weakly, his eyes dropping to the bedroom floor. 'See you around.'

He hadn't expected to be forgiven, he'd almost expected Griff to swear and curse and jump out of bed and hit him with the cricket bat that hung on the wall, the one he'd had signed by Steve Waugh when he was twelve. But the stony silence was worse. It ripped at his insides and hurt like a bastard.

The rest of the day went past in a blur. His mother cried as he kissed her goodbye, and his dad gave his usual gruff farewell, but he heard his voice break a little when he said, 'Take good care of yourself, son.' Harmony simply hugged him but didn't say goodbye. He knew there'd be hell to pay once Hadley found out what had happened. She had already left the reception before the whole fiasco erupted and they'd decided not to tell her until after her honeymoon. He'd deal with that later.

He slowed down as he approached the front gates of Stringybark but he didn't stop. He didn't glance in the rear-view mirror like he usually did one final time before he left. He couldn't. Seeing those gates disappear behind him was too painful to bear.

He refused to even glance sideways as he passed the driveway of the little white cottage further down the road. He didn't say goodbye to Cash. He'd made a promise to his brother and he was going to keep it. He owed him that much.

Thirty-one

Cash took down a glass and watched as the amber liquid ran down the inside edge and filled to the top. The lunchtime crowd was slowly easing, which would give her time to catch up on cleaning and brace herself for the after-work crowd.

As far as jobs went, the money here was good and the hours okay. She'd only been planning on hanging around long enough to save up some money and figure out where she wanted to go next, but she'd been here three months and she still had no real idea. She missed the day spa, but she'd known straightaway that she wouldn't be able to stay after Linc left. She felt partially to blame for everything that had happened and there was no way she could stick around town when everywhere she looked reminded her of Linc.

She hadn't told Savannah the real reason behind turning down her offer to stay, but her friend had known something was wrong. She promised to tell her one day, but it was too raw now. Before she left she'd arranged for Vanessa to open the spa a few times a week. It wasn't ideal but it was enough to keep the Sacred Spirit operational until Savannah could figure out an alternative.

Cash hadn't had a destination in mind when she'd left Rankins Springs, she'd just got in her car and driven. She'd stopped in this little pub at Narrabri for lunch on her way through and seen a bartending job advertised. It had only supposed to be for a few weeks until she figured out a plan, but a few weeks had stretched into three months and she was still here.

It seemed the old Cash was back in operation again. When it came to a breakup, her first instinct was to pack up and move on. Only this time it didn't feel like she was making a fresh start. It hurt. A lot. And more than that, it left her angry. She wasn't sure who she was *more* angry at: herself for being so stupid as to fall for a guy like Linc in the first place, or at Linc for proving she'd been right about the kind of guy he was. And yet he hadn't really proved her right. She knew deep down it had been something real and precious for both of them. Still, when it all fell apart, he'd pushed her away rather than let her in to help, so maybe it hadn't been that important to him after all.

The job came with a room upstairs. It had been tastefully renovated and she lacked for nothing, but it wasn't Savannah's cosy little cottage, and the town, although full of the same down-to-earth country people, wasn't Rankins Springs.

She'd never stayed in any one place for long if she wasn't content, but for the first time ever she just didn't have the energy to move on. Why bother? She didn't have a burning desire to see any particular place, and even though she could have called a few contacts and gotten herself work overseas, the thought of leaving Linc so far behind caused a pain in her chest. That knowledge disturbed her more than she cared to admit. When had she ever let a man hold her back before?

She handed the beer over to the customer and took the money, looking up as another man walked up to the bar.

'G'day Cash.'

'Griff?' Automatically she looked over his shoulder but there was no one else with him. 'What are you doing here?'

'I came to find you.'

Cash blinked uncertainly. Never in her wildest imagination would she have considered the possibility that Griffin Callahan would come casually strolling into the pub where she worked. 'How did you know I was here?' she asked, confused.

'I called Savannah.'

Cash briefly considered pouring herself a stiff drink in order to process what was happening, but she figured she'd need to keep her wits about her. 'Why?'

'Is there someplace we can talk?' Griff asked.

Cash glanced over her shoulder and saw the bar manager in the storeroom. 'Give me a sec and I'll take a break.'

A few minutes later she came around the bar and beckoned Griff to follow her to a table away from the last of the lunchtime customers.

'What made you choose this place?' Griff asked as they settled into their seats.

Cash gave a dismissive shrug. 'It's as good as anywhere.'

'You could have stayed. No one blames you for what happened,' he told her.

His bruising and abrasions had healed and he looked good. No one would ever guess that his brother had beaten the living daylights out of him not so long ago. 'I blame myself,' she said with a sad shake of her head.

'It wasn't about you and me or you and Linc,' he said, holding her troubled gaze. 'It was about Linc. He came home early for Christmas because his business partners had told him he needed to sort his shit out. They could see he was struggling and they wanted him to get help. Linc being Linc wouldn't acknowledge that he had some unresolved issues, and he let them fester until they exploded. What happened wasn't your fault.'

She knew all that, but it didn't make her feel any less guilty. 'He wanted to tell you about me . . . before the other stuff happened,' she said, toying with the coaster on the table. 'I was the one who told him not to. I didn't want things to get any worse between you two, to upset Hadley or ruin your mother's Christmas . . . just so you know. It wasn't his choice not to tell you.'

'Yeah, I get that. It was a shock at first, but I've had time to think about it and it's not like you hadn't tried to let me down gently,' he said drolly, sending her a half-smile. 'I guess I wanted a change—you know? I feel like I've just been standing still forever. Everyone I know's moving on with their life and I'm just doin' the same thing I've been doin' since I left school—workin' the farm. Then you came to town,' he said, glancing up briefly before dropping his gaze once again. 'You were like no one I had really met before. I thought you were a sign or something . . . like, if you want to make a change, here's your shot.'

Cash gave a small grunt of acknowledgment. Oh yeah, she knew all about trying to make changes. 'So why did you track me down?'

Griff clenched his fingers rhythmically on the table top before answering, almost as though weighing up what he wanted to say. 'It's Linc.'

Alarm instantly filled her and she sat a little straighter. 'Is he okay?'

'That's the million-dollar question,' Griff shrugged. 'Mum and Dad are worried about him . . . we're all worried about him. He says he's been getting help and he's doing better, but he moved to Papua New Guinea.'

'Moved there? As in permanently?'

'Apparently they've set up a new office there and he volunteered to run it.'

'Well, I guess that's positive. I mean they wouldn't let him go if they thought he couldn't handle it, right?'

'Yeah, probably not . . . only he's shut everyone out. Mum and Dad spent a bit of time up in Brisbane with him after it all happened, Hadley too, but he rarely answered his phone and barely kept in touch. Now he's up and moved overseas without even telling us.'

'How did you find out?'

'The business. Dad called them to find out what the hell's going on with him and they told us where he was.'

Cash frowned over this news, angry that Linc could be so dismissive of his family's feelings like that. Then she looked up at Griff again. 'What's all this got to do with me?'

'I hate seeing Mum and Dad like this—so worried about him . . . I think the only person who could get through to him is you.'

Cash was shaking her head before he'd even finished talking. 'He left me too, remember? I haven't heard a word from him since. He's not going to listen to anything I have to say—I doubt he'd even answer my phone call.'

'That's why I thought you might go and see him.'

Cash blinked across at him. 'In *PNG*,' she said incredulously.

'I'll take care of the expenses, you'd only have to go over for a few days . . . Please, Cash, I know it's a lot to ask, but could you just try? For Mum and Dad?'

Up until the mention of Lavinia and Bob it had been an adamant 'no', but then she saw their faces, pictured Lavinia crying and Bob looking weary with worry, and a reluctant sigh escaped her lips. She loved this family; Cash couldn't forget how much kindness they'd shown her. She knew that there was no way she could turn her back on them now.

'I think you're wrong about Linc,' she said quietly. 'He made it clear that he didn't want me in his life. We were just a holiday fling.'

'I know my brother better than you think. You're the only one who can get through to him, Cash. Please?'

Thirty-two

Cash cleared customs and walked out to collect her baggage. There was an air of organised chaos to the place. People milled about, speaking loudly in pidgin English, which made her realise that here, as a white, English-speaking Australian, she was very much in the minority. But there was an overall friendly, welcoming atmosphere. She collected her small bag from the carousel before heading out to the arrivals area. She didn't have to search far to spot her name scrawled on a sign held by a stocky Papuan man. He wore her hotel's insignia on his shirt.

'Hello, I'm Cash Sullivan,' she said.

'I am Michael, I'll be looking after you today.'

She could have gone straight to the offices of Standby and just gotten the whole thing over with straightaway, but it seemed wise to take a little time to prepare. She was now feeling extremely nervous about seeing Linc again. The longer she could put it off, the more time she had to work up her courage.

Michael took her bag and they headed out into the bright sunshine. The effect of humidity was instantaneous. It hit her square in the face as they left the airconditioned comfort of the airport building behind. She had left Sydney in autumn weather, but in Port Moresby it was the end of the wet season and still very warm.

The airport was eleven kilometres from the capital and Cash used the car ride to take in the scenery. She'd never been to PNG before, and the travel geek in her was busy soaking up the sights and smells with great enthusiasm, ignoring for the moment the main reason she was here. Flying in, she'd noticed the lush greenness below—so intense it almost hurt to look at it. The green-grey mountains of the Owen Stanley Ranges in the distance, location of the infamous Kokoda Track, was a dominant feature of the landscape.

As they merged into traffic, cars of all shapes and sizes whizzed past them. Cash was fairly sure none of them would be passed for registration back home. Mirrors were held in place with duct tape; windscreens were often non-existent, and most vehicles had mismatched panels. As a rust-coloured car tore past them, blowing copious amounts of black smoke, she wondered how many accidents happened on these roads each day. There was no sign of police and apparently very few traffic rules. Women walked along the side of the road, carrying brightly coloured bags filled with everything from small children to firewood. Some had small stalls set up, selling craft items and food.

Her hotel was right in the centre of Port Moresby. Inside, she could have been anywhere in the world. It was luxurious, clean and not a whisper of pidgin English could be heard. She couldn't help a small gasp of delight as she stepped into her room and saw the breathtaking view of the ocean from her window. The turquoise water beckoned invitingly, but she turned to get together what she'd need for a quick shower.

At the front desk later, she approached the clerk, receiving a wide friendly smile.

'Can you tell me the best way to get to this address?' Cash asked and slid the paper with Standby's details written on it across the desk.

'Certainly,' the young woman said, lifting her hand to catch the attention of a man who stood in the lobby by the front door. 'I'll have someone drive you there.'

'Honestly, I don't mind walking. I'm just not sure how to get here.'

'Oh no, you really shouldn't walk on your own,' she frowned, before her smile reappeared. 'We have drivers.'

There was little point arguing; the man was waiting politely for her to follow him out to a vehicle.

The office was located in a rather modern-looking building only a few blocks from the hotel. Her stomach started kicking up a riot and her hands felt clammy as she entered the elevator and watched the numbers of the floors light up on the screen. The ping announcing her arrival made her pulse leap slightly, but she took a deep breath and let it out slowly, focusing on staying calm.

She found a door with *Standby* stamped across a metal plate in bold, professional letters, and an attractive woman in her early twenties looked up and smiled as Cash walked inside.

'Hello,' Cash greeted her, drawing on every ounce of her fortitude. 'I'm hoping to see Lincoln Callahan if he's available?'

'Do you have an appointment?' she asked, hitting a few keys on the keyboard of her computer.

'No, I don't, but I've flown in from Brisbane. I'm a friend of the family.'

'I'm afraid Mr Callahan is out of the office. He's on site with a client giving a training seminar and isn't expected at the office at all today.'

'Oh.' Damn it. She'd known it would be a risk turning up unannounced, but she'd wanted the element of surprise in case he refused to see her.

A man walked out from a corridor behind the reception desk and looked up at Cash with a curious smile. 'Hello. Richard Mullins, can I help in some way?'

Cash introduced herself. 'I was hoping to see Linc, but I've just heard he's out.'

Richard exchanged a quick glance with the receptionist before turning his attention back to Cash. 'Was it something I might be able to help with instead?'

'No, it was a personal matter actually,' Cash said, her mind racing as to what her next option might be.

'I see,' Richard said slowly, and she could almost see the wheels turning in his head. 'Cash, would you mind coming into my office for a moment? I might be able to sort something out.'

Cash wasn't sure what he could sort out, but she got the feeling that she could trust this man, so she stepped forward and followed him to an office down the hallway.

'Normally I wouldn't pry, but can I ask what your business with Linc is regarding?'

Cash studied the man briefly before deciding to go ahead. She'd come all this way, after all; she might as well take a chance. 'Linc's brother asked me to come over here. The family is very concerned about him. Apparently they've tried to contact him and he's being . . . evasive,' she said, choosing her words carefully.

'I've spoken to Linc's parents. I assured them that we'd keep a close eye on Linc and let them know if anything seemed concerning.'

'I'd feel better if I could speak to him myself,' Cash said candidly.

Richard seemed to consider her for a long while, his arms folded formidably across his chest, but Cash refused to back down, holding his frank gaze with her own until eventually he uncrossed his arms and said, 'Give me the name of your hotel and I'll pass it on to him.'

'All right,' Cash said, standing up. 'But tell him I'll be back tomorrow if he doesn't show. I'm not leaving till I see him.'

Richard gave a slow smile and nodded, 'I believe you, but I can only pass on the message.'

'Thank you,' Cash said, and waited as he opened the door for her, following him back out to reception.

'I'll get someone to take you back to the hotel.'

'I can hail a taxi, or walk, it's not far.'

'Ah, no. I'll have someone drive you. And Miss Sullivan?' he said, taking a business card from the desk and writing something on the back before handing it across to her. 'If you need to go anywhere, use this company, and only this company, for a taxi.'

'I know this place has a bit of a reputation for being dangerous, but is it that bad?'

'Look, it's a great place on the whole and the people are friendly, but Papua New Guinea is known as the land of the unexpected for a reason,' he said gravely. 'Things can turn very quickly, and I take security, especially personal security, very seriously.'

Cash thanked him and slipped the card into her bag.

Linc sat down at his desk to sort out the paperwork from the day's training seminar. It had gone well and he wanted to make sure the assessment and follow-up materials were sent out straightaway. There was a quick knock on his door and Richie walked in and handed him a note.

He stared at the name of the hotel before looking up at his mate with a raised eyebrow. 'You hittin' on me or something?'

Richie scoffed, but pushed away from the doorway where he'd been leaning. 'You had a visitor today. Does the name Cash Sullivan ring any bells?'

Linc sat upright in his chair and Richie gave a chuckle. 'I figured you'd be interested.'

'What the hell is she doing here?'

'Don't ask me, mate. That's where she's stayin',' he said, nodding at the paper Linc held in his hand. 'She seemed pretty determined to catch up.'

It was hard to ignore the way his heart leapt into his throat at the mention of her name, or how hard his pulse seemed to be pounding. He had to be dreaming, surely? How on earth would she have even known he was over here?

He glanced at the papers in front of him, then pushed away from his desk without a backward glance. There was no way he was going to be able to concentrate on anything knowing Cash was right here in Port Moresby. He was kidding himself if he thought he'd be able to stay away. He wasn't proud of the way he'd treated her. At the time, all he'd known was that he needed to get away and sort himself out—try to wrap his head around the fact he'd almost killed his own brother. It had scared him more than anything else in his whole life. It was also the wakeup call he'd desperately needed to kick his arse into getting help.

Richie and Tommo had been concerned about him for months in the lead-up to his return home. They'd been picking up on his irritable mood, but he'd shrugged it off, insulted that they might think he had a problem. Then one day, seemingly out of the blue, he'd been about to get out of his car one morning and found he couldn't. He'd been thinking about how hot it was that day. It had reminded him of Afghanistan. A spilt second later he was back in that street, lying on his back, a dull ringing in his ears blocking out all other sound as he tried to lift his head. He watched as everything seemed to happen in slow motion. A large cloud of smoke and earth cloaked him as debris from vehicles and the surrounding buildings landed on the sidewalk. After the dust cleared he laid his head back in the dirt and peered up to the sky. He was amazed at how blue and cloudless it was. Then he noticed the strong stench of burning flesh, rubber and cordite. The smell triggered his other senses. In the distance, noises started as a soft hum before growing louder; and then things were no longer in slow motion, but speeding up, faster and faster until the whole scene was a chaotic mess of screaming and shouting and the ringing in his ears became unbearable. He saw men lying dead and injured around him, broken and bleeding.

He had no idea how long he'd sat in his car, but he'd almost jumped through the roof when someone had tapped on his window, snapping him out of the flashback. Tommo had opened the car door and talked him down, taking him up to the office where he and Richie had tried to arrange for him to see a doctor. That's when he'd started yelling at them—his mates, men he'd respected and fought beside for too long to remember. They'd issued him with an ultimatum: either get help or they'd reconsider their partnership. He couldn't believe they were being so irrational over some weird, uncharacteristic brain snap. He'd had all kinds of excuses: he hadn't gotten enough sleep the night before, he wasn't eating properly, the business was stressful . . . but then on New Year's Eve it had all come to a head and he'd almost killed Griffin. He'd limped back to Brisbane, like a dog with its tail between its legs, and asked for help.

Since then he'd been seeing doctors and counsellors and had joined a support group for returned servicemen and women, finding the help he needed. He wasn't out of the woods yet—he still had times when he oscillated between anger and depression—but he had the tools and, more importantly, the contacts to get through the worst of it without doing any damage—to himself or anyone else. He understood things a lot better now—things he hadn't wanted to examine or think about before.

The only thing he hadn't completely dealt with was Cash. He and Griff had spoken a few times since the wedding, and while things weren't completely sorted between them, he thought they'd cleared the air of a lot of stuff that'd been hanging over their heads. Linc thought a lot of Griff's resentment stemmed from something else; he wasn't convinced he'd been the sole reason for his brother's bad mood over the Christmas break. But Griff would have to sort out his own demons—Linc had enough of his own to worry about just now.

Walking away from Cash had been so much harder than he'd anticipated. He'd been desperate to get away from Stringybark, from the faces of his family who were looking at him like he was some kind of stranger. On reflection, they probably hadn't been looking at him like that, but that's what he'd seen through his fog of guilt and shame. He hadn't been able to stand the idea of Cash looking at him with the same disappointed disgust he was feeling for himself. So he'd left.

He hadn't stopped thinking about her though. He couldn't if he tried. She was the last thing he thought about at night and the first thing he thought of when he woke up. He knew part of his decision to take the PNG job was to stop himself doing something stupid like going off to find her and begging her to take him back. There was no way she would after what had happened—he was certain about that.

Cash had no idea how Linc would react to her showing up on his doorstep like this, but she knew she couldn't leave without trying to see him. She was anxious and jittery, not sure whether to stay in the hotel and wait to see whether he turned up, or to go out sightseeing and risk missing him. She decided she needed some exercise to calm her nerves.

The cool water of the sparkling hotel pool washed over her heated skin as she dove beneath the surface, and for a moment all sounds were muffled by a cocooning silence. After exhausting herself doing lap after lap, Cash rested her folded arms along the side of the pool and closed her eyes, enjoying the afternoon sunshine on her face.

Eventually a cloud came across and blocked the light and Cash reluctantly opened her eyes, only to find someone standing above her, their bone-coloured trousers filling her vision. Startled, she lifted her gaze higher, taking in the olive-green polo shirt with *Standby* stamped across the pocket and finally coming to rest on the unreadable expression of the face she'd dreamed about for months.

For a moment they both simply stared at each other, Cash busy drinking in the sight of him greedily, while Linc seemed to be waiting, his body held rigid, watching her.

Cash swallowed past a dry lump in her throat. 'Hello, Linc.'

His head tilted slightly, and for a moment Cash didn't think he was going to say anything.

'What are you doing here, Cash?' he finally asked.

'I could ask you the same thing,' she said, recovering her wits at his unexpected appearance.

'I work here,' he told her bluntly.

'Or are you hiding?'

His face tightened and he folded his arms across his chest as he glared at her, unamused by the remark. 'I don't have to explain myself, Cash. Now what are you doing here?'

Cash narrowed her gaze at his closed body language, deciding that the best form of defence was a good offence, and pushed herself up and out of the pool, streaming water onto the warm concrete beneath her feet. She saw his eyes darken slightly as his gaze took a quick tour of her bikini-clad body before he focused them once more on her face. *Good,* she thought, *he isn't completely immune to me then.* Cash leaned over and snagged her towel off the sun lounge, patting her face dry. 'Griff came to see me. Your parents are worried about you, Linc.'

'My parents don't need to worry. I've told them that.'

'Well, it mustn't have convinced them.'

'So they thought sending you over here would be a good idea?'

That stung a bit more than she might have anticipated. Cash hid the hurt his remark caused, dropping the towel onto the lounge and placing her hands on her hips to face him. 'I guess they're just that desperate. I did warn them that you wouldn't listen to anything I had to say—after all, it was only sex to pass the time, and I was just another notch in your belt, right?' She turned away from him to slip on her shoes and pick up her towel.

Screw Griff and his emotional blackmail. She didn't need to be put through this rejection all over again. 'Call your parents, Linc. They deserve that much.' She didn't look back; she was too angry at herself for having held on to the tiny bit of hope seeing him again had brought. When would she ever learn?

She shut the door to her room and tossed the towel over the back of the chair, heading for the bathroom. A knock on the door stopped her mid-stride. Cash closed her eyes and thought about ignoring it. She didn't want to hear Linc's excuses. She didn't want to put herself through that again. If only falling *out* of love was as easy as falling in love had seemed to be. The knocking came again, this time louder, and Cash gritted her teeth before opening it. 'What?'

Linc seemed slightly taken aback by her aggressive tone but recovered quickly. 'We haven't finished our discussion,' not waiting to be invited in before pushing past.

'Oh please, come on in,' she said, closing the door and turning to glare at him.

'I owe you an apology. I'm sorry for leaving the way I did.'

'It's not about what happened between us. I'm here to tell you your parents are worried sick about you and you need to get over yourself and call them.'

'Get over myself?'

Cash sighed impatiently. 'Okay, I know what you've been going through has been tough. I realise it would have taken you a long time to come to terms with what happened, and I'm fairly sure there's been no miracle cure for post-traumatic stress, but you can't shut out the people who love you. That's not fair when all they've ever wanted to do was help you. They deserve to get a call now and then to say "hi", so they're reassured that you're getting there. They don't expect you to be a bouncing ray of sunshine, but they at least need to hear your voice and know that you're doing okay.'

'It's taken most of this time to convince *myself* I was okay. I didn't need the added pressure of trying to convince them as well.'

'I can understand that it's been hard, but they'll handle the fact that it's going to take time if you keep them posted.'

'Yeah, I know.' His shoulders slumped a little as he turned his head towards the view from her window. 'It's just hard you know,' he said, glancing across at her. 'They've always treated me like I was some big hero . . . then to have them discover that I'm not . . . I tried to tell them . . . I guess I just can't face their disappointment.'

'What happened was not a weakness. It was a result of being too strong for too long. I wish you could see your family from the outside, like I can. Your parents would move mountains for any of their kids. There is nothing you could do to make them disappointed.'

'Look,' he said, turning back to face her, 'I came up here to tell you you were wrong.' At her raised eyebrow he continued, 'You were never just sex to pass the time or a notch on my *anything*,' he told her, holding her gaze with a glare that almost dared her to look away. 'It happened so fast that I couldn't think past what was going on with Griff and everything that was going on with me . . . I didn't mean to make you feel as though you meant nothing.'

Cash felt her throat tighten at the low, earnest tone of his voice, before forcing a blasé shrug, 'We both knew what it was going in.'

'Yeah, we did, only somewhere along the line it all got a bit blurry. I wanted to ask you to move to Brisbane with me, but I heard Savannah's call about wanting you to stay. I was still working out how to ask you when everything blew up in my face.'

He had wanted her to move in with him? A little leap of joy caught her off guard.

'It was always more than just a bit of fun.'

'Was,' she said softly and held her breath as she saw his eyes darken.

Before she could blink, he swooped down and caught her lips in a swift, urgent kiss. There was nothing gentle about it, it was almost desperate, and she reacted in kind. All the months of hurt and pain she'd lived with after he'd left burst out of her in an almost frenzied response. He walked her backwards until she was up again the wall, moulding herself to his body. His hands held her head and the kiss became deeper. God, she'd missed him. Cash's hands impatiently went to his shirt, tugging it free from his trousers. She ran her hands up his sides and around his back, her nails scraping gently and sparking a shiver through his body that made her smile against his lips.

With a grunt, Linc pulled away slightly and rid himself of his shirt, before lifting her, holding her bikini clad backside in his hands as she wrapped her legs around his waist. They fell to the bed, lips locked as hands moved to undo buttons and remove excess clothing.

Later, they both lay panting as they stared up at the ceiling.

'I swear, I wasn't intending on that happening when I followed you up here,' he said, breaking the quiet of the room a few moments later. He rolled his head sideways to look at her. 'But I'm sure glad it did.'

Thirty-three

'It was a long way to come just to pass on a message from Griff,' he said a little while later, toying with her fingers as he held her hand.

'I had no plans to be anywhere else,' she said casually, which made him lift his gaze to hers.

'Is that the only reason you came here?'

He got a smug sense of satisfaction when she couldn't hold his look. A little spark of hope began to flicker inside him.

'I guess I wanted to see for myself that you were okay,' she admitted.

'I missed you, Cash.'

'Really?' she said curtly. 'Is that why I heard from you all those times since you left?'

The spark flickered and died away. 'I didn't think you'd want to hear from me.'

'Seriously?' she said, removing her hand from his. 'You didn't think I'd be just as worried about you as everyone else was, after everything we'd been through?'

'I guess I just didn't think you'd be too eager to see me after I'd left without a goodbye.'

'So you just decided not to bother?'

'I'd already agreed to come over here, I couldn't change my mind.'

'They don't have phones?' she said, sitting up and swinging her legs over the edge of the bed.

God, she was still the most beautiful women he'd ever laid eyes on. He was briefly distracted by the intricate tattoos wrapped around her back and sides, before snapping himself out of it. 'You're right. I didn't try hard enough.' Another thing to add to his growing list of failings. 'I know it sounds selfish, but I've been really trying to focus on getting my own shit together before I try to rebuild any of the other bridges I burned.'

She'd been draping the towel around her, tucking it in at the front as he spoke, but he saw her shoulders slump as he finished and he held his breath.

'I know,' she finally said, turning slightly to look at him. 'And it's not selfish. I think everyone realised you needed time to sort things out. I guess we all felt hurt that you didn't think we'd understand.'

Linc sat up, rubbing the back of his neck as he let out a sigh. 'I honestly didn't consider how everyone else would take it. I was trying so hard just to get through each day.'

'You need to see this from your family's point of view too, Linc. They're fixers. That's what they do. Your dad can fix a broken tractor, mend a fence, patch up whatever's broken around the farm,' she said. 'And your mum, she comforts everyone and tends to all the scrapes and scratches. They're not used to standing by and watching while one of their kids is hurting. They've felt helpless.'

'I understand that. I do,' he said, looking at her steadily, 'but I was in a really bad place. You feel all alone, even when you know you're not. You lose yourself . . . It's hard to explain to someone else when half the time you can't even explain it to yourself.'

He saw her nod slowly and knew she was trying to understand. It was a bastard of a thing to deal with, and even though he'd come a long way in a relatively short time, he knew it was going to be a long road ahead. He'd have to work with it for the rest of his life. Linc got to his feet, not caring that he was naked, and saw her eyes widen a little as he moved towards her. 'I really am sorry, Cash. I never meant to hurt you.'

Her eyes fixed upon his solemnly. 'I know. And I'm glad you've been getting the help you needed. You look better . . . healthier.'

He'd been spending a lot of time outdoors since he got here. He'd taken up hiking and rock climbing and went on early morning runs—it all helped to keep his mind clear. He felt better mentally and physically than he had in years.

'If I hadn't been so busy ignoring all the warning signs, I could have saved everyone a lot of grief.'

He looked down at his arm, where she had gently placed her hand. 'You're getting help now, and that's the main thing.'

'I'm glad you're here.' He really had missed her, but he'd been so scared of rejection that he hadn't let himself believe she would give him another shot. Yet here she was, and now he knew beyond a shadow of a doubt that he'd do everything he could to make sure she stayed in his life. He couldn't lose her again.

She seemed to hesitate at his words and his heart thudded in his chest. Maybe she didn't feel the same way. Maybe he'd hurt her too badly for her to forgive him.

'It was really good to see you again too, Linc,' she said softly.

'But?' he asked, feeling his hopes sink like a rock.

'But I don't know,' she shrugged. 'I didn't really think beyond finding you and giving you a serve about ignoring your family,' she admitted with a half-smile. 'I don't really know where this could possibly go.'

'Nothing's changed since we were back in the Springs,' he argued.

'Everything's changed, Linc,' she said, shaking her head at him and stepping away. 'You're over here. It can't work when we live in different countries. Living in Brisbane was one thing, this is something else entirely.'

'I can't leave straightaway, but I could work something out with the guys and we could find someone to take over for me.'

'So this was only ever temporary?' she asked.

'The original plan was to be here for a couple of years until we'd established ourselves, but that doesn't mean I can't make a new plan now.'

'Do you like it here?'

'It has its challenges,' he hedged.

'But do you like it?' she pushed.

'Yeah, I like it. The country's beautiful and the people are great . . . It has a lot of problems, but business-wise it's the ideal place to have an office. We're getting most of our client base from here and we're gaining a pretty good reputation.'

'That's great,' she said smiling.

'But that doesn't mean I *have* to be here.' Although being the only one out of the three not married with children, it made sense that he be the one to uproot his life and move overseas. Still, they could work something out—he was sure of it.

'Yes, it does, Linc,' she corrected. 'You need stability in your life right now, and your partners have been more than understanding so far, but I'm pretty sure they would take a dim view of rearranging everything just so you can be with some woman.'

'She isn't *some* woman,' he said, tugging on her hand to make her look up at him. 'She's *my* woman. The woman I'm in love with.' He saw her swallow hard and stare at him and he held his breath. 'Stay here with me, Cash,' he said quietly. 'You said once before you could find work anywhere, or don't work—it doesn't worry me—but just stay.'

The woman I'm in love with, Linc had said and Cash felt her throat close up at his words. It was still there—everything she'd felt for this man before the whole wedding fiasco had torn them apart was still *there.* She'd felt the chemistry the moment she'd glanced up and seen him by the edge of the pool. She hadn't expected that to have faded, but it was the other emotions, the ones not connected to his raw sex appeal, that had momentarily stolen her breath away. The realisation that she still loved him, and that hollow, empty feeling inside at the thought of saying goodbye to him. This was what she'd really come here for, besides passing on Griff's message—to see if she'd somehow imagined everything that had happened between them. If she got here and felt nothing, then she'd at least be able to walk away and know she could start someplace all over again. If she felt something, then . . . well, she hadn't quite known what would happen if that were the case. She hadn't been overly confident in predicting Linc's reaction.

She had to be crazy. Move to another country for this man? Maybe they were both crazy. *Why not?* a little voice questioned. It wasn't as though she'd never made a spur of the moment decision before. She'd packed up and moved based on far less reliable relationships than this. But now it counted. This time there was more than a casual fling at stake. This time her heart was on the line.

Savannah had been trying to tell her for a long time she was heading down a destructive path. Cash had always thought of partying and men as things to make her feel good, to fill that void where her family should have been. It wasn't until she'd seen Savannah and George together, and then met the Callahans, that it had hit her how much better her life could be.

She'd changed, and no one was more surprised by the transformation than she was. There'd been only one thing missing over the last three months, and she was looking at all five foot nine inches of him.

'I'd have conditions,' she said, managing to sound relatively calm despite the thundering of blood that had begun coursing through her veins.

Linc's slow smile made her stomach flip. 'Okay. Let's hear them.'

'Firstly, you wouldn't be keeping me,' she stressed. 'I'll find a job.'

'Providing I check it out and think it's safe,' he added.

'These are *my* conditions,' she reminded him.

'I work in risk management and security—I'm pretty sure I know what I'm talking about here.'

'Fine,' she huffed. 'I'll find a job in a safe part of town,' she conceded, 'and contribute to all expenses.' He opened his mouth to protest but she held up a hand. 'Secondly, you'll call your parents and let them know you're okay.'

'Okay.'

'I'm not finished yet,' she told him. 'Thirdly, you will never, and I mean *ever*, try and handle anything else alone.' She took him by surprise, pushing his chest until he sat back down on the edge of the bed. She sat down beside him and took his hand. 'If we're going to do this, then you have to tell me when things are getting on top of you, and you have to tell me what to do to help. If that means you need some space, or you have to get out and go for a run, that's fine, but I don't want to be shut out. It's all or nothing,' she said and heard her voice shake a little. 'Is that something you can do?'

'That's definitely something I can do,' Linc said, moving his hand so that he could tug her closer. 'I agree to all those terms. So we have a deal?'

Cash gave a small chuckle. For a life-changing moment, it had all happened rather fast. 'I guess we do,' she smiled as his lips covered her own.

Maybe this was where life had been trying to lead her all this time.

And maybe she hadn't ended up with the *wrong* Callahan after all.

Acknowledgements

In 2017 I was honoured to be an Australia Day Ambassador and invited out to a place called Carrathool, in the Riverina district of New South Wales. The people were amazing and the landscape was breathtaking. From the air, I got a whole new appreciation for the vastness of our country and the sheer magnitude of land that is used for farming and agriculture. Our farmers are absolutely vital to our everyday lives, and they work so incredibly hard and under extreme conditions a lot of the time. The stress these people deal with on a daily basis—financial, mental and health-wise—often goes largely unnoticed by mainstream Australia. Our farmers and their families are at the constant mercy of Mother Nature, large corporations, government bureaucracy and the rise and fall of the Australian dollar. They stake not only their livelihood every season, but also the fate of every single person who depends on buying food for their table. Buying Australian produce has a positive roll-on effect for employment not only in the rural communities, but across all of Australia, supporting trucking companies, truck drivers, produce stores, cafés, restaurants and more. We need to support our rural communities whenever and wherever we can, so I ask, if you see a way to help by buying Australian produce or donating to a trusted appeal to buy feed for animals, please do so.

A big thanks to my fellow authors and friends, Bramwell Connolly and Keith McArdle, who have always been there to help out and offer advice. Thank you to Anthony Moorhouse for allowing me to borrow his profession for Linc. You make me want to change my career so I can work for Dynamiq . . . although I'm not great with jungles . . . or hostile countries . . . or dealing with a crisis for that matter, so maybe I'll just leave it to you guys!

To Karly's Angels, the creative, amazing brainstorming gang who help me out with titles and names and a host of other things—thank you, guys!

Thanks also to Trevor Lynch, as well as John and Gloria Hunter, for their insight into Papua New Guinea.

Brent Parsons—what a guy! I was lucky enough to present this fella with an Australia Day award in 2017 for his part in organising a massive event in his community which brought thousands of people to the reopening of the local pub. He was also my go-to man for everything farming, although if there's anything incorrect, it'll be my doing—authors tend to bend a few rules now and again to suit the plot!

Thank you to the lovely Fiona Palmer, friend, question answerer and awesome author. Thank you for your support and friendship over the years.

Lyn Mattick, friend, sister, brainstormer and organiser—thank you for everything you do for me, and a huge thanks as usual to my husband, parents, kids, brothers, aunties, uncles and cousins who all continue to support me through this incredible journey. I'm very lucky to be surrounded by so many amazing people.

Thank you to everyone I met during my time out in Rankins Springs, Carrathool and surrounding areas. It was such a huge honour to be part of your Australia Day celebrations and I will forever be grateful for the lovely friendships I came away with.

If you or someone you know has recently left the military and needs somewhere to turn, please contact Soldier On: www.soldieron.org.au.

OUT NOW

Mr Right Now

KARLY LANE

Book 2 of THE CALLAHANS OF STRINGYBARK CREEK series

Griffin Callahan and Olivia Dawson were inseparable. Everyone in town knew it. But when Griff went off to ag college, Liv told him it was over and fled her family's farm to study law. Griff had never understood her reasons but eventually accepted that first loves don't last. Until now.

Currently back on the farm to help her twin brother with the harvest, Liv is the same gorgeous, laughing, hazel-eyed girl he'd always loved. Yet Griff can sense a difference, an uncertainty playing beneath the surface that wasn't there before.

Amidst crossed wires, drunken declarations, and families on a mission, will Griff and Liv finally have a second chance? Or will the old saying—*If you love someone set them free*—become their reality?

ISBN 978 1 76063 266 3

One

Griffin Callahan climbed down from the tractor and swore as he stared at the tyres submerged in the soft soil. Great. This was all he needed. He closed his eyes for a minute, giving in to the frustration he'd been fighting off all morning.

After a dry spell, the rains had finally arrived, filling the dams and the tanks and nourishing the pasture to feed weary livestock. The only problem was, once the rain had started, it hadn't known when to stop.

The weather had delayed seeding and Griff was eager to get moving. He'd walked the paddock yesterday and thought it had dried out enough to risk it. He'd been working steadily most of the morning but then his luck had given out and the tractor had run into a boggy spot.

Griff swore again and climbed back into the cabin to radio for his dad to bring out the other tractor as a tow. He seriously didn't need this right now. They were already behind schedule. He wanted to take advantage of the rain and plant some oats as feed for the cattle, and there was spraying to do before the next lot of wheat and canola could go in.

He knew there was nothing he could do to control the weather, of course—being at the mercy of the elements came with the territory of being a farmer—but sometimes he hated the uncertainty of this life. He tried to imagine a job where he went to work and everything ran smoothly, where he didn't have to worry about whether there was rain or no rain, he just did his job, got paid and went home. He couldn't picture it. It seemed too far from the realm of his reality.

He took a photo and posted it on Instagram, adding one or two descriptive hashtags about his predicament, then sat back in the cabin to wait for help to arrive. If nothing else, at least his mates would have a brief moment of enjoyment and a few would sympathise. Misery loves company.

It was peaceful again now that the engine was off. He rested his head back against the seat and closed his eyes. The lonely call of a crow echoed across the wide-open land that stretched out all around him. In the distance a cow called for her calf and reminded him that they'd soon be needing to drench, mark and ear-tag again. There was always something to do. It wasn't that he didn't like this work; far from it, it was what he'd always wanted to do.

Farming was in his blood, as it was in his dad's and *his* dad's before him. But recently a restlessness had grown in him—for what he wasn't sure, but he knew he needed a change of some sort in his life.

He'd thought that change had been the arrival of Cash Sullivan to their sleepy little town last year. She was like nothing the place had ever seen before—sexy, rebellious, a mystery woman. He'd wanted Cash—wanted that taste of something different, to be more than good old dependable Griffin. He'd wanted to be like his older brother, Linc.

Linc was the family hero, the commando who'd spent his adult life defending the country and fighting wars. Linc had come home last Christmas and stolen Cash Sullivan right from under Griff's nose.

If he was honest about it, though, Griff had known deep down that he and Cash were never going to be a thing. She'd tried to tell him that, but he'd been blinded by hurt pride and mixed up by this uncharacteristic restlessness that had taken hold of him. So when he'd walked in and discovered Cash in Linc's arms on New Year's Eve, at his little sister's wedding no less, the growing resentment he'd been harbouring towards his brother had sent Griff into a blind rage. What he hadn't been aware of was his brother's own internal struggles. Griff's anger had unleashed a furious violence in Linc that had seen him beat Griffin into unconsciousness.

Ending up in hospital hadn't been the ideal way to spend the first day of a new year—neither had watching his whole family implode. Griff hadn't realised the strain his brother had been under over the past few years, suffering post-traumatic stress disorder after his years as a commando. It had been a shock to realise Linc wasn't the invincible hero that Griff had somehow always thought him to be. It had changed his whole perception of things. Still, it'd probably been for the best that things had all come to a head between them out here. He hated to think what might have happened had Linc been pushed too far by a complete stranger on the street somewhere. As bad as it was, things would have been worse had his brother snapped around someone else. He might have ended up in jail rather than in therapy.

The approaching growl of a large engine alerted him to his father's arrival and Griff wearily dragged himself from the cabin to await the inevitable lecture. It didn't matter that Griff was twenty-seven years old and had been pretty much running the place for the past few years—when it came to stuffing up, you were apparently never too old to get a sermon from your dad on *what you should have done*.

'I told you it was too wet.'

'It was all right yesterday,' Griff muttered, trying to keep his cool.

'One day you'll learn the art of patience. You're always in such a damn hurry.'

'Yeah, well, the bills and the weather aren't exactly patient either, are they?'

'One more day would have saved you a morning of stuffin' around though, wouldn't it?'

Griffin took after his old man, which was why they argued so much, but that was where the similarities ended. Linc was the one who took after their dad in looks. Griff was more like their mother's side of the family, taller than both his father and brother and, in his opinion, far better looking, although Linc would no doubt disagree.

The two brothers had always been like chalk and cheese in everything, even down to the type of women they preferred. In his day Linc had worn the stereotypical military man-whore medal, happy to play the field and play hard. His line of work had made it impossible to maintain any kind of long-term relationship. Griff, on the other hand, had only had two serious girlfriends. He'd been shy and tongue-tied around girls as a kid, and that hadn't changed much as a grown man. He wasn't after anything complicated; he just wanted a marriage like his parents', built on love, trust and a good, solid partnership.

He'd thought he'd found that with his previous relationships, the first starting way back in high school with Olivia Dawson—his neighbour and best friend's twin sister. They'd grown up next door and everyone had thought they'd end up together, but when Griff had gone away to agricultural college Liv had broken up with him. He'd been heartbroken and utterly confused. Later, he'd met Tiffany and for three years they'd been inseparable, but then she'd got a job offer too good to pass up—overseas. Maybe if he'd been willing to leave Stringybark Creek, he'd have been able to save the relationship, but Stringybark was in his blood—farming here was the only thing he'd ever seen himself doing.

He hadn't been celibate since then. He was a healthy red-blooded male after all. He'd been seeing Ashley from the pub on and off, but it was just a casual thing. She was nice enough, but she wasn't into exclusivity and he really wasn't into sharing, so it was never going to go anywhere. Nope, it seemed like he was destined to become a crabby old bachelor farmer who lived on the same property as his parents for the rest of his life. Fantastic. If he hadn't felt like shit before, he certainly did now, thanks to that rosy image of his future.

He finished attaching the strap to the rear of the tractor and waited for his dad to start pulling. For a minute Griff thought the machine might be in too deep and they'd have to call in an excavator to dig the bloody thing out, but after a few more tries, the wheels gained traction and the tractor was finally pulled from its muddy resting place.

At least one thing's gone right today then, he thought, climbing back into the cabin and heading home to the shed. Looked like he'd be spending another day on maintenance instead of out in the field where he needed to be.

Great start to the day.

Two

Olivia Dawson stared out the window of her office overlooking Sydney Harbour and knew she should be appreciating the way the water was extra blue and sparkling today, but she was too busy processing the review meeting she'd just had with her boss. She felt ill. She'd received a reprimand and a warning that if she didn't lift her game she'd be replaced on one of the biggest accounts the firm managed.

Olivia had spent her entire life behaving in exactly the right way. Her worst fear in school had been having the teacher call out her name in class for doing something wrong. Not that it had ever happened, but she'd lived in fear that one day it might. She'd always handed in her homework and assignments on time; she'd never skipped school and she'd never lied to her parents—except for the times she'd covered for her twin brother, Ollie. Like when he and Griffin Callahan had decided to skip school and hitch a ride into Griffith when their cricket hero came to town to promote his new book. That neither of them even liked to read hadn't deterred them. But fibbing because your twin begged you to didn't really count as lying to your parents, given you weren't the one who had actually done anything wrong.

Olivia sighed as she realised that even after all these years she was still a goody-two-shoes. This was why her boss had seemed so bewildered. He couldn't quite wrap his head around her sudden personality change.

Some rebel, she thought miserably. *At the first sign of trouble you're sitting here like a quivering mess.*

'I don't understand what happened in there today, Olivia,' Mr Rothers had said, sounding utterly perplexed. She couldn't blame him really, it *wasn't* like her . . . the old her, that was.

She'd been wrestling with frustration for a while now, but it had taken her last trip home at Christmas to realise she needed to make a change. She was tired of being Olivia, 'the good girl'. Where had it got her? She ignored the little voice that was quite happily listing the things it had got her: a decent job, a great apartment, a new car, savings in her bank account. *Other than that,* she thought irritably.

Where was the excitement? She'd excelled in a very complex field, and yet when she tried to explain to someone what it was she actually did, she could almost see their eyes glaze over, and she couldn't really blame them. Most people usually switched off once she told them she was a corporate lawyer. She usually got a nod and a vague smile, followed by, 'That sounds interesting.' But it really didn't. Not to anyone who wasn't in her field.

She specialised in structuring mergers, acquisitions and finance operations. She was hired to assess, plan and implement value-adding processes to improve the financial function and operational processes of a firm.

Since Christmas her life had been in turmoil. She wasn't sure who she was any more. Who did she want to be? Her old self had seemed destined to climb the corporate ladder right to the top. Her employers wanted her to head that way, but it was no longer making her happy. She wanted to be more like her best friend, Hadley Callahan—war correspondent, globetrotter and general all-round amazing person. Hadley had always been Olivia's hero—the bravest person Olivia knew. Even back in kindergarten nothing had scared Hadley. She'd stand up to the bigger kids in the playground when they tried to bully them; she'd throw away a chance at winning a ribbon on athletic days, not even flinching when the PE teacher yelled at her, just so she could keep Olivia company at the rear of the running pack. She was smart, pretty and had a heart of gold—there was nothing Hadley couldn't do. Unlike Olivia. The only thing Olivia was good at was getting excellent grades and doing what she was told.

Until now. Telling their biggest client that he was being an unreasonable jerk hadn't been the smartest move. But he really had been a jerk—for weeks now they'd been bending over backwards to accommodate his demands. The old Olivia would have meekly bitten her tongue and stayed silent. In hindsight, that would have been sensible, but would Hadley have sat there and let the man not only dictate what was going to happen, but do it with a smug smirk because he knew he was the company's biggest client? No, she would *not* have.

So Olivia had decided to embrace her inner Hadley and stand up to the bully. She had imagined the rest of the boardroom would applaud her, give a standing ovation at her courage . . . Sadly, the reality hadn't been nearly so epic: an uncomfortable silence, followed by a lot of awkward paper shuffling, and then Mr Rothers had excused himself and Olivia so they could speak privately. It had been humiliating, to say the least.

This would *not* have happened to Hadley.

Hadley's world was perfect: she'd just married her long-time celebrity reporter boyfriend in a lavish New Year's Eve wedding. Magazines and TV news had covered the event, celebrating the two darlings of the newsroom on their special day. Olivia was happy for her friend, she really was, but the wedding had brought home just how lonely Olivia really was.

It hadn't helped that as a bridesmaid she'd been paired with Hadley's brother, Griffin Callahan. Olivia let out a small sigh and closed her eyes.

Griffin was a year older than Hadley and Olivia, and he and Olivia's twin brother, Oliver, were best friends. They'd grown up next door, and for years she'd only ever been his best friend's sister. He'd barely given her the time of day. It wasn't until high school that Griff had finally begun to notice her. He'd kissed her at a school disco, when she was in Year Nine, and that had been the beginning of a teenage love affair she'd thought would last forever.

It was funny how sometimes just thinking about a time in your life could almost transport you there. When she thought of Griffin back then, she could feel the warm sun on her shoulders and smell the faint scent of chlorine and coconut oil sunscreen. She remembered the feel of beaded water and warm lips on smooth skin. He'd been her first true love.

Of course, teenage love was very different to any other kind of love, she reminded herself. Everything was heightened with raging hormones and the first taste of grown-up emotions. It was new and exciting and completely unrealistic. Maybe that's why you always remembered your first love with such reverence. It was untarnished by adult responsibilities and expectations.

She opened her eyes and shook her head. It was pointless, she thought irritably, dwelling on the past like this. Not to mention irrelevant, as she remembered the last time she'd seen Griffin. It was after she'd gone and made a complete fool of herself at Hadley's wedding reception. Olivia groaned aloud at the memory, quickly stopping it before the drunken scene could replay itself on a never-ending loop as it liked to do whenever she felt particularly depressed. What *had* happened to the professional, intelligent woman she'd worked so hard and diligently to become?

Olivia reached for a file on her desk. Her phone rang and Olivia frowned as she picked it up and saw the name on the screen. Ollie. She swiped the green answer button.

'Liv,' Ollie said urgently, 'Dad's had an accident.'

COMING DECEMBER 2019

Return to Stringybark Creek

KARLY LANE

Book 3 of THE CALLAHANS OF STRINGYBARK CREEK series

When top-flight journalists Hadley Callahan and Mitch Samuals married two years ago, theirs had been declared the celebrity wedding of the year. But, now, Hadley unexpectedly returns to Stringybark Creek alone to tell her parents one major piece of news while determinedly hiding another even more explosive secret.

Hadley's big society wedding had killed any hopes that Oliver Dawson, the Callahans' neighbour and Griff Callahan's best friend, had nurtured since his teenage years when Hadley was his best friend's little sister and thus out-of-bounds.

While Hadley's in town, the shocking suicide of one of their old school friends brings them together as they mourn their loss. Hadley and Ollie begin a campaign to raise awareness of rural mental health, both wanting to make a difference.

With Mitch putting pressure on Hadley to keep quiet, and the secret she's keeping causing her great anguish, Hadley's feelings for Ollie take her by surprise. But her life is so messed up at the moment—what future could they possibly have together?

Return to Stringybark Creek concludes the Callahan family trilogy with a delightfully irresistible story of loyalty, hope and the importance of staying true to yourself.

ISBN 978 1 76052 923 9